The Lazarus Widow

THE LAZARUS WIDOW

Bill Knox
and Martin Edwards

Constable · London

First published in Great Britain 1999
by Constable & Company Limited
3 The Lanchesters, 162 Fulham Palace Road
London W6 9ER
Copyright © Bill Knox 1999
The right of Bill Knox to be
identified as the author of this work
has been asserted by him in accordance
with the Copyright, Designs and Patents Act 1988
ISBN 0 094 79680 7
Set in Palatino 10 pt by
SetSystems Ltd, Saffron Walden, Essex
Printed and bound in Great Britain
by MPG Books Ltd, Bodmin, Cornwall

A CIP catalogue record for this book
is available from the British Library

This fiction story, like others in the Colin Thane series, varies in some procedural detail from the real-life Scottish Crime Squad's operational methods.

This is at the direct request of the detective officers concerned. There are valid reasons which they have explained to me and I am grateful for their help.

There is a real-life Riverman. His name is George Parsonage, legendary son of a legendary father. We have been friends a long time.

B. K., Glasgow.

Preface

Until a few days before his sudden death, Bill Knox had been hard at work on the manuscript of *The Lazarus Widow*. The story – which he regarded as being among his best – was well advanced, but incomplete. Bill's method of writing was to polish each chapter before proceeding to the next. He was an assured and immensely experienced story-teller who did not find it necessary to write synopses or plan his books in detail before starting. The only clues to his intended resolution of the story were a few enigmatic handwritten notes scribbled in a pad and three press clippings. Coupled with a shoal of red herrings in the manuscript, therefore, Bill left a conundrum to match the best of his fictional puzzles.

I had the privilege to be asked by Bill's editor, Tara Lawrence, and his widow Myra, to solve the mystery of *The Lazarus Widow* and complete the book. It has certainly proved to be one of the most fascinating experiences of my own writing career. Fortunately, I have needed to make few changes to the chapters Bill wrote, simply because he was such a professional, one-draft writer. None of us can be sure how he meant to finish the book, but I hope that he would have approved of the way I have tackled the challenge. I would like to record my particular thanks to Myra for her enthusiastic support; she and Bill were married for almost fifty years and the background information she has supplied has been most welcome. The first Colin Thane novel, *Deadline for a Dream* (1957), was dedicated to Myra; so is this, the last entry in a long-running and deservedly popular series.

Martin Edwards

1

The Riverman was almost part of the scenery. His old-fashioned rowing boat operated on the upper reaches of the Clyde, and, when he could, he rescued the living.

More often, he harvested the dead.

Noon on a sunny Monday in mid-September found the Riverman on his way downriver again, knowing exactly where he was going – and why. As always, he rowed standing upright, facing the bow and using easy, economical strokes to cut into the flat greasy water. There was no need to hurry. This was a date he had noted in his diary eight days earlier, and he probably had at least half an hour to spare.

Medium height and muscular, blue-eyed and grey-haired, with powerfully built arms and shoulders, the Riverman was in his late forties. He wore an open-neck red plaid shirt, faded denims with a broad leather seaman's belt. He didn't wear socks, and his feet were in grubby lace-up trainers. When a small boy yelled a greeting from one of the piers, the Riverman grinned a reply. Only three months back, he had hauled the same small boy out of the river after finding him white-faced with fear and close to drowning, clinging desperately to what remained of a home-made raft.

The same thing had almost happened to the Riverman at that age. Kids living beside water would always build rafts and risk drowning. Some would always die that way. He had learned not to weep when he found them.

The sunlight pleasantly warm on his back, he continued on at the same easy stroke while the sun glinted on the ranks of office windows and factory roofs on both sides of modern Glasgow's river. Times had changed for the Clyde. The few remaining operating quays along this stretch were almost empty, most of their tall dockside cranes dismantled. What little was left of deep sea shipping life now lurked downriver beside the bulk quays and container terminals. That was also where most of the very little left of Scotland's once world-famed shipbuilding industry clung to a precarious existence.

A fish rose in mid-stream, the fat, silvery body splashing down again in a way that sent out broad ripples, and the Riverman grunted in pleasure. As man went into retreat, nature was making a comeback. Swans had returned to the upper Clyde, along with other birds the river had not seen for a long time. A few adventurous seals had been spotted. On the land, there were paved riverside walks, cafes and night-time live music where the cranes and cargo warehouses had once ruled.

Eyes narrowed against the sun's glitter on the oily water, the Riverman finally reached his goal, a little way down and across from the familiar north bulk of Yorkhill Quay. A few more strokes brought his boat nearer to the south bank. He shipped his oars as the wooden hull bumped a protruding stump of weed-fringed timber where there had once been a long-gone jetty. The Riverman tossed a line around the stump and allowed the boat to drift until the line tightened and brought the little craft to a halt, then he settled down near the stern and opened the lunch basket at his feet, ate a meat sandwich and sipped coffee from a flask. His wife made up a packed lunch for him most days.

A small coaster throbbed past going upriver, and her siren gave a mild toot of a greeting. A moment later, the little ship's rippling wash made the rowing boat bob, and the Riverman raised a hand in a greeting. He knew the coaster's skipper.

Time passed. The Riverman chewed another sandwich, glanced at his watch, and was about to pour another cup of coffee from his flask when a small, new swirl in the water caught his eye. He paused. That kind of swirl was not caused by a fish.

The Riverman stoppered his flask, closed the lunch basket, and waited. In another minute the body surfaced, floating low, moving a little with the current, face up, the way a woman's body surfaced. The Riverman untied his boat from the stump, picked up the oars, and rowed over.

The dead woman had long black hair now laced with thin green strands of ribbon weed from the river bottom. She had probably been pretty, and she wore a black plastic coat which gave a glimpse of a light-coloured dress beneath. A black high-heeled shoe still clung to one foot, the other foot was bare.

The Riverman nodded to himself, satisfied. The police report in his pocket said she was Vikki Austin, thirty-six years old, a shop assistant, a single parent with two children. She had simply walked out of a late-night party at a riverside club and jumped into the Clyde. She had lost her job earlier that day.

Two more half-strokes of the starboard oar brought the River-man close alongside. Bending over the gunwale, he gripped the dead woman's shoulders and used a single heave to bring her aboard his broad-beamed boat. When he lowered the body down, water dribbled from her clothes across the unvarnished stern sheets.

'Rest in peace, lass,' he said softly. 'It wasn't me who kept you waiting.'

He picked up his oars to start back upriver, then stopped and stared. Another bubbling swirl had begun to show on the water only a stone's throw away. He waited, he watched, and a second body broke the surface – face down, meaning a male. The Riverman swore under his breath. He hadn't been told about this one.

He rowed a few strokes, then allowed his boat to drift the rest of the way until this new body bumped alongside. Frowning, still puzzled, thumbs tucked into his leather belt, he looked down and considered what he'd found. The dead man had been medium height and medium build, balding, probably middle-aged, and wearing a good quality blue pinstripe suit. He had expensive looking lace-up black leather shoes. Dark river ooze smudged across most of his head and face.

'Better take you in, friend' mused the Riverman resignedly. 'Somebody will be looking for you.'

He bent over the gunwale for a second time, gripped the dead man below the shoulders, heaved, then grunted at the effort to bring him aboard. This one weighed considerably more than the woman. But at last they lay side by side at the bottom of the boat, the water coming from their clothes mingling.

Because he felt it mattered, the Riverman squatted down and adjusted the clothing on both bodies to give them more dignity. Then he retrieved his lunchbox, took out the mobile telephone which lay buried below his sandwiches, and began punching buttons. There were things to do.

Fifteen minutes later, his rowing boat lay hauled out of the

11

water on a nearby ferry slip. Two police cars and a mortuary van had arrived and his bodies had been taken aboard the mortuary van, destined for the City Mortuary.

'Finished?' queried a divisonal police sergeant who had been turned out to see what was going on.

'For now,' agreed the Riverman, munching a sandwich.

Once they'd been landed and he had gone through the formalities of handover, recovered bodies were mainly someone else's worry. Another police car was arriving. The Riverman smiled. This one was towing one of his boat trailers.

That meant he could be driven home in comfort. To a fresh cup of coffee.

The next day, Tuesday, brought more of the same clear blue skies which usually mark September as the best month for the wise tourist to visit Scotland.

Detective Superintendent Colin Thane wasn't a tourist and certainly didn't feel like one. He had started off the morning with the hope that for once he would get on top of his work schedule. Instead, he drove the motorway route towards the city centre knowing that Tuesday was rapidly shaping into a download of trouble where things could only get worse.

A tall, well-built grey-eyed man in his early forties, Colin Thane was deputy commander of the Scottish Crime Squad. This time, the first warning of what might lie ahead had been a Strathclyde division mid-morning telephone call to the Squad's headquarters on the fringe of Glasgow. The divisonal officer had been brief, cheerful – because it wasn't his case – and to the point. An eleven-day search in which every UK police force had been asked to assist had ended. An unidentified body recovered from the Clyde the previous day had now been identified as that of Samuel Baker, described by the Squad as 'wanted for questioning'.

Which wasn't really an end – more a new beginning. An overnight autopsy report that Baker had been a murder victim was an embarrassment, for several people.

Including Thane.

Samuel Baker, a bankrupt insurance agent who had done prison time for fraud, had been a man few people would have

12

found it easy to like. But he had volunteered to turn informer in a major Crime Squad operation. In return, he had been guaranteed immunity from prosecution, a large bundle of Spanish pesetas and a new identity abroad. Fortunately, he hadn't reached the stage of getting his hands on the pesetas. They were still lying in an old shoebox in the main Crime Squad safe.

'Hard luck, Baker,' murmured Colin Thane. 'You'd have liked the Costas.'

The detective was at the wheel of the black two-litre Ford Mondeo which was one of his favourites from the Squad's transport pool. This morning the motorway route was clogged with traffic and to make it worse he was stuck behind an ancient van pouring stinking black exhaust smoke.

Except that there was suddenly a gap in the traffic ahead.

Thane grabbed his chance. Dropping a gear, accelerating hard, he left his lane and overtook, sweeping past the smoker. Except that the gap beyond was less than Thane had calculated, and he had to weave into his lane again, coming close to shaving the van's nose. He eased on the accelerator and gave a quick backward gesture of apology towards the van driver. The other driver replied by mouthing an insult aimed squarely at Thane's rear view mirror.

'And up yours!' Thane snarled back, cancelling the apology. But it had been an 'almost' accident, near enough to leave his mouth suddenly dry. Thane sighed and resigned himself to the traffic again, his thoughts switching. Murder always set its own priorities, he had already set some inquiries moving by telephone, and Thane's own starter, meeting the Riverman, would be no hardship.

They'd known each other for – yes, a long time. His mouth shaped a wry grin. at the thought.

Detective Superintendent Colin Thane was a man with regular features, thick dark hair with just a few hints of grey around the temples and a start of crowfoot lines around the eyes. He was wearing a favourite lightweight Lovat suit with a grey shirt and a knitted blue tie, and his shoes were a pair of comfortably old brown leather moccasins.

How long had he known the Riverman? Long enough for them both to have gained some weight, long enough for it to begin to show. But maybe not too much else had changed.

Thane smiled and his eyes twinkled.

Professionally, that smile and those grey eyes could combine in a trap for the unwary. Behind them, Thane had a reputation for being bleakly willing to back a hunch. He wasn't ever likely to win any kind of a prize for general diplomacy.

It added up to just the way he was made – a way that could equally attract trouble or results.

Sunlight baked the car as Thane drove the Kingston Bridge route over the Clyde to the north side of Glasgow. He kept to the M8 for another short spell to avoid the city centre, then took an exit which brought him out and down below the thirteenth century spire of Glasgow Cathedral. From there, he avoided more traffic in a curve of a route which brought him back towards the Clyde, then slowed and turned onto a narrow, easy to miss vehicle track before the old King's Bridge. The Ford swayed along a short length of potholed carriageway, then Thane steered in at a small parking area and stopped the car.

Colin Thane had used the same parking area often enough before. But it was always hard to accept he was so near to the heart of the city. A Parks Department garden area of flowers, shrubs and neatly raked paths ran down to the edge of the broad, lazily flowing Clyde. Across the water, beyond King's Bridge, the modern skyline was where the high-rise housing blocks of the new Gorbals district had taken over from Glasgow's oldest and most notorious tenement slums.

True, some of the new skyline blocks had already fallen victims to a mix of drugs, despair and vandalism. Others had even been demolished. But over on Colin Thane's side of the river there were people strolling in the sunlight, some walking dogs, women pushing prams. They were using a path which went past a large, well-maintained boathouse at the river's edge.

A small private path from the boathouse climbed a gentle slope to a modest bungalow with a fenced-in garden. Signs on both boathouse and bungalow read Glasgow Humane Society. Thane left the Ford and went towards the boathouse, where a trio of dinghies were moored in line beside a large launch and some rowing boats. Another launch and a punt, both up on chocks and their hulls being revarnished, lay inside the building.

'Hey, Colin!' Appearing from further back in the boathouse,

14

the Riverman waved a greeting. 'Give me another minute, will you?'

'Can do.' Thane grinned and returned the wave.

The Riverman disappeared inside. Thane walked on, passing an open-air gallery collection of metal artworks, some abstract, others taking the shapes of ships and fantasy animals. When he reached the boathouse, he stepped aboard the verandah deck and leaned on its rail. A racing shell went sculling past. It was crewed by two girls.

He'd been a young beat cop when he'd first visited this place and had met the man he'd come to talk with – who had then called himself an apprentice at his profession. The recognised Riverman of that time, official title the full-time officer of the Glasgow Humane Society, had been the so-called apprentice's father. And things had stayed that way until father retired and son had formally taken over.

More fragments of background came into Thane's mind while the racing shell vanished from sight downstream .

The Glasgow Humane Society operated with one paid, full-time officer, a handful of boats – and a proud history which went back in the late eighteenth century. That was when a Glasgow merchant, sickened at the steady toll of drownings in the Clyde, had gifted what had been the considerable sum of £200 to the city's Faculty of Surgeons for the setting up of a rescue and recovery service. Somehow managing to stay totally independent, the infant Glasgow Humane Society spent its first years installing rescue equipment at locations along the river. What began as a few lifebuoys and ropes hanging on hooks at key locations grew to become a number of small rescue boats. Then at last the Society had managed to employ its first full-time lifesaving officer.

Right up to the present, the importance of the Society's role hadn't diminished. In a combined total of seventy years all-weather service, the present Riverman and his father had on their own saved over two thousand people – men, women and children – from drowning in the Clyde. Between them, too, they had recovered a similar number of bodies. Along the way, father and son between them had been awarded an impressive collection of medals for personal bravery.

15

In an emergency, the routine was simple enough. Whenever a lifesaving was reported, the emergency services would telephone the Humane Society – and from that moment on speed of response mattered in terms of seconds saved. One of the Riverman's standby boats, mounted on a trailer, could be collected by police car and rushed to the scene. If the call-out came during the night, the Riverman would leave his bed and change from pyjamas into outdoor clothes along the way.

Modesty rated behind saving lives.

Thane heard footsteps and turned. Wiping his hands on an oily rag, wearing a black sweatshirt and old jeans, the Riverman was back.

'Good to see you, Colin.' The man's welcoming grin emphasised the slight gap between two of his front teeth. The rest was a weather-beaten face, a strong nose, firm cheekbones, and deep-set eyes which always seemed to be half-hooded against the glare from the river. 'So – how's thief-catching?'

'Never short of trade,' confessed Thane. 'What about your scene?'

'Enough to keep me busy.' The Riverman looked past the detective, puzzled. 'Where's that wee red-haired police girl who usually comes with you?' He gave a mock frown. 'Don't tell me you've had another economy purge and had her culled?'

'Any day now, but not yet.' Thane wondered how Detective Sergeant Sandra Craig would have liked the 'wee red-haired police girl' description. 'She's at a meeting.'

'These days, half the world spends its time at meetings.' The Riverman tossed the oily rag into a waste can. 'Well, I was cleaning out the fuel system on one of the outboards, but it can wait. Get to why you're here. When you 'phoned, you said it was about yesterday.'

'True.' Thane nodded.

'But the woman I brought out was what could be called a routine drowning?'

'Routine.' That was harsh reality. 'But the autopsy report on the man – '

'Says murder,' sniffed his companion. 'I heard. Except you won't want that shouted around?'

'Not yet,' agreed Thane stonily.

'You'll have no problem with that from me.' The Riverman

rubbed a hand along his chin, leaving a new oily stain. 'I talked to the mortuary people, then someone sent me a fax of the autopsy report. It says yes, Baker drowned. But first he was hit on the back of the head, blunt instrument style. His skull showed a hairline fracture.'

'Meaning that he had been attacked,' nodded Thane. 'And probably unconscious but still alive when he was heaved into the water.'

'He wouldn't be the first.' Frowning, the Riverman leaned on the rail beside Thane. 'But normally, when there's a killing like this, I see an ordinary divisional murder team move in. So why does finding Baker bring your top gun Squad galloping in?'

'I could just say you don't need to know.' Thane eyed him mildly.

'And whatever you want from me, I could just tell you to go to hell,' countered the Humane Society officer cheerfully. They'd played the same game before. 'So?'

'So the usual – I tell you, you forget you heard.' Thane surrendered. 'We grabbed Baker during a combined Crime Squad, Customs and Excise ploy. The operation broke up a liquor and tobacco smuggling scam and Baker probably could have faced five years jail time – '

'Big deal.' The Riverman was not impressed. 'You said probably. What's the rest?'

'Baker had already served one jail term for fraud, he had decided he couldn't take another,' said Thane dryly. 'So he offered us a trade – something a damned sight bigger than a few truckloads of duty free booze and fags.'

'Just another public-spirited citizen at heart?' suggested the Riverman caustically.

'What else?' Thane grimaced, remembered Baker's tearful, wriggling panic. The one-time insurance agent had been prepared to make any kind of trade to escape a return to the grim, stale reek of Barlinnie Prison. 'If we forgot the charges and threw in some extra fringe benefits, he'd tell us everything he knew on a major financial scam happening under our noses – one we didn't know about.'

'And you agreed?'

'Yes.' Thane pursed his lips. It was a deal he regretted. 'Baker admitted he was only a hired casual help, good at posing as a

17

company executive. Mainly, he carried a briefcase and did what he was told.' He shrugged, because this was where things became uncertain. 'Sometimes he'd been sent abroad, courier style. Sometimes he guessed he was carrying cash. Sometimes all he had to deliver was a computer floppy disc.'

'But there was a problem?' asked the Riverman.

'For us, yes. He had damned little fact to back any of it,' admitted Thane wryly. 'If he was telling the truth, the people he worked for are nobody's fools. They operate with word of mouth instructions about pick-ups and deliveries – '

The Riverman grunted.' Sounds like a variation on the Three Wise Monkeys. But you thought he might be kosher?'

'Enough to tell him we'd do the deal – but that we needed hard fact.' With Baker pleading, almost grovelling, they'd allowed him two weeks to come up with more facts and had given him a Crime Squad all-hours contact number. At the end of the two-week deadline, a Glasgow evening meet was arranged in the foyer of Royal Concert Hall at the start of an evening concert, the Royal Scottish National Orchestra with a middle-brow programme of Strauss waltzes. Thane remembered that detail because Strauss waltzes were about the peak of his personal cultural level and he'd even thought briefly of going along with his wife.

'Then when Baker didn't show, you thought he'd done a runner,' said the Humane Society officer grimly, and sucked on that little gap between his front teeth. 'And this all stays under wraps?'

'As much as possible.' For a moment, Thane saw his own reflection on the water, then it had rippled away. 'Strathclyde's police media unit will put out a very dull press release – they are good at very dull press releases – sometime today, guaranteed to bore. Usual wording – the body of a man recovered from the river, apparent drowning, inquiries continuing.' He paused for a moment as a small pack of yelling children rushed past on the path, chased by a large, delighted mongrel dog. 'We'll hold back on Baker's identity for a spell. But his wife made a formal identification this morning.'

'Rough for her,' said the Riverman with a genuine sympathy. 'Were they close?'

'Not very.' Less than that. Thane had talked with Muriel Baker twice in the days since her husband went missing. 'It seems they shared a roof, not much more.' But a mortuary i.d. was a grim experience for anyone, several times worse than grim after a body had been rotting in a river, and Thane didn't need a reminder that another visit to Muriel Baker was next on his list

'Sad.' The Riverman sighed. 'Still, not my business. So – ' he raised a bushy, questioning eyebrow ' – what is?'

'You're an expert,' said Thane flatly. 'If you get enough detail about when and where someone drowns in the river then you can forecast when and where they'll surface again. True?'

'More or less. Give or take.' The Humane Society officer's blue eyes were cautious.' But – '

'Can you do the same thing in reverse? This time, you know when and where the body was found. We can make a guess at when he went missing. Can you make another guess – at where he maybe went in?'

'It would be rough estimate style, Colin. Very rough.' The Riverman frowned, sucked his lips, then reluctantly nodded. 'For you, I'll give it a try. But no guarantees.'

'None asked.' Thane gave him a grateful beam. 'How long will you need?'

'Give me a day – that's if I don't get too many call-outs. Mostly, I'll be relying on what is stored in my personal database. But I'll also need a full copy of the autopsy report and some other bits and pieces.'

'You'll get them.' Thane straightened up from the boathouse rail. 'We got careless over this one. For me, that makes this close to personal.'

'I'll do my best.' The Riverman gave him a friendly slap on the arm. 'Look – before you go, I want to show you something.'

He guided Thane out of the boathouse and along to the grassy patch of riverbank. Then he stopped and pointed.

'What do you think?' he asked simply.

The large metal heron which stood glinting in the sunlight had been fashioned out of welded metal rods and feathered with strips of copper. From slim neck and cruel beak to power-ful wings poised ready for flight, the Riverman had caught the total essence of the bird which was one of the kings of the river.

'Well?' asked the man earnestly. 'Be honest.'

19

'Uh – what is it meant to be?' asked Thane innocently. 'Some kind of – ah – weirdo Concorde?' Then, as the Riverman's expression collapsed in dismay, the detective made a soothing noise. 'All right, it's maybe a heron. It's good!'

'Damn you for an unfeeling Philistine plod! One day I'll take a welding torch to your dangly bits,' snarled the Riverman, while Thane's grin widened. 'You know damned well it's a heron. It's for a group collection of riverbird sculptures I've been asked to exhibit in Paris next month.'

'All right, it's probably a heron.' Thane's chuckle healed the wound. Going over, he examined the metal bird and its delicately detailed facets. 'Good enough for the French.'

The Riverman's metal sculptures were highly respected by art experts. He exhibited regularly at home and overseas – and away from the calls of the river, the Humane Society officer wore another hat as an arts lecturer at one of the city's colleges. As a part-time academic, he had a classroom studio with a panoramic window towards the Clyde. But he never forgot his other hat – even when lecturing, he always carried his portable 'phone and was ready to respond to any emergency call-out.

'Cop-style praise could go to my head,' said the Riverman bleakly. Then he gave a sour chuckle. 'Get on your way, man. I know what you want, I'll do my best.'

They parted, Thane walking back towards his car. In the distance, the two girls with the racing shell were sculling upriver again, fast enough for their shell to leave a small, creaming wake. He stopped at the Ford's door, watched for another moment, then got aboard the car and set it moving.

A vital aspect of the hunt for Sam Baker's killer now depended on the Riverman and his database.

It was roughly a half-hour's travel from Glasgow to Kirkintilloch, the sleepy burgh town where Sam Baker had lived. That gave Thane some much-needed thinking time as he drove towards his destination, first through the crawl of city traffic, then on a fast by-pass route where the sunlight arrived filtered through a tunnel layer of exhaust smog.

There were a few things he hadn't told the Riverman, mainly because they didn't concern him. Starting with the way Sam

Baker had first appeared on the scene, at the very climax of the joint Crime Squad and Customs operation. He was one of close on a dozen minor villains arrested in a late-night raid on a warehouse near to Hampden, Scotland's national football stadium. As a Squad target, it had been under observation for more than a month, and the raiding team found it piled roof-high with uncustomed crates of beers, wines and spirits. Two newly arrived road container wagons crammed with cigarettes and bulk tobacco completed a seizure with a duty-paid value of close on two million pounds sterling.

There was little skill required bringing duty-due goods into Britain. Typically nonsensical European Union regulations had made a mockery out of the UK Customs system. Budget motivated government cutbacks had drastically downsized the skilled teams of Customs rummagers and investigators available. By air and by ferry, by the Chunnel or over the Irish border, smuggling traffic was booming – one estimate was it ran at around fifteen million pounds sterling of uncustomed goods every month. A normally level-headed opposition MP had claimed that the annual trade in uncustomed goods could have squared the national debt of two African countries.

During the warehouse raid, a frightened Baker had been found hiding inside an empty wine barrel. His initial story that he was just a van driver collapsed when others identified him as the smuggling team's ledger man – and his personal black hole became deeper when the Scottish Criminal Records Office computer produced his previous conviction for fraud and embezzlement. Then Baker had made his offer—

'Hell!' Thane braked the car to a last-minute halt as a pedestrian crossing light ahead turned red, then drew a deep relieved breath as a pre-teens schoolgirl carrying a hockey bag strode out into the road. Her eyes met Thane's, she gave an angelic smile, one hand came up in a casually obscene greeting which didn't come from any schools hockey rule book, then she reached the other pavement.

He swore under his breath, had to laugh, then set the car moving again as the lights went back to green.

The offer –

He had decided to gamble that Baker might be telling the truth about his courier role in the financial fraud operation when the man earnestly produced a much-used passport covered in visas and entry and exit stamps. Then there had been two personal bank books with fat credit balances, balances unlikely to be creamed off by a smuggler's book-keeper.

Pressured for more details about his courier trips, Baker came up with a list of dates, deliveries and pick-ups – with inevitably untraceable contact names and telephone numbers which were either public call boxes or stolen mobile 'phones.

Then, unexpectedly, he produced a gun he'd been given. The oiled and gleaming metal of an unregistered Colt automatic with a full magazine had to be taken seriously. This one arrived almost gift-wrapped in a parcel made up of a thick, dark grey coloured wax paper tied with household string – there was still a widespread underworld fantasy belief that a man couldn't be charged with carrying an illegal firearm if it came parcelled.

Throughout, Baker was a man it would have been hard to like. But he appeared to be trying hard to keep his part of the bargain. He made a daily check-in telephone call. He twice met with Crime Squad officers, insisting that he was making progress. He had spoken to Thane on his last telephone call, made with one day left of the fourteen he had been given – and, with an eager degree of returning confidence, had claimed he was on the brink of success.

Colin Thane found it easy to remember the man's final words. Thane had been encouraging him along, emphasising the safeguards in a witness protection scheme – and Baker didn't think much of some aspects of the deal.

'Here, I've got a laugh for you, Mr Thane,' he had said with a nervous whinny of a giggle. 'What do you need if you've got ten cops up to their necks in sand?' The whinny came again. 'You need more sand, that's what!'

Thane had said nothing.

Sam Baker didn't show the next evening, had quite simply vanished. His powder blue two-door Nissan coupé had vanished, still hadn't been spotted.

And when the one-time insurance agent's body had finally surfaced in the Clyde his pockets had been empty except for a pocket comb, a sodden handkerchief, and a soggy pack of chewing gum. Eleven days in the river had wrinkled the skin on his fingers, washerwoman style. But Glasgow's mortuary knew

22

a medical technician who had developed a speciality skill in retrieving fingerprints using injections of liquid wax. Then a matching check with SCRO files had done the rest.

And now Colin Thane was on his way to see a woman who would have to come terms with being a widow. Even if her marriage had burned out for long enough.

· 'You poor, stupid bastard, Baker,' said Thane softly, making it an almost weary benediction. 'You made a total mess of it.'

The road topped a low rise, passed a farm, a golf course, and a railway station, and went through a village which had two steepled churches. Then the snaking tarmac curved downhill into the little town which was his destination. Kirkintilloch, a quiet little Dumbartonshire burgh town had a population of under fifty thousand and its origins could be traced back to Roman times. But now it was at least as proud of the shops in its new town centre and its scatter of new small housing estates. As a town, it didn't claim to be the eleventh wonder of the world. But its inhabitants clung fiercely to their independence from their mighty neighbour city. The rest included an almost forgotten length of the Forth and Clyde Canal, a prize-winning gardening club and Kirkintilloch Rob Roy, a successsful little junior league football team named after a legendary Highland cattle rustling bandit.

Thane drove through towards Legion Grove, one of the quiet tree-lined avenues on the older side of town, the view out across flat farming country towards the Campsie Hills. The small grey stone villa he wanted was halfway along Legion Grove and set in a modest walled garden. A uniformed constable was on duty at its open gate, and as Thane slowed the man saluted and waved him through.

The Ford crunched along a length of gravel driveway, then Thane drew in at the end of a small line of parked cars. One was a Crime Squad vehicle, stopped behind a local police patrol car. Then he stared. A white Volkswagen Golf was parked further along the line. He hadn't expected it to be there. Nor to see the attractive redhead who had appeared from the house and was loping over towards him.

'Sir.' Detective Sergeant Sandra Craig arrived as Thane climbed out of the Ford and greeted him with a quick grin. 'I just beat you to it.'

'I thought you went to a Federation meeting,' frowned Thane, puzzled.

Sandra Craig, his personal sergeant, had been elected as the Crime Squad's representative delegate to the Scottish Police Federation. Her Federation meetings were sacred. 'What went wrong?'

'Nothing, sir.' She shook her head in a way that let the sunlight turn that hair to the colour of rich copper. 'There wasn't much on the agenda, the chairman thought he could still grab a game of golf, so we broke early.'

'Good.' Thane was genuinely glad to have her back.

Still in her twenties, Sandra Craig was tall and slim, with attractive looks and green eyes. Her red hair was nature's warning of a temper to match. Although she didn't know it, Sandra Craig was already marked down as future Accelerated Promotion material. For the moment, dressed in one of her favourite working outfits of a light blue shirt topped by a blue corduroy waistcoat, faded but tailored blue denims and a broad, metal-studded leather belt, her feet in black lace-up training shoes, she looked ready to cope with most things likely to come her way.

'Spoken with Muriel Baker?' asked Thane, as they crunched together across the gravel towards the stone pillars of the front door.

'Just enough to let her know who I was, sir. A couple of friends are with her – there's also a neighbour in the kitchen brewing tea and making general helping noises.' Sandra Craig shook her head, those green eyes slightly puzzled 'I don't think Mrs Baker is totally heartbroken.'

'Maybe not, sergeant.'

Thane led the way up the stone steps and in through the open front door into a simply furnished hallway. A trio of police officers were standing halfway along the hallway, and their murmur of conversation ended as Thane approached. Two of the three were Crime Squad detective constables. Beauty and the Beast, a petite blonde sugar plum fairy of a girl and a hairy giant of a man, formed a regular working partnership – and they'd been with Muriel Baker at the City Mortuary in Glasgow. The third officer, in uniform, was a local chief inspector.

'Chief Inspector Arnott, sir,' said Beauty, introducing the local man.

'Bill Arnott,' said the man. 'Courtesy help, superintendent.'

They shook hands, Colin Thane with concealed relief. It made a difference when a local force stayed co-operative – and it wasn't always that way. He turned back to Beauty. 'How was it at the mortuary?'

'Mrs Baker wasn't too bad, sir.' The blonde glanced at her massive companion for confirmation. 'We thought we might get tears.'

'But she coped all right.' The Beast gave a sympathetic scowl. For such a large man, he could be surprisingly gentle in his ways. 'Saw the body, confirmed it was her husband, then just wanted back here.' He shrugged. 'You told us not to push her. We didn't.'

'Some people only weep in private,' mused the County man. He thumbed towards a room door off the hall. 'She's in the lounge, superintendent, waiting. Her friends are still with her. I was going to chase them, but she insisted they stayed.'

'Names?' queried Thane.

Sandra Craig had them in her notebook. He had expected that. 'The younger one is a Trudi Andrews, the other is a Lizbeth Rankin, sir. They arrived together in Trudi Andrews' car, a red Renault four-door.'

'Right.' He beckoned at the redhead, gestured to the others to stay, and went over to the lounge door. As he knocked, he caught a glimpse of a grey-haired woman appear further back in the hall, look in his direction, then vanish again – the tea-making neighbour was still around.

There was always a tea-making neighbour. Thane took a deep breath, then opened the lounge door and went with Sandra Craig into a shabby but clean room heavily smelling of furniture polish. He looked at its three occupants while his sergeant closed the door behind her. Baker's widow, a thin-faced, angular, but not unattractive woman in her mid-forties, wore her mousey coloured hair in a French pleat and a black sweater with a plain grey skirt. She was sitting in a high-backed tapestry chair. Her two visitors shared a matching couch next to her, Lizbeth Rankin smartly dressed in grey and with jet black hair, was smoking a

cigarette and looked about the same age as Muriel Baker. Much
younger and wearing a knitted blue two-piece, Trudi Andrews
was an attractive brunette, cropped razor-styled hair streaked
with blonde highlights. A tray with used cups, saucers and a
teapot sat on a small table beside the couch.

'Mrs Baker.' Quietly, Thane crossed over and laid a hand on
the woman's shoulder. 'Muriel, my condolences.'

'Thank you, superintendent.' Muriel Baker nodded
unemotionally, her expression hard to read, fingering the thin
wedding ring which was her only jewellery. She waited silently
while Sandra Craig murmured introductions then looked at
Thane again and said simply, 'You tried to warn me.'

Thane searched for words, but Lizbeth Rankin cut in before he
had a chance to use them.

'What the hell has been going on here, superintendent?' the
raven-haired woman demanded fiercely. She leaned forward
and mashed out her cigarette in an ashtray, acid sarcasm in her
voice, anger on her plump face. 'Muriel says her beloved husband was in trouble yet again. But what happens? First you
arrest him, then you let him go again.' She snorted. 'Sam tells
Muriel there's nothing to worry about – then vanishes. When
you do manage to find him, he's in the river, very dead.'

'Liz.' It came from Muriel Baker, an odd blend of protest and
plea. 'Remember your blood pressure'.

'Stuff my blood pressure.' She aimed a fierce scowl at Thane.
'Sam Baker wasn't any kind of prize, superintendent. Most of
the time he was an out-and-out bastard. But he was her husband,
for God's sake!'

'Mr Baker had been helping in a police investigation,' said
Thane warily.

'She already knows that much,' snapped Lizbeth Rankin. 'But
what kind of investigation?'

'Sorry.' He shook his head. 'I can't tell you.'

'You're saying that Sam Baker was on the side of law and
order?' Trudi Andrews almost laughed at the thought. 'Him?
The man was a total waste of space – and that's putting it
mildly!'

'Ease back, Trudi,' murmured Lizbeth Rankin. Her mood had
suddenly cooled, there was a new, warning glint in her eyes. 'I
feel the same, but we've said enough. It doesn't help Muriel.'

26

'No, it doesn't.' Whatever else she had been going to say, the younger woman coloured, stopped, and shook her head. 'I – Muriel, I'm sorry.'

'Don't be, Trudi.' Muriel Baker managed a small twist of a smile which took in both women. 'You and Liz are here – that's what matters to me now.'

There was a sudden silence in the room, a silence with its own underlying tension. A vehicle door slammed in the driveway outside. A police radio crackled and the rays of sunlight pouring in through the windows caught a slow spiral of dust motes floating in the air. Thane pursed his lips, waiting in this unhappy, shabby room where there were no books, no photographs, only a few pieces of nondescript china in a glass-fronted cabinet, a single mass-produced Peter Scott bird print above the fireplace and faded plum velvet curtains at those windows.

'It's always good to have friends.' Sandra Craig came to the rescue, as if reading Thane's mind.' How long have you known these ladies, Mrs Baker?'

'It seems like for ever, sergeant – Liz the longest.' Muriel Baker glanced affectionately towards her friend. 'We met when we worked in the same office – which is also where I met Sam. In fact, he dated Liz for a spell before he decided to marry me.'

'My good luck,' muttered Lizbeth Rankin grimly, brushing a fleck of tobacco ash from her skirt.

'I'm later on the scene,' volunteered Trudi Andrews. She brought her fingertips up to her chin and rested them there. 'When Sam Baker ran his insurance agency, I was his secretary.' She saw the question coming. 'I smelled trouble ahead, superintendent. So I got out a couple of months before the business folded – and I didn't weep when he was jailed for fraud. But – ' she gave a small, quick smile towards Muriel Baker ' – by then, I'd got to know Muriel and Liz. One of the things they did was to make sure I wasn't dragged down by Sam's crookery.' She paused, looked at Sandra Craig, and smiled. 'Yes. you're right, sergeant. It's always good to have friends.'

Thane had positioned himself behind Muriel Baker's high-backed chair, and posed another question to Lizbeth Rankin. 'How did you know Baker was dead?'

'Muriel telephoned to both of us,' she said simply. 'We'd

spoken with her at least once a day since Sam disappeared, superintendent. Trudi lives in Ayrshire, and drove straight up to collect me in Glasgow. Then we came over together.' She glanced at her wrist watch. 'Trudi, I think it is time we moved.'

'Now?' For a moment, Trudi Andrews seemed ready to argue.

'Now,' pronounced the raven-haired woman firmly. 'The police aren't here to see us. Muriel knows we'll be back whenever she needs us.'

'True.' Trudi Andrews looked away and sighed. 'Just one last thing, superintendent. Did you know Baker sometimes beat her up?'

'Enough, Trudi. Leave it,' said Muriel Baker firmly, getting to her feet. She paused, and once again Thane sensed that silent interchange between the three. 'We can talk more next time.'

Her two guests rose, said their goodbyes and left the room. A slight nod from Thane had been enough for Sandra Craig to leave with them. When the lounge door had once more closed, Baker's widow returned to her chair.

'Do you smoke, superintendent?' she asked suddenly.

'I stopped.' He gave her a small grin. 'It wasn't easy.'

'I thought I had finished with them. Until this morning.' There was a cigarette box and a matching lighter on the small table beside her. Tiredness on her sharp face, the woman took a cigarette from the box, lit it, and took a long, deep draw, then let the tobacco smoke escape slowly. When she spoke again, her voice was resigned. 'So – he's dead. At least there's no more guessing about that.'

'None.' He waited.

'Everything I told you stays unchanged, Mr Thane.' She drew on the cigarette again. 'We married fourteen years ago, but it stopped mattering a long time ago. We still shared a roof, he used this place as a bed-and-breakfast, but apart from that he went his own way – and I went mine.' She shook her head in a way that made her mousey French pleat swing. 'So why the hell did I come close to tears at that mortuary?'

'Because of what might have been?' suggested Thane gently. Any cop heard the same kind of story. He went over and settled on the couch opposite her. 'Now my people have to find out who killed him – and why. That means we'll need to take you through your story again, from the beginning. Maybe several times. You understand?'

'Yes.' She nodded. 'I probably owe him that much.'

The neighbour-making-tea arrived a moment later, beaming at being useful and bringing two large mugs of her latest brew. After she'd gone, Thane took a thirsty gulp from his mug before he went over to the lounge door, made sure it was properly closed, then came back to pull the couch nearer to Muriel Baker's chair.

'Here we go,' he declared, sitting down. 'Don't try to rush.'

Starting at the beginning, never hurrying, backtracking any time he felt it necessary, Thane took Muriel Baker through her story in fine detail from the time of Baker's arrest in the warehouse raid until her husband's disappearance. Then on from there, until the moment when she was told that a body had been found and she was needed to identify it.

It took a full forty minutes. When they'd finished, he went back to the beginning again, questioning, gathering more detail, taking no notes – that would be someone else's job later – but mentally filing any aspect that could be worth pursuing.

That took another half hour. At the end of it all, he drank the last cold dregs of tea in his mug, sat back, and considered what he had. On the plus side, Muriel Baker's first and second versions varied in some aspects – but none that mattered. The variations, on the other hand, were just enough to make him certain that the woman facing him, her tiring voice, long drained of emotion, was telling the truth as she remembered it.

No, Sam Baker's lifestyle seldom included telling her anything he was involved in. Muriel Baker had come to accept a pattern in which he would pack a suitcase, disappear for a few days, then return and dump some dirty washing on the bathroom floor. Once a month, he also dumped a small envelope with housekeeping cash on the kitchen table. The amount was meagre – and he had beaten her when she had asked for an increase.

'Always punching to the stomach,' she said simply. 'That way, the bruises didn't show if anyone looked in. And he told me I'd be wasting my time going to the police – most of them still hid from domestic violence cases.'

Thane deliberately didn't comment. Women officers didn't

think that way. Nor did new generation cops, men and women alike – police culture had changed. But it could still be too near the truth with some older males.

Muriel Baker had given up worrrying about what her husband did when he went away. She knew there were occasionally other women, sometimes caught a scent of their perfume lingering on his discarded washing. She knew he spent a lot of his time between London, Glasgow, and other cities. She knew he went abroad, she knew he gambled. When he lost, she knew the best plan was to stay well clear of him.

In the last two weeks before Sam Baker vanished he had said nothing about having made any kind of deal with the police. But he had been progressively more nervous and more foul-tempered – at the same time there had also been occasional moments when she had seen him almost in tears.

'Why?' asked Thane.

Muriel Baker shook her head. 'I only asked him once. He threw a frying pan at me.' Her voice was brittle.' He missed.'

Ten days earlier, a police search team had checked through the house and the brick-built garage at its rear.

'If you want to do it again, go ahead,' she invited.

There was one last question on Thane's mind. 'Liz and Trudi – you'd call them good friends? They'd do most things to help you?'

'Yes.' That quick caution flared in her eyes again. 'Of course.'

'Then why did you stay with Baker all this time?' he asked bluntly. 'We're talking about a man who treated you like dirt. Yet you knew you had Liz and Trudi ready to help you. Why didn't you get out, leave the man?'

'I don't know, superintendent,' she said simply. 'Maybe I was too much of a coward.'

Then, for the first time, Colin Thane saw her in tears.

Quietly, he left the room. The hallway outside was empty, but he could hear voices and knew where to look. When they've got time on their hands, most cops, male or female, gravitate towards the nearest kitchen – and he found Sandra Craig along with Beauty and the Beast packed in there with Bill Arnott, and three of Kirkintilloch's finest.

They were drinking tea and rapidly emptying a tin of biscuits the friendly neighbour had placed on the kitchen table. Thane arrived as a howl of laughter greeted the pay-off line to a story which involved Snowwhite, Pluto and Quasimodo and a book of record breakers. Snowwhite and Pluto made it, Quasimodo having to give way to a certain notorious assistant chief constable known in every Scottish force as the Poisoned Chalice because of the way he'd been inherited from a previous Chief Constable.

Everyone knew the story, it was still ritual that everyone laughed. Every cop who wanted to survive what life could throw at them could trot out at least a couple of joke book-type stories.

'Sir?' Arnott saw Thane first and flushed.

'Try telling it using Tony Blair instead of Pluto,' he said mildly, defusing any worry about his reaction. 'Now how about getting back to work?'

He assigned Beauty and the Beast, plus one of the local men, to another combing search within the house, then gave Arnott and the remaining two Kirkintilloch officers the task of repeating the check through garage and garden.

'You and I – ' he thumbed at Sandra Craig ' – we do Baker's room. If we need to, we take it apart.'

The group split and went its various ways. Sam Baker's bedroom was on the upper floor, large and overlooking the front garden, and as they reached the top of the stairs Thane paused for a moment.

'Any problems with Liz and Trudi?'

'None, sir.' Sandra Craig shook her head. 'Like they said, they thought Baker was the original bastard. They tried hard enough to get her to leave him.'

'Why didn't she?'

'Some women are built that way, sir,' said his sergeant stonily.

He saw it was as clear an answer as he was going to get.

Sam Baker's room had obviously been a private kingdom. The faded shabby air of the rest of the house had gone, giving way to comfort and some luxury. A large television set and video recorder, satellite box attached, shared part of one wall, along with a stocked drinks cabinet and CD player. The room had wall-to-wall carpet, the window curtains were unfaded, and a large airline calendar had been tacked beside the bed. A black leather captain's chair showed all the signs of regular use. The rest of the furniture included a dressing table which had its polished top covered in old ring marks left by glasses.

There was an established Crime Squad way about searching a room. A drawer was simply taken out and its contents emptied on the floor. Carpets were rolled back, bedding was hauled clear and the underside of any mattress checked. Any clothing in Baker's wardrobe was taken out, the pockets examined. When a rack of CD discs was accidentally knocked over and went flying, it simply meant one more task simplified.

A few personal papers, stuffed in the bottom of an envelope, were still under the mattress where Thane had left them. The level in a brandy bottle had dropped, but he decided not to ask why. A small tin box in the wardrobe, one he'd forced open with a credit card last time, still contained a rolled 'emergency kit' bundle of twenty-pound notes, along with a Swedish-made spring-back knife and a spare set of Nissan car keys.

'There's still something wrong, sir,' declared Sandra Craig, looking around, a puzzled note in her voice. 'I'm not sure, but – '

'It's what isn't here,' said Thane flatly. 'Enough to get by on, yes. Spare clothes, yes. But shortages – '

'Because there's somewhere else?'

He nodded. It had to be that way. They went through what they had yet again, came across a couple of inked but anonymous 'phone numbers on the wall beside the telephone and a cleaner's tag on a jacket. A trace of white powder on the carpet beside the bed was probably talcum, but Sandra Craig painstakingly collected a sample while Thane stuffed the envelope of personal papers into his pocket.

'That's it.' He took a last look around. Beauty and the Beast could put things together again, and it was a long time since he'd eaten. 'Meal break, sergeant?'

'Sir!' The redhead beamed and almost beat him to the room door.

They located Beauty and the Beast on the ground floor, working their way through a gloryhole cupboard but with nothing special to report. Outside, Bill Arnott and his men were almost finished rummaging in the garage, going through the contents of a couple of tool cabinets.

'Anything?' queried Thane as he and Sandra Craig went in.

'Just the usual junk you'd expect, superintendent,' said the local chief inspector. He thumbed at the cupboards. 'And that's a pretty poor collection of tools – I wouldn't imagine he did much of his own car maintenance.'

'But he wrapped parcels,' mused Sandra Craig. Going over to a shelf, she lifted a handful of crumpled fragments of the grey waxed paper Baker had used around his pistol. 'Not exactly tidy, was he?'

There was a large white stain on the oil-stained concrete of the garage floor. Going nearer, Thane rubbed a foot along the edge of the bleached area. It had bubbled and flaked around its edges as the substance which had caused the stain had dried almost to a powder.

'Something spilled,' suggested one of Arnott's men.

'That wins a prize for original thought,' said Arnott sarcastically. 'Now you'll tell me it was something nasty. Right?' He grimaced at Thane. 'We just can't get decent help these days.'

His men grinned.

'I'll leave you to finish here,' said Thane. 'But do me a favour – keep a friendly eye on Muriel Baker.'

Then, Sandra Craig at his heels again, he left the garage.

Five minutes later, Thane driving his Ford and his sergeant following in her white VW Golf, left Legion Grove. This time, Thane took the old Glasgow Road out of town and, still leading, turned off on a side road. The side road took them to the Forth and Clyde Canal, then followed its route, close to the canal's old towpath. After about two minutes, the Ford pulled in at a large, busy car park and the VW murmured to a halt beside it. Then he and his sergeant walked the rest of the way along a track towards an eye-catching granite building.

The Lock Gate Restaurant had begun life in early Victorian times as a lock-keeper's cottage. Then, when most canal traffic died after World War One, it had been semi-derelict and neglected for almost half a century until new owners came along with sufficient money to gamble on establishing their new restaurant, then make it grow, make it expand, and make it a success.

As always, the Lock Gate was obviously busy and looked as if every table inside was probably filled. But the warm sunlight had tempted many customers to settle for the umbrella-covered outdoor tables beside the canal. That was where there was the

33

additional attraction of two brightly painted canal barges, both decked with flags, fitted out as dinner boats for the evening trade and moored at a stone-flagged wharf.

'Food.' The word came from Sandra Craig like a muttered prayer of thanks while she moistened her lips.' Whatever it's like, it's food!'

Thane grinned and steered his sergeant towards a vacant table. She had to be fed at regular intervals. Yet it was one of life's mysteries that no matter what Sandra Craig ate or how much she ate, her weight didn't gain a pound in the process.

'Yes,' she purred as they found an outdoor table near the canal bank not far from the big glass windows of the restaurant. 'This is fine. Like to pass me that menu, boss?'

He did. She grabbed the menu card, made a drooling noise then beamed at a waitress who appeared beside them.

'Onion soup with croutons, then the large cheeseburger with French fries and ketchup,' she ordered. happily 'What's Canal Boat Pudding?'

'Syrup covered fruit dumpling.' The waitress gave a friendly wink. 'Wall to wall calories.'

'I'll have it. And a starter bottle of beer.' Beaming, Sandra Craig handed the menu to Thane. 'Fancy the same, sir?'

Thane thought of his wife, thought of his waistline, shook his head, and settled for the beer and an Aberdeen Angus beef-burger The beers came within moments, straight from a cool cabinet. He sat back, took a swallow from his bottle, and watched his sergeant take a first mouthful from her own bottle, then the way the beer left a fine, tantalising line of froth on her lips.

'Beautiful,' she sighed.

'I'm not arguing.' Thane sat back in his chair and considered the scene, from the rows of parked cars to the patrons eating at other outdoor tables along the canal bank.

He took a more leisurely sip of beer and let it trickle down his throat. 'So – what did you make of the coven?'

'They're not exactly Macbeth's witches, sir,' his sergeant protested. 'But – ' she hesitated and frowned a little ' – all right, I think they're holding back on something.'

'I had that feeling,' murmured Thane. 'What kind of something?'

34

'I don't know.' Sandra Craig shook her head. 'But it's there, shared between them.' She nursed her beer in both hands, holding it just short of her mouth. 'They're edgy, that's all.'

They sat in silence until the food arrived. As the waitress placed the plates in front of them then left, the red-headed sergeant beamed. 'Sir – '

'Not now,' said Thane quietly, surprise in his voice. 'Look to your left, inside the restaurant. Keep it casual, like you don't notice anything.'

He heard her slow intake of breath. A couple had just risen from a window seat table inside the main restaurant, allowing them to see some of the other tables further back. Lizbeth Rankin and Trudi Andrews sat at one of them, accompanied by two men. They had drinks in front of them, and Trudi Andrews was laughing at a remark from one of the men.

Thane switched his attention to their companions. The man next to Trudi Andrews was tall, thin and probably in his late thirties, with dark hair and a sallow complexion. He wore a safari-style sports jacket with a collar and tie. His companion, beaming at Lizbeth Rankin, was older, around fifty, with thinning fair hair and a small bristle of a moustache. Thick set, slightly smaller than the other man, he wore a tweed jacket and an open-neck green shirt. The jacket had leather elbow patches.

'What the hell are they doing here?' muttered Sandra Craig. 'When they left, Trudi told me they were heading back to Glasgow.'

'So she lied – or they changed their minds,' murmured Thane.

Either way, it was no crime. He concentrated on the men again. Nothing about either of them jogged any memory, but their confident, easy-going attitude towards the two women gave him the feeling they weren't strangers. 'Any mention made of boyfriends?'

'Not to me, sir. We weren't exactly discussing social life.' The redhead glanced hopefully at the food in front of her.' Does it have to be any of our business?'

'No.' But he didn't like coincidences, whatever shape they came in. Thane sucked his teeth. 'So start eating. We don't notice them unless they notice us.'

Sandra Craig sighed her relief and got to work, while Thane took a first bite at his beefburger. While he was chewing, the window seat was filled by a new couple and he again lost most of his view of the tables behind them. Nothing happened that registered. But after a few more minutes he was hit by a growing doubt, half-rose in his seat, then cursed under his breath as he sat down again. Trudi Andrews and Liz Rankin were still at their table, but both men had gone.

He told Sandra Craig. First they watched the outside of the restaurant, hoping they might spot the pair leaving. Then, less hopefully, they switched their attention towards the car park. A few vehicles came and went, but there was still no sign of either man.

'Let's make sure of what we've got, sir.' Sandra Craig chewed at a mouthful of cheeseburger, bobbed up to make her own check on the inside table, then settled again with a groan. 'The coven pair are getting ready to go!'

'Then so are we.' Thane laid some cash beside his plate to cover their bill. 'What is Trudi Andrews driving?'

'A red four-door Renault.' His sergeant had the registration number.

'This could be none of our damned business, but I want to find out.' He shoved back his chair and got to his feet. 'Back to our own wheels and we take both cars. If they meet up with that pair again, then we split. I'll follow the men. You stick with the coven.'

Sandra Craig rose, used a paper napkin to salvage what was left of her cheeseburger, then hurried to follow Thane as he weaved back through the tables to the car park.

Two minutes later, Detective Superintendent Colin Thane gave a howling curse as he saw his Ford. Both front tyres had collapsed, the sidewalls slashed. A similar treatment had been meted out to his sergeant's Golf. But they weren't alone. At least another four neighbouring parked cars had been similarly damaged.

The knife probably used to slash all of the tyres had been abandoned beside the Golf. A small Stanley hobby knife with a scalpel-like steel blade, its red plastic handle had been given a thicker grip using several turns of black insulating tape, it was sharp enough to rip through any tyre wall in seconds. Knives like it came in sets of three, sealed in plastic and were available in every hardware store in the land. Apart from their wide use as hobby knives, they were ideal gang weapons.

36

'Bag it,' said Thane wearily. The slashings were no casual outbreak of vandalism, but guessing was one thing, proving another.

'There go the coven pair.' Sandra Craig was looking past him. Over at the far side of the car park a red Renault four-door was gently driving away. When Thane didn't answer, she dropped the Stanley knife into a plastic bag, sealed the bag and looked at him with a caution born of experience. 'What now, sir?'

'We find out if Kirkintilloch's finest know a good tyre replacement depot,' said Thane stonily. 'And while we wait, we go back and you can eat your killer Canal Boat Pudding! I paid for it!'

A tiny green light was winking on the Ford's radio console, meaning a call waiting. Getting in, Thane reached for the handset. The Squad's radios used encrypted low-band transmission, safe from evesdroppers, and in seconds a familiar growl in his ear meant he was connected to Jack Hart, the detective chief superintendent who ranked as Squad commander.

'Wherever you've been, wherever you were going, make your way back here, Colin,' said Hart in a voice like vinegar. 'This whole damned Sam Baker business is getting out of hand. And I'm dumping it in your lap.'

Somehow, Thane wasn't too surprised.

2

Beauty and the Beast were first to arrive, aboard a black two litre Audi coupé which was fairly new to the Crime Squad pool. A Kirkintilloch patrol car followed hot on their heels, bringing Bill Arnott – and the local chief inspector made no secret that he disliked his divisional crime statistics being given an extra upward tilt.

'Yet we don't know for sure that you were being targeted, superintendent,' he declared hopefully. 'It – well, these things happen, don't they? This could have been some idiot who – who – '

'Who didn't like his Canal Bank Pudding?' suggested Sandra Craig sweetly, and ignored the glare that Arnott threw her way.

37

Colin Thane sighed. Bill Arnott had to defend his corner, and the local man had some kind of a case. A total of eight parked cars had been found with slashed tyres, a small grouping that might be random, might be not. An attempt was under way to trace their owners over at the Lock Gate Restaurant. So far, they had no witnesses.

'I could put out a tracer request on the Renault that Trudi Andrews is driving,' suggested Arnott, trying to be more helpful.

'No.' Firmly, Thane shook his head. He'd had the same thought and had fought it down. Instead, he had decided to ring-fence anything involving Muriel Baker and her two friends. An instinct told him they should be handled with care – and also told him that he needed to know the real questions to ask them before he even tried for answers.

In the same way, he had to accept that the men who had been at that table with the two women were well away. That didn't mean he was finished with them. But for the moment they could wait.

He had Arnott renew his promise to keep that low-key round-the-clock surveillance on Muriel Baker. Then he pulled rank to commandeer the black Audi from Beauty and the Beast and detailed them to help Sandra Craig organise replacement tyres for the Ford and the VW Golf and carry out another restaurant area trawl for possible witnesses. That done, he gave his sergeant the task of pulling together whatever she could about Muriel Baker, Lizbeth Rankin and Trudi Andrews.

It meant Thane was on his own when he started back for Glasgow – and that in turn allowed him to think his way through the task of assembling a starter-pack plan of action. He grimaced. Apart from involving the Riverman, there was nothing in what he had put together which would gain any particular prize for initiative or originality. But that was reality in the early-days slogging which the detectives on three out of four police investigations regularly had to endure.

It was late afternoon when the Audi reached the Glasgow's city boundary. By then, after being unbroken blue for days, the sky had begun to acquire a first thin line of grey stratus rain clouds coming in from the west. More stratus cloud began building

38

during the further half hour it took to reach Crime Squad headquarters, now south-west of the city.

A few months had passed since the Squad had made the move from its previous cramped base to this new headquarters, so usefully close to the main spine of the Scottish motorways network and to Glasgow International Airport.

Before then, the Squad had been accommodated in quarters hidden at the rear of a Glasgow police training area where their nearest neighbours had been the Strathclyde Police mounted branch. The only thing in its favour had been a guaranteed free supply of horse manure for any cop with rose-growing ambitions. Thane knew plenty of local villains who would have said forget the roses – that the best thing to do with any cop was to feed him plenty of the same horse manure.

But horses and horse manure had been left behind in the move. The Squad's new location was a big, anonymous two-storey brick building surrounded by a high metal security fence. The building looked no different from the rest of its scattered neighbours in a modern business estate. In fact, one neighbour was an equally anonymous Customs and Excise anti-smuggling unit – the unit they'd teamed with in the warehouse raid – but all the others were genuine business operations.

There was nothing to mark the Squad's existence, apart from the occasional sight of a police uniform arriving or departing, or the way in which any marked police car vanished out of sight into a shielded central compound area. With a few exceptions, any visitors who called had been invited – had to be. There were CCTV security cameras and a small forest of communications aerials on the building's roof, but both were commonplace at a location only minutes away from an international airport.

Colin Thane's return had been spotted by the duty officer monitoring the main gate security cameras. The gate rolled open with the purr of electric motors, then purred shut again the moment the Audi was through. With a feeling near to being home again, Thane stopped his borrowed car in one of the individually marked parking bays then sighed and sat back for a moment, looking around.

A posting to the Scottish Crime Squad was the kind of chance any real cop dreamed about, though few ever realised. A small unit, its total strength only around ninety men and women, its people were hand-picked from Scotland's eight regional police forces. With a few particular exceptions, most served for a maximum of three years then were rotated back to their parent forces – usually fighting tooth and nail against being returned.

Being Crime Squad was a very different form of policing. It was a unit financed directly from central government and free from local ties or the kinds of restrictions too often imposed by old-style regional boundaries. As a squad, it mostly chose its own targets, which were always major. It tackled them in its own way – which meant using its own methods.

More often than not, a case was finished before a local cop knew much more than that a Crime Squad team might be in his territory. Or it might be when Crime Squad officers dropped off prisoners at some police station with a polite request for a receipt.

That part was necessary. The Scottish Crime Squad had no holding cells of its own and didn't want them. In the same way, no prisoner – and very few witnesses – ever saw inside that two-storey building. It helped fuel what was near to a nervous fear at even their name – and the ways of the Squad's members were hard to match, starting with a blend of undercover work and surveillance, part of a deliberately low profile approach. When an operation ended, much of the credit when a case came to court was quietly passed on to a local force.

But another set of rumours would circulate in prisons and spread from there out to the underworld. In terms of psychological warfare, it certainly helped.

Colin Thane suddenly came back to the present at the sight of a first spot of rain on his car's windscreen. There were only a few more spots, then the light September shower died away. But it had ended his reverie – he got out and walked the short distance across the tarmac yard to the key-pad controlled entrance door to the main building.

Two detective constables came ambling out as he reached it. Neither looked old enough to have reached shaving age, and they were dressed as what they were supposed to be – young neds, Glasgow's trademark label for two-a-penny plain layabout thugs.

'Sir.' They gave him a cheerful half salute.

'Picked him up?' asked Thane.

'Picked him up, locked him up, boss,' nodded the taller of the two.

'Good.' Thane had been at the briefing that morning when it was agreed the pair should end a three weeks old surveillance operation by nailing a paedophile ex-athlete running a small stable of under-age rent boys. 'Any problems?'

'No, sir,' the tall DC threw a grin at his companion. 'We made sure we kept our backs to a wall.'

'Want to know something?' asked Thane stonily. 'I can do without comedian cops.'

He went into the building, then crossed an entrance hall with potted plants and wall to-wall carpeting. The reception desk, a long curve of polished wood, fronted an array of monitor screens showing endless flickering rota pictures from the outside security cameras. The Crime Squad had reason to be proud of their new base – a further case for not bringing in villains from outside who might have questionable habits.

Behind the curve, a small group of men and women, mostly in uniform, were at work at computer terminals or call-centre style telephone stations. A constable in her twenties, a petite brunette with a rainbow-hued black eye, saw him, smiled, and came over.

'Commander Hart's secretary phoned down a message for you, superintendent,' she said cheerfully. 'The commander is meeting with someone right now. She'll collect you when he's free.'

'I'll be around.' Thane inspected the black eye, a souvenir of an unarmed combat training session that had gone wrong – gleefully wrong for almost everyone else. After the black eye, the brunette had nearly killed the instructor. He frowned, then gave a sympathetic nod. 'Your eye is improving.'

'Tell that to my husband,' she said tartly.

Grinning, Thane headed towards the stairway which led to the upper floor and his own office, then stopped, glared towards the typing pool area further back, and gave a resigned sigh. A lanky, long-jawed, all too familiar figure in grubby overalls and rubber boots was sprawled back in one of the typing chairs, drinking a mug of coffee. Jock Dawson, the Squad's dog handler, was lazily watching a teenage police cadet offer biscuits to the giant black and tan German shepherd dog lying at his feet. The

German shepherd, a fierce-looking animal named Rajah, lay on his back with his legs in the air, an open invitation for his stomach to be rubbed. A second police dog, a young labrador bitch named Goldie, lay curled up in a cozy, sleeping ball of golden fur on the carpet an arm's length away

'Jock – ' Thane made his voice a low-pitched growl ' – get that pair out of here! Commander Hart doesn't want them in the building.'

'Sir.' Jock Dawson sighed and shifted a little in his chair. Beside him the German shepherd brought his head round enough to glare at Thane and yawn. The labrador twitched her tail twice in friendly style, but otherwise didn't stir. The dog handler gave a hopeful smile. 'As soon as I've finished my refreshment break. Uh . . . the Federation says – '

'Stuff the Federation,' snarled Thane. 'Do it now!'

He headed up the stairway, where the walls were decorated with framed photographs of old convict sailing ship hulks from a bygone age. Jack Hart, who owned the collection and kept adding to it through car boot sales, thought that scrapping prison hulks was just one more good idea needlessly abandoned. Like it had been with hanging. Like it had been with flogging, and a few other items. At the top of the stairs, Thane looked back down again. As he'd expected, neither Dawson nor his dogs had moved. Dawson didn't like being rushed. That was the main reason why the Crime Squad had been landed with him in the first place.

But an unexpected bonus had been discovering that Dawson and his dogs could more than earn their keep any time the going got tough. They might have been landed with them. Now even Jack Hart would have battled to keep them.

Thane's office was along the corridor to the right at the top of the stairs, where more government issue plants in plastic pots were intended as part of the New Millennium decor for a police administration area. When he got there, the door was lying open, and a small, thin-faced man, looking as though he needed at very least a shave and a clean shirt, was perched on the edge of his desk and talking on the telephone. Thane was seen a moment later.

'He just walked in. I'll tell him.' Detective Inspector Phil Moss ended the conversation by hanging up, then gave Thane a glad nod of welcome. 'Hell, Colin, that switchboard lot knew you were out, but they kept putting calls through to your extension.' He scowled. 'Do I look like an answering service?'

'Not the kind I'd use,' said Thane. 'Was there anything that mattered?'

'That last one was from a cop named Arnott who says he met you at Kirkintilloch,' said Moss sourly, and came down off the desk. 'They've turned up some witness who saw a blue Transit van leave the car park where your tyres were slashed. No description of the driver, but the van was in a hurry to leave. It scraped another vehicle on the way out, but just kept on going.'

'That's no surprise.' Thane pulled off his jacket, hung it on a hook behind his desk, then settled with a sigh into his leather armchair. The old armchair was now at its third location. Originally, he had inherited the chair when he became detective chief inspector at Glasgow's Millside division. Beating the system, his chair had moved out with him – smuggled away in the back of a patrol van after dark – when he'd been promoted and posted to the Scottish Crime Squad. When the Squad moved and all furniture was replaced, he had surreptitiously moved the armchair again and got rid of the brand new issue chair which waited. Personal office possessions mattered to a cop – too few of them remained permanent.

Now? He shrugged and raised a questioning eyebrow towards Moss. 'Phil, have you any notion why I was hauled back?'

'Peasants like me never get told anything' Moss shook his head. 'Except that something isn't making our beloved commander too happy. The last time I saw him was about an hour ago. I saw him passing, I said hello, and he damned nearly bit my head off.' He scratched at his scrawny chest. 'I know about the tyre slashings. What else happened in sunny downtown Kirkintilloch?'

'Maybe more problems.' Ruefully, Thane told him.

'Women and trouble usually go together. What else would you expect?' Moss gave an embattled bachelor grunt. 'Any better luck with the Riverman?'

'He'll try.' Before Thane had gone out, he had talked with Phil Moss about what he had in mind. 'But he'll need until tomorrow.' He considered the small pile of new fax and telephone messages on his desk. 'Anything here that matters?'

'Not a lot.' Moss paused for an instant and released a low rumble of a belch. 'Strathclyde's press office – '

'Media services section,' corrected Thane with a mock frown. 'Stay with the times, Phil.'

'Same mob in disguise. Hot and cold fairytales!' Moss made it plain this wasn't a day when he felt particularly kindly toward anyone. 'Anyway, they've put out that press release about Baker's body been found in the river. No name, basic details, dull as they could make it. Radio Clyde have used it a couple of times in their on-the-hour news round-ups, and the late evening papers will have it.'

'Good.' Thane found the faxed copy, glanced through it, and was happy. The unidentified body of a man fished out of the Clyde didn't make headlines, but someone somewhere was going to be very interested. He shuffled through the rest, then glanced up.' Still no lead on Baker's Nissan?'

'Still no lead, and a team still trying.' Moss glanced at his wristwatch, large and old-fashioned with an expanding metal bracelet which had seen better days.' I'll make more threatening noises to encourage them. Then – ' he looked pointedly at Thane ' – then I've the usual suspects to chase about case reports.'

'Guilty.' Thane had paperwork hidden in his desk drawers, some of it going back over a couple of weeks. There were even team expense sheets he should have signed. When they weren't paid, he wouldn't be popular. 'But I'll work at them soon – that's a promise.'

'And a promise that sounds like a tape recording.' Moss gave his senior officer a disbelieving scowl and left, closing the door hard behind him. A minute later, a new rumbling belch sounded from the tiny office down the corridor where the shuffling detective inspector had his personal lair.

Thane chuckled at the sound. Detective Inspector Phil Moss was another inheritance that went back to Milllside Division days. Wiry, always untidy and in his late fifties, Moss had already been a DI – and his stomach ulcer almost a legend – when Thane had arrived at Millside. They had become close friends, with Moss finding himself adopted as an honorary uncle by Thane's children.

And Phil Moss hadn't really changed since then. His thinning, mousey hair badly needed a trim and he still looked as though he had slept in his clothes then had forgotten to shave. Yet, for reasons no male could really understand, most women were instinctively and sympathetically drawn towards him. At least one old lady had stopped him in the street and given him money to 'buy a cup of something hot'. A succession of landladies had tried to coax him into bed or marriage – sometimes both, and not just for the possible security that might eventually come with a police pension or even the police widow's variety.

But the same Phil Moss was also an abrasive, acid-tongued cop, always happy to wade into a back-street punch-up regardless of the size of the opposition. Equally important, Phil Moss could at times almost enjoy the report work which Thane could literally loath.

As a team, they had been briefly split when Thane moved to the Crime Squad and Moss had gone off for overdue and not particularly successful stomach surgery. After that, Moss had been invalided to an indoors headquarters post – but within a few months, and right in the middle of another crisis time, the small, bleak-eyed detective had somehow managed a transfer to the Crime Squad.

Where his skills were needed maybe more than ever.

There were skills and skills. Thane heard a deep-throated barking from outside. He left his desk, went over to the window, and saw Jock Dawson ambling across the building's central courtyard followed by the two dogs. Several squad cars were always parked in that area, one of them being Jack Hart's official Jaguar. As always, the giant German shepherd reached the commander's car, sniffed at one of the front wheels, then raised a leg and relieved himself in spectacular style. But Jock Dawson had always claimed those dogs could read his mind.

Thane went back to the messages on his desk. They were update reports from some of the several police forces and law enforcement agencies now working on what had become the Baker murder inquiry. One group were continuing the hunt for Baker's missing car. Another group, including Criminal Intelligence, were bringing together every recorded mention of the man, from known associates to general background. It included the period when he served prison time and went on to include a list of creditors who had lost money when he went bankrupt – all the way down to the cost of a meal at a carry-out Chinese restaurant.

Electronically stored records, computerised files – it was the way most modern criminals were eventually tracked down. Even if, so far, there was not a computer that would handcuff a suspect and drag him out to a waiting police van.

That was maybe for next year.

Thane was still sorting through the scatter in front of him when there was a knock at his office door. As he looked up, the door opened.

'God wants you for a sunbeam – or something. And he means right now,' the well-groomed middle-aged brunette who looked in said it stonily. 'Take a tip, Colin. Don't keep him waiting.'

'Thanks for the warning, Maggie.' Thane grimaced his thanks and rose. Maggie Fyffe was Commander Hart's personal secretary. She was also a cop's widow and not afraid of anything that wore trousers, but a very accurate barometer of Hart's moods. 'Want to tell me what his problem is?'

'Would I rob him of that pleasure?' There was a trace of irritation in her words. 'There are times when the man is totally impossible. So heel, boy!'

Thane followed as her high heels clipped a way back along the corridor and on past her room to Jack Hart's private office. She knocked lightly on the ribbed glass door, opened it, gestured Thane through, but stayed outside as she closed it again. That left him facing Jack Hart. The Squad commander, immaculate in an expensively tailored dark blue suit, white shirt and carefully knotted dark red tie, was behind his large bleached walnut desk.

'Sir.' Thane started with on-duty formality.

'Ah, the return of the wanderer!' said Jack Hart sarcastically, then thawed. 'Sit down, Colin. I'm having a bad day, and you make the place look untidy. Do you know what the price of car tyres does to our budget?'

'I might know a friendly fence who could give us a good deal,' said Thane with a small grin.

'Colin, today I don't want funnies. Right?' Hart, a man in his early fifties with thinning grey hair and a lined, sad-eyed face, had a quiet voice which could hold a cutting edge. He watched as Thane took the chair already placed opposite the desk, then sighed. 'I've just said goodbye to a Crown Office clown who came to suggest that we should trim ten per cent off our budget.' His words became a low snarl. 'Ten per cent? On present form, they'd probably use it to send our better class villains off on holiday breaks to Spain!'

'Like we were going to do with Sam Baker,' mused Thane.

'I haven't forgotten.' Hart picked up a pencil from his desk, looked at it, then impatiently slapped it down again. 'You know that I totally backed you on Baker. Well, it now looks as if we were very right.'

'Because of the way he was murdered?'

'Partly.' Hart stopped as his office door opened again and Maggie Fyffe came in. She was carrying a small tray, which she placed on the Squad commander's desk. A lot could be learned from the way coffee break visitors were treated. This time, things didn't look totally good. She was using plain brown pottery mugs, with a single sugar coated doughnut on a plate for Hart, who nodded his thanks.

He waited until Maggie Fyffe had left, then leaned forward with his elbows on his desk. 'Baker's wife that was, widow that is – you think she didn't seem to know much about how he earned a living?'

'It looked that way,' said Thane carefully.

Hart munched, they sipped coffee, and Colin Thane considered the Squad's commander. In the police world, Jack Hart ranked as a detective chief superintendent, but with an autonomous power and authority that went much higher. His next step up – if he wanted it and when he wanted it – would see him appointed assistant chief constable in one of the largest forces. And the force that got him would be lucky.

Hart continued demolishing his doughnut in a scatter of crumbs and sugar coating and Thane killed time by looking around the big executive-style office. As always, a prized antique-style police helmet had its place on top of one filing cabinet and one of Hart's latest acquisitions, a long-bladed, brass-handled cutlass, was mounted behind his desk. Up until mid-Victorian times, a sword-like cutlass had been part of a Scottish beat cop's equipment – but then, so had a water key for shutting down burst water pipes, a pole for lighting gas lamps and, to complete the Christmas tree effect, a shovel and a small broom to sweep a clearway for pedestrians at street crossings where horsedrawn traffic was heavy.

Balancing that, one whole wall of Jack Hart's office was covered by a large-scale map of Scotland which reached to take in the Outer Isles. At their last location, a similar map had been studded with pins to mark Crime Squad target operations under way. But now, New Millennium-style, electronics had taken over. Press a button and lights would glow or wink in a variety of colours. Hart and Maggie Fyffe were supposed to know what the different lighting codes meant – nobody else did.

'Right.' Hart took a final swallow of coffee, slid his coffee mug aside and brushed some stray flecks of sugar from his jacket front. 'Here's the bottom line to date. I had a telephone call at about noon today from a government junior minister. He invited me to lunch, but I said I couldn't make it.'

'Your long spoon was in for repair?'

Hart nodded soberly. 'There's no such thing as a free lunch. That goes double for politicians – particularly that one. So then we talked. He knew a "someone" who had been very glad to hear that our Sam Baker was dead.'

'How did his "someone" know so early?' Thane frowned.

'Because there's a certain Fraud Squad cop who has a good memory and a valid reason to tell him.' Hart leaned forward. 'Our sensitive soul lives in Edinburgh. He's a friend of the junior minister, and ready to talk. But he wants a guarantee of total anonymity – he points us in the right direction, then we forget he exists.'

'And?'

'I said yes.' Hart smiled in a wolfish way. 'He'll come through from Edinburgh tomorrow, and you'll meet him here, ten a.m. A Fraud Squad officer will be along too. Use my office. I've an Interpol meeting in Brussels tomorrow.'

'But – ' Thane knew his mouth had fallen open.

'In your usual diplomatic way you now want to ask if I'm tiptoeing through the politicians,' said Hart softly.

'Are you?' asked Thane bluntly.

'When insulting a senior officer, the correct form is "Are you, sir?"' frowned Hart, unperturbed. 'You haven't asked, but our

48

sensitive soul's name is Sir Andrew Silverhill. You've – uh – heard of him?'

Thane swallowed and gave a nod. An Olympic gold medalist of a few decades back, charity worker and church leader, the man known as Andy Silverhill was a living legend. If he was involved—

'Before you ask, I don't know the full story.' Suddenly, Jack Hart was totally businesslike. 'But it sounds as if, given the chance, he would have nailed Sam Baker's hide to the wall.'

Methodically, they took it from there. Every possible lead relating to the smuggling team had been followed, and it had emerged as a relatively modest operation. Even while Baker claimed to be working for the Crime Squad a small team of officers had begun digging back into his total past.

With little success. The bankrupt one-time insurance agent emerged as colourless, without real friends or close relatives. If he had a weakness it involved gambling – mostly on horses. There were wide gaps when he would simply disappear for a week or so. Sometimes, when he reappeared, he could have a newly acquired tan. Following him hadn't worked. Baker would do nothing for hours – then suddenly disappear.

Sam Baker had been nervous. Sam Baker had been frightened. But it was as if Kirkintilloch was only a small segment of his life, that the rest – the rest that mattered – had existed somewhere else.

And now he was on a mortuary slab.

'I read the autopsy report,' said Hart. He spotted a few grains of sugar on his desk top, moistened a forefinger, and mopped them up. 'It said there were other tests under way. Been in touch with them yet?'

'I thought I'd ask Phil Moss – '

'Moss could do it standing on his head,' agreed Hart. 'But the way this is building, I'd rather you showed the flag. A lot of people could eventually be interested in this one – I'm getting noises that a few already are.' His mind moved on. 'Still nothing on Baker's missing car?'

Thane shook his head.

'Then what's left – the Riverman?'

'If we're lucky,' There was still a mouthful of now cold coffee left in Thane's mug, and he drank it

'And Baker's widow? Her friends? These men?' demanded Hart.

'Sandra's working on that, with help. She may come up with something. Either way, I'll move in more people.'

'Which leaves you.' Hart built a steeple with his fingertips and considered Thane over the top of it. 'Colin, you've some other cases on your existing workload.'

Thane nodded. They included a practised team with a new method for ripping bank cash dispenser machines out of filling station forecourt walls. All it took was some planning and a fork-lift tractor. Right beside it was a drugs wholesaling operation, mostly into heroin and using a legitimate frozen food door-to-door delivery service's warehousing operation as their base. There were others in various stages of ripening.

'Either put them on the back burner or farm them out. As of now, Baker has total priority – and keep me posted. Right?'

Thane nodded. The signal was flying that the session was over. Shoving back his chair, he got to his feet.

Finding Phil Moss wasn't difficult. He was in the main duty room, growling at the two detective constables who had become part of Thane's small private team. Ernie Vass, the older of the pair, was a solidly built individual in his thirties who chain-smoked small Dutch cheroots. He was married, and his past included serving as a CID officer in Aberdeen – that after being eased out of the Grampian force's traffic department for bending one police car too many. Teamed with him – a marriage of total opposites – Dougie Lennox, was slim and tall with a boyish face and fair, curly hair. Lennox had arrived after being on Edinburgh CID's murder team – and brought with him the reputation for a relentless pursuit of every female over the age of consent who came his way.

Thane was seen. The growling noises stopped as he went over.

'Something happening?' he asked.

'Nothing vital,' said Moss, with a vinegar-like glance which encompassed Vass and Lennox. 'These two are more interested in when they'll get their leave.'

'When and if,' said Thane stonily and drew a sour glance from both men. They were due off on leave, Vass and his wife planning a 'harbour lights' trip back to their Aberdeen haunts,

Dougie Lennox booked on a sex and sangria singles break to Ibiza. But their leaves depended on relief officers who so far hadn't arrived.

'Sir – ' began Lennox.

'Not now. Later.' Thane shook his head. 'Phil – '

He beckoned and led Moss across to a window which showed a first few specks of rain from a sky now filled with grey clouds. It was a between-shifts time of the afternoon and, except for the two DCs, they were the only people in the duty room.

'From the look on your face, we've a problem,' murmured Moss. 'And I mean more than just our beloved commander.'

'Which wins you a prize,' confirmed Thane sadly.

Hands in his pockets, he looked past Moss and for the first time noticed that the duty room was at last beginning to lose its brand new look and was taking on a patina of general wear. Above all, compared with their former quarters, this duty room had ample, uncrowded space to house everything from desks and computer terminals to large, busy noticeboards and dog-eared wall charts. An open partitioned sector along a length of one wall was occupied by a professionally lit make-up mirror beside a bank of TV and audio recording and playback facilities. Nearby, a line of secure cupboards and lockable grey metal filing cabinets held some of the specialised equipment used by Squad officers, men and women alike, in surveillance operations. Then there were the two basic items which were vital to any police duty room – a large microwave oven and a wall-mounted thirty-cup coffee percolator.

There was a gleaming, well-equipped canteen in the basement of the building, but that was never quite the same – Thane came back to what mattered.

'Starting now and Sam Baker becomes our total priority,' he told Moss bluntly. 'Except we're not really talking Baker, but he remains the way into the rest of it. We're talking Tablets of Stone. Clear enough, Phil?'

'Crystal clear!' said Moss sarcastically. 'Says who, apart from Himself?'

'Sir Andrew Silverhill.' Thane saw the blink of disbelief that crossed Moss's thin, leathery face. 'He's coming here tomorrow morning, brought by a minder. So wear a clean shirt and stand closer to your razor.'

51

'Andy Silverhill!' Moss gave a soft, tuneless whistle. ' Hell, when I was a child I got his autograph – '

'You were never a child,' said Thane acidly. 'You were adult-size when you fell off a production line.'

'Silverhill,' persisted Moss. 'Why?'

'I don't know.' Thane shook his head. 'But he matters. His friends matter, damn them. So we double-check everything, Phil – including the p.m. report.' Then he got in just ahead of Moss. 'I know. You checked the p.m. report. I'll do it this time – and that wasn't my idea.'

'Enjoy ... and you're welcome.' Moss scowled at the rain on the window, and pursed his thin lips. 'I was thinking – Jock Dawson and his dogs aren't doing anything. We could send him over to Kirkintilloch to have a look around that canalside, then take that pair for a swagger around Baker's house.'

Thane nodded agreement. There was little chance of any result from it, but even showing willingness could sometimes matter.

They went on from there, agreeing a Records check on Baker's widow and her two friends, organising extra officers anywhere they might be needed during the overnight period ahead. That included the continued priority of locating Baker's missing powder blue Nissan. That meant, in turn, widening the search to take in most of Central Scotland, combing yet again through the inevitable airport, ferry and rail parking lots, then the less obvious possibilities like vehicle scrap yards – and even, because it wasn't unknown, a search of police vehicle compounds for what might be hidden and forgotten.

It amounted to a long list. In the night ahead, scores of officers in plenty of police divisions would be out searching, plodding, and cursing. It was what beat men still called 'pulling padlocks'. A monotony that went with the job.

'Then we've these two.' Thane thumbed at Vass and Lennox. The two DCs had drifted away, Vass smoking one of his cheroots, Lennox looking half-asleep. 'Put them to work, Phil. I want them to run another check on anyone listed as being a known associate of Baker.'

'Asking what?'

'About Baker's other life.' Thane sucked on his teeth. 'The other life he lived away from his wife, away from the Kirkintilloch nest. All along, that's what has mattered. So we're back to the same old questions.'

'Meaning what did he do, where did he go?' Moss nodded. 'So we try to find somebody who knows maybe just enough to give us a lead – I'll get them started.' He rubbed a thumb along the faint stubble on his chin.' But why the hell haven't we heard from Sandra?'

They both knew the answer. As soon as her team had anything worth reporting, they'd hear. Until then, the red-haired, often fierce-tempered Detective Sergeant Sandra Craig just didn't believe in wasting time.

Fifteen minutes and a scatter of organising-type telephone calls later, Colin Thane left Crime Squad headquarters and again headed in towards Glasgow. One of the 'phone calls had been to the City Mortuary, where an unusually fraught-sounding atttendant checked then confirmed that Doc Williams, the police surgeon, was still around and would stay to meet him there. The other call had been to Thane's home.

But it was after four p.m., school was out for the day, and the number engaged. His daughter and son both regarded use of the telephone as somewhere ahead of food and drink on the life-needs scale.

Neither of the cars was back from Kirkintilloch, and he once more borrowed the black Audi. He was on his own again, the rain keeping up a steady tattoo on the car roof while the windscreen wipers kept to their hypnotic sweep. With his only company the soft crackle of static from the car's radio, he had a chance to think, to put together what had been done to date and assemble the priorities from what came next.

Andy Silverhill – all right, Sir Andrew Silverhill – was a totally unexpected addition to the scene, the complication of a living legend he could well have done without. Whatever his involvement might be ... and Thane had his own hero-worshipping memories of an Olympic champion.

Some of the memories were still in his mind as he reached the city, drove through its busy, rain-soaked streets, and approached the City Mortuary, a red brick building close to the High Court of Justiciary – sensibly close, being where many of the Mortuary's reports would eventually end.

Parking was never easy around the Mortuary area. Thane squeezed the Audi into a space with a Parking Prohibited notice, sharing it with another car. It was only when he had switched off and was about to get out into the wet that he recognised the other vehicle.

He swore pungently. The vintage black Daimler limousine, an immaculate veteran, was only too well known around Scottish police forces. It meant that Professor John MacMaster, who held the Regius Chair of Forensic Medicine at Glasgow University, was in attendance. Yet why, when the Sam Baker autopsy had been carried out by Doc Williams and the police surgeon had certified and signed the 'On Soul and Conscience' report?

There were always other autopsies, other cases with problems. But Thane had a nasty gut feeling that he could forget that hope.

He got out of the Audi, loped through the steady downpour of rain, reached the main door of the mortuary, and went into a wide tiled corridor. He'd only taken a few more steps when a window hatch in the corridor wall banged open. The duty attendant stuck his head out and saw their visitor.

'You're expected, Mr Thane.' He beamed a greeting.' Nice to see someone alive now and again. How's it going, sir?'

'Not too bad, Fred,' replied Thane mildly 'I'm still perpendicular.'

'And what more can anyone ask?' the man cackled. 'Wait a moment.' The hatch slammed shut again. Thane heard him use a telephone, the soft ting as the instrument was replaced, then Fred, a small, balding man, emerged from a door further along and beckoned.

'Fred – ' Thane didn't hurry ' – does Doc Williams have company?'

'Too right.' The attendant winked. 'Professor MacMaster arrived an hour or so ago. He just appeared – which didn't make the Doc's day.'

'It wouldn't,' said Thane neutrally, then followed the man along a corridor which had a harsh, antiseptic odour.

'I've a new joke for you, Mr Thane,' said the man cheerfully. 'I've a new fun-word for you. Do you know what a sitcom is?'

'No, Freddy.' Thane managed not to groan. Mortuary jokes were usually old and always dreadful – like the tea they kept brewing in a blackened metal teapot in the staff kitchen. If you didn't know the pay-off line the best thing to do was to get it over quickly. 'Go on.'

'Sitcom – Single income, two children, oppressive mortgage!' The man beamed, and Thane forced the obligatory laugh.

They reached a door marked Private where his escort gave a quick double knock, opened it, and waved Thane through into a large room with white tiled walls and a hose-down tiled floor. It contained two autopsy tables with stainless tops, floor-level drains, and a surrounding fringe of benches and forensic equipment. As the door closed behind him, he saw that only one table was in use, the body on it covered by a sheet. Two men stood beside the table and in the background a technician worked quietly at an electronic rig.

'Good to see you again, detective superintendent.' Elderly, tall, and skeletally thin, Professor John MacMaster was a forensic legend who wore an old-fashioned white hospital workcoat over a dark business suit.

'Professor.' Thane nodded. MacMaster had watery blue eyes, ill-fitting, occasionally clacking false teeth, and a frosty formality of a smile which had frozen obedience into decades of University medical students. One of those students had matured as the middle-aged police surgeon now standing beside MacMaster – something the Regius Professor never allowed Doc Williams to forget. Thane looked from one to the other. 'What's going on?'

'Crown Office in Edinburgh, superintendent.' MacMaster showed his teeth in another mirthless smile and indicated the sheet-covered body. 'They feel that a second opinion might be helpful. There could be sensitive aspects of this death, they wanted everything to be – ah – '

'Watertight?' suggested Doc Williams stonily. He was slim, dark-haired and immaculate as always, and wore modern hospital theatre greens with ankle-length rubber boots. He knew his job, few better – and he combined his status as an expert witness with being a star on the Rotary after dinner speakers circuit.

'Watertight?' MacMaster converted a scowl into a thin, self-deprecating smile. 'Very droll. Mainly, of course, it was a matter of our formally agreeing what had already been established. But – ah – we moved on a little from there.'

Doc Williams had eased slightly behind the Regius Professor. He gave a tight grimace towards Thane, the type which didn't need translating.

'I've read the initial autopsy report,' said Thane slowly. 'What's changed?'

'Nothing – as far as the rather simplistic conclusions go.' MacMaster stepped nearer to the autopsy table, flicked back a corner of the sheet, and exposed Baker's head and slack-jawed face and the start of his naked body. What the post mortem work had done, added to the earlier river damage, wasn't pretty. The dome of the skull had been removed, as neatly as slicing off the top of an egg. 'A hairline fracture of the skull was located – about here.' MacMaster gestured a short curve of an arc on the right temple. 'It was caused by a single blow, and the weapon used was a hammer or something of the sort. The – ah – impact of the blow would render him deeply unconscious.'

'But it didn't kill him, Colin,' bravely interjected Doc Williams. 'That's for sure.'

'Important to remember it, superintendent. Before we project a possibility on from there.' The Regius Professor gave one of his frightening on-and-off smiles and rested his fingertips on the autopsy table's stainless steel top. 'Let me explain, keeping everything as simple and as non-medical as possible – '

'The old bastard never changes,' murmured Doc Williams, so softly that only Thane could hear.

For a moment, Professor MacMaster's face seemed to freeze, and Thane wondered if his hearing was better than Doc Williams realised. But it passed. Tapping the metal table top, demanding attention, MacMaster went into lecturing mode.

Death by drowning was an asphyxial death, with post-mortem signs to match – and while on the one hand a victim could drown face-down in just three inches of water, the intensity of a struggle to survive, with continued attempts to breath, left its own traces.

'When a victim has fallen into water in an unconscious state, the principle evidence of that is in the lungs and respiratory passages.' MacMaster used a long, bony finger like a pointer.

56

'But respiration will only continue at a low level. There will not be the same pattern of lesions or of cerebral haemorrhage.'

Then there was the text-book test. Water entering the lungs passed to the left side of the heart – and as a result, blood from anyone drowned in salt water presented an elevation of chloride content which could be up forty per cent. Drowning in fresh water similarly reduced chloride content.

'Based on experience, I agree that the man Baker drowned in the waters of a tidal river. I also agree that death most likely took place around eleven days ago, as you estimate, superintendent. But now – ' MacMaster swept back the entire sheet from the body beside him ' – we have other matters to consider. There are a number of definite post-mortem bruisings around the trunk and shoulders of this cadaver. Would you like me to hazard a totally unscientific opinion?'

'Based on long experience,' muttered Doc Williams viciously.

'Go ahead,' invited Thane quickly.

'This man was still alive but unconscious when he went into the river. The bruisings indicate to me that he may have been placed inside a car – even in the boot of a car. That a door or the boot lid burst open with the force of water that resulted when the car rolled into the water and sunk, that the bruises were caused as this man, by then dead, floated free.' MacMaster paused and beamed. 'Naturally, Doctor Williams would have reached the same conclusions if given a little longer to complete his examination.'

Thane looked from the Regius Professor to the dead Sam Baker and swore softly.

'One other thing, perhaps only incidental,' added MacMaster, giving that pleased smile again. 'An illustration.' He turned to a workbench beside him, switched on an ultra-violet hand lamp, brought it over, and played the strange bluish light on Baker's left arm. 'Look closely, superintendent. More bruising, caused by injection needles – modest in number, of course. But – ah – your victim appears to have been a fairly regular mainliner.'

'We've started blood tests,' contributed Doc Williams doggedly. 'They'll take time, but if we're lucky we may still be able to tell you what he used.'

MacMaster had laid down the lamp. He beckoned the technician, and as the man came over and replaced the sheet over the body, the Regius Professor glanced at his wristwatch and began to unbutton his hospital coat.

'I'm due to lecture a lowing herd of University students,' he explained, folding the coat over his arm. 'But – ah – I'm sure my colleague can guide you through any remaining elemental details, superintendent.'

'Professsor – ' Thane held up a hand as MacMaster turned for the door ' – tell me one thing. How well do you know Andy Silverhill?'

'Silverhill?' MacMaster hesitated then gave a small, tight smile. 'Well enough, superintendent. We – ah – sometimes golf together. Satisfied?'

Thane nodded, watched him leave, then turned as he heard Doc Williams give a snort.

'The trouble is, he's still always right,' complained the police surgeon. 'I'll go along with him that your man was probably believed dead and was dumped in a car. Before you ask, the Forensic Bureau got his clothes in the usual way. We haven't heard from them yet, but I wouldn't look for any miracles there.'

Thane politely refused the offer of a mug of mortuary tea, then managed to dodge the hovering attendant as he left the building. There was still a drizzle of rain falling, but as soon as he was in the open he stopped to take a deep breath of the smog-tainted air – and felt better for it.

The ancient Daimler limousine had gone. When Thane got back to the Audi, it had collected a parking ticket, which he stuffed in his pocket. He got aboard, saw the green call-light was on, and radioed Crime Squad control. Yes, he was told, they wanted him. Another moment and he was speaking with Phil Moss.

'I tried to get you at the mortuary,' complained Moss over the set's soft static hum. 'All lines engaged – if they're all dead in there, who does the talking?'

'Problems?' asked Thane.

'Two.' Moss didn't waste words. 'Sandra called in. She hit trouble.'

'What kind?'

'A break-in at the Rankin woman's home. It was trashed, but nothing stolen. Sandra thinks she knows why, and she's heading out of town to Trudi Andrews' place, in case the same thing happened there. Either way, she wants the local cops to keep an overnight eye on both places.'

'Fix it, Phil.' When Detective Sergeant Sandra Craig asked for help, Thane didn't argue. 'What else?'

'The Riverman phoned. He was looking for you.' This time, Moss was less certain in his attitude. 'He had visitors at the boathouse. They tried to quiz him about what happened when he found Baker.'

'And?'

'He chased them.' Moss gave a graveyard chuckle. 'He threatened to put the sharp end of a boathook through one visitor's guts, then belted the other on the head with a boat thwart, whatever the hell that is! But when I offered to get people over, he said no – no way. Not if we wanted his help.'

'We'd maybe damage his reputation as a neutral,' said Thane sourly.' And we need him more than ever.' He told Moss about the Regius Professor's theory.

'That old devil MacMaster usually means what he says,' admitted Moss. 'So if the Riverman can backtrack us to where Baker went in, maybe we could find the car as a bonus?'

'Maybe.' Thane sighed. 'But do nothing about the boathouse, Phil. I'll go over to see the Riverman right now, try to talk sense into him.'

'You, talking sense? It'll be like the blind leading the blind,' grunted Moss. 'How about you taking along some personal back-up?'

'Oh ye of little faith,' countered Thane. 'No need.'

'Your choice.' Moss didn't argue. 'In case it slipped your memory, you've a wife waiting at home. Mary 'phoned. She said you were supposed to call her.'

'Damn.' Thane sighed. He'd meant to try again. 'I tried, but – '

'No problem,' said the scrawny detective inspector with a surprising cheerfulness. 'In fact, I've to come round and eat with you tonight. I always say that wife of yours is a decent woman – and God knows why she chose you as a husband!'

'Go to hell,' snarled Thane. When he got home to eat, if he got home to eat, he was now condemned to an ulcer-friendly meal. Fries and calory-rich sweets would be off limits. It would more likely be steamed fish and a milk pudding.

'Nice to know I'm wanted,' chuckled Moss. 'I said I'd make it around seven.'

Thane met the start of the homebound evening rat-run traffic as he drove out of the city. He followed the line of the river towards King's Bridge and the Humane Society boathouse and checked a couple of local radio news bulletins while he travelled. Most of their time slots were taken up by reports of a fire at the new Scottish Parliament over in Edinburgh, which didn't break his heart. Jumping channels, he listened to each right through and heard no mention of the Body Found item put out by Strathclyde's press office.

It often happened that way. The hour by hour importance of any news item depended on the competition. What the police media squad were still offering as just another Clyde drowning – even duller, one with a nameless victim – no longer rated as worth a mention.

When Thane reached his destination, he took the Audi down the same side road track he'd used earlier and stopped at the same parking space near the Humane Society boathouse landing stage. The weather was clearing, only a trace of rain still falling, and the sun was reappearing as he left the unmarked car and began walking along the path towards the boathouse.

It took a minute or so before he realised that there was no one else in sight and that he had the path to himself, which was unusual. Puzzled, still walking, he was suddenly alert – and at the same moment two men stepped out from some bushes and appeared on the path ahead. They didn't move, watching him approach.

'You, pal,' growled one of the men suddenly,' where are you heading?'

'The boathouse,' said Thane neutrally, keeping going. 'Who's asking?'

Both men were in their early thirties and unshaven. One had a deep scar down his face, the other had a tiny attempt at a moustache and a gold ear ring on his left ear. Both wore the standard daytime rig of a Glasgow ned – grubby football-type tee shirts and faded denim jeans. Their feet were in heavy lace-up boots, the industrial safety type which offered the fighting bonus of hidden steel toe-caps.

'Why the boathouse, pal?' said the scar-faced man softly. 'What's your business there?'

'Personal, with the Riverman.' Suddenly, Thane knew he might now have reason to regret turning down Moss's suggestion of back-up. Oh hell. Oh, ye of little faith –

'Forget it, mister,' growled the second man. 'Turn around. No visitors today.'

'Do me a favour,' murmured Thane. 'Get lost.'

'No visitors – we're turning you round.'

'Don't even think it,' said Thane grimly.

Their eyes told him a split second before it happened. The scar-faced man came in, holding a rubber cosh he had dragged from his hip pocket. His partner, only a pace or so behind him, had a spike-faced brass knuckle-duster in his right fist.

'We warned you!' The cosh swung in a vicious arc.

Except Thane had side-stepped, was no longer there. As the cosh came up again, he went in close to his attacker, rammed a knee into the man's crotch, heard a whoop of agony, then, as the crew-cut head folded down, Thane slammed an elbow hard into the scarred face in a way that brought a jet of blood from the man's nose and that attacker staggered back. Then it was the man with the knuckle-duster's turn. Thane avoided a savage kick, blocked a blow from the knuckle-duster, and in return pistoned his right fist into the second attacker's middle. He heard a yelp, then saw the thin moustache twist in pain as the man fell back.

The scar-faced attacker lurched in again and once more Thane tried to dodge the swing of that rubber cosh. This time, he wasn't so lucky and the cosh partly connected with his upper arm with enough force to be numbing.

'Not him, you bampots!' The warning roar came from a third figure now rushing towards them from the boathouse direction. Thick set, similarly dressed, the third figure roared again. 'He's a cop – a boss cop, you dumb great idiots! Give over!'

The two men fell back, panting, suddenly contrite, one clutching his middle, the other with blood still pouring down his face.

'You all right then, Mr Thane?' asked the newcomer, reaching him.

61

'Yes.' Breathing heavily,Thane looked at the burly, earnest figure and relaxed a little. 'Do these two headbangers belong to you, Tank?'

'Aye, sort of, Mr Thane.' Tank Grant was embarrassed and showed it. Thane knew him, he knew Thane. They had clashed in a few back-street brawls, Thane had arrested him twice, then Phil Moss had put Tank into a hospital bed by ramming him into a metal door. There had never been hard feelings on either side.

'Running an escort service now, Tank?' asked Thane dryly.

'Just – uh – doing the Riverman a wee favour,' explained Grant unhappily.

He pointed to the nearest of his pair. 'Go get the Man. Now!' As the man trotted off towards the boathouse, Grant turned back to Thane.' We heard there was this wee bit of bother earlier, Mr Thane. See these two that went for you? The Riverman's father hauled both of them out of the water years ago.' He grunted. 'He shouldn't have bothered.'

'And you?' Thane's arm was still numb, but he decided that otherwise he was still intact.

'Me?' Tank Grant gave a serious scowl. 'A few months back, he pulled my oldest kid out of the river. Danny looked dead, but the Riverman gave him the full artificial respiration bit, saved the silly wee sod's life. I owe him. So – ' he grinned hopefully ' – well, if I was still in the army, we'd be volunteers, right?'

'How did you hear about the trouble?'

'Local kids.' The man shrugged. 'You know how it is.'

Thane did. And, looking past the man, he saw the Riverman already hurrying from the boathouse.

'We'll – uh – be more careful next time, Mr Thane,' promised Tank Grant. 'Fair enough? We'll still be around but more careful, right? This is our patch.'

'Make it very careful,' said Thane soberly. 'No more vigilante stuff.'

The Riverman reached him a moment later and Tank Grant thankfully eased away.

'They meant well, Colin,' said the Riverman, giving Thane his gap-toothed grin. 'And you hurt them more than they hurt you.' He gestured with his hands. 'They – well, just wanted to help.'

'So what happened here?' asked Thane bluntly.

'Two men, ties and cheap suits, turned up. It was less than an hour after the first radio news after I brought in that body.'

'And then?'

The Riverman's eyes hardened a little at the memory. The two visitors had claimed the unidentified dead man he'd brought in might be a missing friend. What had he looked like? Had the police found any clues that might help identify him?

'Then they lost patience and tried shoving me about,' the Riverman frowned. 'One waved a knife around. That didn't make me happy.'

'And you brained one with a chunk of wood, then threatened to gut the other with a boathook?' Thane grinned. Whatever the situation, he'd have backed the Riverman.

'Only threatened,' protested the muscular Humane Society officer. 'It would have been like using a harpoon on butter!'

'Can you describe them?'

'Not easy,' confessed the Riverman. 'Average height, average build, both mid-thirties.'

'Hair?'

'Dark, close-clipped – a number three clipper.' The Riverman saw Thane's surprise. 'I like to keep up to date in trivia detail, Colin.'

'Would you recognise them again?'

'Yes.' The Riverman reached into his shirt pocket, brought out a carefully folded piece of paper, and handed it over. 'I thought this might help.'

Two pencil sketched faces looked out at Thane. Ordinary enough faces, hard around mouths and eyes. They meant nothing – and they weren't the men he'd seen at the Kirkintilloch restaurant.

'Thanks.' He refolded the paper and put it in his own pocket. 'Anything else?'

'They had transport – parked it where you've left your car.' The man shook his head. 'Sorry, I couldn't get the licence number. They didn't hang around when they left. But they had an old Peugeot station wagon, metallic green in colour. Does that help?'

Thane nodded. The way things were shaping so far, anything did.

'I'm coming up with some good database material on your floating bodies puzzle,' volunteered the Riverman. 'But I still need time. Suppose I have it ready for noon tomorrow?'

Thane promised he'd be there.

3

He blamed Phil Moss.

Phil Moss, who had solemnly assured Mary Thane that her detective superintendent husband would be home by seven that evening. Phil Moss, who had also declared that would be the ideal time to arrange their meal. And the reality? At eight, Colin Thane was still stranded in the Crime Squad building, and when he did try to 'phone home, it was inevitable that the line seemed permanently engaged. When he did manage to escape, he knew his welcome could be burned at the edges.

There was only one consolation. His Ford had been returned from Kirkintilloch, and someone out there had been generous when it came to replacing his slashed front tyres. The Ford now had a new set of treads all round – and Thane decided to ignore the transport pool sergeant's pointed sarcasm that some Kirkintilloch cop would now have a low-mileage set of rear tyres as a private freeby bonus. Who would foot the bill was something accountants could argue about.

Thane had only intended a mere passing through look-in at headquarters before leaving for home. Instead, he met a minor flood of situations, all demanding attention – and, for once, no DI Moss to cope with them. Unusually, Phil Moss had walked out with the simple announcement that he had people to see. When he left, he had signed off for the night.

'That's all I know. But I've some good news, boss,' declared Ernie Vass. The bulky Aberdeenshire detective constable clenched a cheroot happily in his teeth. 'It's positive – my holiday relief will be here tomorrow, first thing!'.

'Good,' said Thane absently. He thumbed at their other leave candidate. Dougie Lennox, hovering in the background, looked less happy. 'What about him?'

'Still waiting, boss.' Vass looked over at his fellow DC and the cheroot gave a sympathetic waggle. 'Still, something might still turn up.'

'Might.' Thane tried to sound encouraging, then set to work.

On top of the latest bundle of messages on his desk were two notes of radio calls from Sandra Craig. Both declared that his sergeant would 'call again later' – the redhead's way of saying she was busy and didn't want to be annoyed.

Meantime, Criminal Records had a full computer search into anything they had on file on Muriel Baker and her two coven friends. There wasn't much – but one surprise was that the friendship between the newly widowed Muriel and the raven-haired Liz Rankin went back more years than Thane had antici-pated – back to when they were both still in their early twenties. They had both been arrested during a drugs raid at a city dance hall. Together, they had admitted being found in possession of 'illegal substances intended for personal use'.

Two tabs of cannabis didn't exactly amount to a crime wave, and they had been admonished. It had happened at a time when cannabis had become almost a fashion accessory, and the court's response had been only a warning slap on the wrist.

That had been Muriel's only formally recorded transgression. But then, another few years later, Liz Rankin had again been in court. This time she had been fined for heaving a complete wedding cake through a second-floor window at the height of a drunken wedding reception. It hadn't helped that the cake had landed on the head of the local beat constable, sent to cool things down after complaints from neighbours.

That left Trudi Andrews. The baby of the coven had once received a suspended seven days jail sentence, similar to a 'go away and don't do it again' verdict. She had attacked a late-night prowler who tried peering in her bedroom window. After-wards, he had needed serious hospital treatment.

No big deal situations. But they were enough to mark the trio as women who should not be ignored.

A little later, Jock Dawson brought his dogs back after their show-the-flag patrol around Muriel Baker's home area of Kirkin-tilloch. The dog handler had nothing that mattered to report, but produced an overtime sheet he wanted initialled. Other Squad members came and went, each at some stage of a long list of follow-up inquiries that continued to yield nothing new. The Riverman's pencil sketches of his two strangers were photo-copied then sent over to Strathclyde's Identification Bureau. The faxed all forces appeal for information on any blue Transit van with bodywork damage was repeated with an add-on about a metallic green Peugeot shooting brake and upgraded to Special Search status.

Then, with the time already past seven o'clock, Sandra Craig radioed in again. Her call was patched through to Thane's desk 'phone.

'So where the hell are you?' demanded Thane sourly.

'Still south of Ayr, sir.' Like Thane, she didn't sound in any mood for taking prisoners. 'We're finished here.'

'Good.' Ayr, the Burns Country holiday town on the Clyde coast, was about thirty-five miles away by road. Thane glanced at his watch. 'Then you should be back in less than an hour?'

'We're due a meal-break first, sir.' The redhead gave him no chance to argue. 'You'll remember. The latest Federation guide-lines agreed with the Association of Chief Police Officers insist – '

'Whatever you say,' capitulated Thane, in no mood for the kind of negotiation that could happen when Sandra went into Squad delegate mode. 'So how did it go?'

'Unspectacular.' For a moment, there was a faint hum of static somewhere between her car and Squad headquarters, then her voice was back again. 'No break-in down at Trudi Andrews' place. From Kirkintilloch, her first stop was to drop Liz Rankin off near her home in Glasgow. Then she headed for Ayr, did some shopping locally, and wasn't long back home when we arrived. She said that she hadn't been contacted by anyone since she arrived – '

'So she can say she didn't know about Liz having visitors,' accepted Thane. 'All right, what about the Rankin break-in?'

'Front door forced, clean and professional.' She paused again, and Thane heard a chewing noise. There was either a hungry mouse at work somewhere on the line, or a starving sergeant had started on one of her emergency stock of chocolate bars. 'It has all the looks of a quick in-and-out job, every room turned upside down. Some jewellery is missing, some cash has gone. But they didn't touch a near-to-new digital TV or a Sky satellite box.'

66

Things that wouldn't have been left in any ordinary, opportunist break-in. They both knew it.

'Neighbours?'

'Either out at work or pensioners too busy watching TV, sir. Heard nothing, saw nothing, until one woman returned from a shopping trip and saw the front door lying open.'

'Typical.' Thane made it a growl. As break-ins went, it could have been lifted from a standard Crime Prevention script. All of which, at least on the surface, seemed routine enough. 'What's Liz Rankin saying about it?'

'A lot!' Sandra Craig gave an almost admiring chuckle. 'What she thinks of today's world and what it contains. Her personal Pilgrim's Progress etched in acid!'

Remembering Liz Rankin's CRO sheet and what it hinted, Thane could believe her. 'And friend Trudi?'

'Much the same, sir. I was asking, not stirring.' Meaning his sergeant had avoided mentioning the real reasons why she was visiting them at their homes, had probably blamed Thane for wanting more general background. Blaming him was her favourite theme, something she had developed to a fine art.

Liz Rankin still worked in insurance in Glasgow, and had come up through the ranks into personal accounts management. From once being Sam Baker' secretary, Trudi Andrews was now employed in the Ayr office of an estate agency as a well-paid house sales negotiator.

Had they gone anywhere after leaving Muriel Baker's home? The question had been put mildly, and both women had volunteered that they'd had a meal at the Lock Gate canalside restaurant.

'What else did they say about being there?' Thane waited for her answer. It mattered.

'They obviously didn't know we'd been outside, so I didn't tell them.' Sandra Craig paused and frowned.' Liz just said they ate there and left it at that. Trudi volunteered how a couple of men tried to pick them up. According to Trudi, she and Liz gave them the deep freeze treatment – eventually the pair realised they weren't getting anywhere and left.'

Thane cursed under his breath. It was the kind of simple, easy to believe story which could torpedo a lot of possibilities.

'What do you think?' he asked.

'It might be that way,' said the redhead warily. 'Just an attempt pick-up.'

Thane grunted. 'And does that explain why our tyres were slashed?'

'No, sir.' Sandra sighed. 'I – uh – there's also something I thought you'd like to know. According to one of her neighbours, Trudi has a new regular boyfriend called Gary.'

'Sergeant, you've made my day,' said Thane gloomily. 'Be in first thing tomorrow, as usual – and goodnight.'

He hung up before she could reply.

'Trouble, Colin?' asked an amused voice close to his ear. He turned and faced a grin from a slim golden tanned woman with short dark hair. Crisply smart in a knee-length tailored brown skirt and a white linen shirt-blouse, Tina Redder was a detective chief inspector of uncertain age who operated a Crime Squad drugs team. The grin took on a slightly malicious edge. 'Let me guess, dear friend of mine!. That was your Baby Sergeant reporting in.'

'Yes.' Thane saw Tina Redder's grin widen.

There was little love lost between DCI and sergeant. Tina Redder had first launched the Baby Sergeant label, and Sandra had countered by tagging Tina as the Broomstick Lady. The truth behind that, agreed by every male, was that the Broomstick Lady had, without challenge, the best looking legs in the Squad. Tina Redder knew it, and usually wore the highest of high heels to emphasise the fact.

Even Sandra was willing to admit that the Broomstick Lady knew her job inside out – and odd moments of weakness, usually when she didn't think anyone else was listening, Tina Redder had been heard to return the compliment.

But neither did it in the other's hearing.

'What's Baby Sergeant done this time?' Tina Redder gave a vinegar-sweet purr, her eyes twinkling dangerously. 'Is it something simple where I'd want to help?'

'When she needs help, I'll let you know,' said Thane. This was one between-females war he wasn't going into. He sighed and tried to avoid looking at her legs, which wasn't easy. 'Do me a favour, Tina. Stay off her back.'

'You've got it wrong, Colin.' The Broomstick Lady chuckled.

'That girl needs a sympathetic, more experienced female around. Someone like me – even if she doesn't know it!'

Then someone was shouting outside in the corridor, saying that the DCI was wanted on her 'phone. As she left, he took his chance and fled.

Colin Thane drove to his home on the south side of the city through the slow, gradual twilight that was a feature of Scotland's northern September evenings. Most of the way, he listened to a Golden Oldies radio show soothingly built around the late, great Francis Albert Sinatra. Clear of the city, into suburbia land, he twice exchanged headlamp flashes with other vehicles. One was driven by a uniform branch inspector who had committed the heinous crime of being a little too rude to an assistant chief constable and seemed condemned to perpetual night shift. The other vehicle looked like a florist's van but was being used by a plain-clothes team targeted on break-ins. The van driver was ex-Millside division, and gave Thane an 'old times' wave.

Then he had arrived. Home was a small bungalow in a street of houses that were all identical except for an occasional extra porch or a satellite dish here or a new paint job there. He turned the Ford in at his driveway entrance, stopped, got out of the car, spent a moment's hate on a neighbour who had the time to pander to rose bushes, and looked around with the proprietorial pride that came from still getting used to the fact that he'd paid off the mortgage. Then as he opened the front door a large tan and white Boxer dog named Clyde dived out towards him.

Man and dog went through the usual brief frantic tussle that established they knew each other, then Thane went in.

Mary Thane was in the kitchen. She was dark-haired and atttractive, she had been working over pans at the stove, but she stopped and glared at him.

'You're late,' she accused.

'That's possible,' admitted Thane and fielded a well-flung washing up cloth. 'At least you noticed.'

'I noticed.' Mary thawed and let him kiss her nose while Clyde, once more assured the world was intact, retreated to his basket in a corner.

'Phil here?' asked Thane, splashing water on his hands and face at the kitchen sink.

'Here, and arrived on time.'

'He's being fed for free.' Thane found a hand towel and used it.

Mary was wearing loose-fitting chino trousers and a tie-belted grey silk blouse. He looked at her again. His wife had been a hospital casualty room nurse and he had been a young beat cop when they'd met and married. Now she was part-time manager at a local health clinic, as well as being mother of their two adolescent children. Yet somehow she didn't seem to have changed along the way. That included still taking size twelve dresses – necessary, she said, because she couldn't afford anything new.

She watched as he replaced the towel. 'Rough day?'

'I've had better,' he confessed. The house seemed quiet. 'Where's everyone?'

'Front room. You can sort them out – if you and Phil ever want to eat.' She thumbed him on his way.

He found Phil Moss hunkered down on the lounge carpet, with the two junior Thanes as an enthralled audience. Tommy, older by a mere couple of years, was at the large, awkward and pimple-faced stage. His sister Kate already had much of her mother's colouring and good looks with signs of more to come. Thane's arrival hadn't been noticed as they concentrated on Moss's expertise with a short length of borrowed school plastic ruler and two pennies, one penny showing heads, the other tails.

Moss flicked the ruler. The pennies shot up and landed separately on the carpet. Tommy and Kate peered and groaned.

'Both tails,' declared Moss. One hand clawed up the small scatter of staked pennies lying in front of him. 'So you two lose!' Then he saw Thane and nodded a greeting. 'Some add-on further education, Colin.'

Thane swallowed. Pitch and toss was one of the oldest, most vicious gambling games in the world. He'd seen pitch and toss cause a riot outside a football ground. He'd been at racetracks where punters with real money didn't give a damn about the horses compared with what happened to two little coins on a stick. Phil Moss's roots were in Lanarkshire, where striking

70

miners had in the past organised pitside pitch and toss schools with hundreds of players.

'One thing to remember, you two.' Moss frowned at his audience and simultaneously dropped his winnings into a pocket. 'Gambling is usually against the law – if you play with money in sight. But if you keep your own mental scoreboard, then what you do afterwards is different. Right?'

'Right,' they chorused sadly.

Moss handed the school ruler back to Kate. Then he winked, got to his feet as Thane beckoned, and followed him out of the room.

'Keeping your winnings?' scowled Thane.

'That's the real world,' said Moss, unperturbed. 'Some day, they'll thank me.'

They ate in the kitchen with Mary, as the children had already been fed. Pandering to Moss's ulcer, there was a herb flavoured chicken casserole and the sweet that followed was a plain apple tart with ice cream. Mary backed the menu with three small budget-priced cans of white wine, then sighed when Moss gave a politely restrained belch.

'Phil, I'll only tell you this once more,' she appealed. 'You could get that ulcer fixed without any more surgery. Things have moved on. There's a drug treatment, antiobiotic style. I could speak to a specialist who sometimes consults at our clinic – '

'No way!' Moss stiffened. 'Mary, I'd sooner trust a damned vet – ' he nodded approval as Clyde's stump-like tail quivered at the magic word ' – yes, a good, honest-to-God vet. No-one in a white coat is ever again getting near my plumbing. Not ever!'

'I tried.' Mary sighed and got to her feet. 'You two can wash up. There's a TV weepie show I don't want to miss.' She left them, and Thane did most of the washing and stacking, knowing it was better that way than relying on Moss's bachelor systems.

At the finish, he opened a cupboard and produced two tumblers and the remains of a bottle of twelve-year-old Oban Single Malt. He poured their drinks, and they took them back to the kitchen table and settled down.

'So – ' Thane sipped his whisky. Until then, they hadn't talked shop. 'Why did you disappear this afternoon?'

71

'Call it tidying.' Moss tasted his own drink and gave a contented murmur. 'Strathclyde's lab people are finished with Baker's clothing, nothing special to report, except they located what was left of a cleaning tag inside a jacket pocket. They're working on it – but it will be tomorrow before they've any results from the drug test samples from the mortuary.' Setting down his glass, Moss ticked other items on his fingers. 'That stain on Baker's garage floor is industrial solvent – more on that also later. Scenes of Crime say they've no unaccounted finger-prints at Baker's home. They also went back to the booze warehouse and tried there again – no change.

'But after that, I did some research digging on tomorrow's visitor – '

'Andy Silverhill?' Thane blinked. 'Why?'

'Call him Sir Andrew,' corrected Moss with a gnome-like grin. 'And as for why – why not?' He took a quick swallow of whisky, burped and kept the glass nursed in his hand. 'First I looked in on someone who owes me a favour in Special Branch. Then I saw an ex-cop who has come back into SCRO as a civilian, and I finished off visiting a couple of newspaper cuttings morgues – but everything off-the-record, guaranteed!'

'Well?' Thane tried to read the lined calm face opposite him. 'What did you get?'

'I'm not sure.' Moss grimaced. 'Before Andy Silverhill got his Olympic medal, he was on the wild side. That changed him – all round. But – ' he paused uncertainly.

'But what?' Thane seized on his lieutenant's hesitancy.

'Something happened about eighteen months ago,' said Moss carefully. 'One story was that he had heart trouble, another that it was more like a nervous breakdown. He backed out of hosting a royal visit, he resigned from a few charities.'

'Nothing more?'

'One or two photographs, before and after.' Moss shrugged. 'He'd aged a lot.'

'And we're looking at possible fraud, maybe mega-fraud.' Thane drank the rest of his whisky in a long, slow swallow. He brought over the bottle and topped up both glasses. 'All right. My turn.'

He brought Moss abreast with his side of things, ranging from

72

MacMaster at the City Mortuary to his brush with the River-man's unofficial posse. Then there was Sandra Craig's report from Ayr and various other pieces to be added. A long, thin spill of chicken casserole had left an eye-catching stain down Moss's shirt. But Moss didn't seem to notice anything unusual and gave occasional, punctuating grunts of surprise or derision.

Tomorrow they had Sir Andrew Silverhill. Then back to the Riverman. But tomorrow was when they had to focus in on Sam Baker's background again – a background which was still more shadow than substance.

They had people who had seen Baker, they had people who had spoken with Baker – yet what they had to date told them very little about the Sam Baker who mattered. Thane talked his way through much of it again, deliberately using Moss as a sounding board.

'We need more about Baker's past.' His fingers restlessly tapped the tabletop in emphasis 'Things like his insurance agency before it went belly-up. After that, there's his time in prison – then who did he meet when he came out? And how did he get into liquor smuggling? Along that route somewhere are some of the answers we need.'

'Well – ' Moss frowned, sucked his teeth, then surprised Thane ' – yes, you could be right.' Then he gave a quick, gnome-like grin. 'But quote me on that, and I'll deny it.'

It was close on midnight and Clyde was snoring in his basket by the time they decided that there was nothing more that could be done before morning. Moss left on foot, turning down the offer of a lift home. They both knew that, being Moss, he would quickly 'just happen' to come across a prowling night shift patrol car.

Phil Moss had spent a lifetime learning that kind of little detail.

The rest of the house was silent. Thane locked the front door, went back into the kitchen, looked down at his snoring dog for a moment, then put out the lights and went upstairs. There was only silence as he went past Tommy and Kate's bedroom doors, but there was still an edge of light showing under the main bedroom door. When he went in, Mary looked up from the pillows. She had been reading, using the bedlamp.

'You two took long enough.' His wife yawned a criticism. 'If you have to set the world to rights, have neither of you heard of office hours?'

'We've got problems.' Thane grimaced an apology and began changing into the pyjama trousers laid out on his side of the bed. Mary, he noticed, was wearing the jacket. 'You shouldn't have stayed awake.'

'Think of the scintillating conversation I'd miss.' She yawned again. 'You're bad enough. But I know what Phil Moss needs.'

'A wife?' Thane slipped into bed beside her, conscious of her warmth and her soft perfume.

'A wife?' She chuckled and the bedlight was switched off. 'No, with him we're talking a serious keeper with a choke chain and collar. Forget Phil – ' she moved nearer ' – I've enough problems with what I've got. Where are you?'

They found each other a moment later.

Next morning, Wednesday, there were still dark rain clouds around but the streets were dry. Showered, shaved and dressed, thinking of Andy Silverhill as he chose one of his best white shirts and a knitted maroon tie, Colin Thane teamed them with his grey suit and his usual scuffed mocassins. Downstairs, wrapped in her dressing gown, Mary had coffee ready and fed fragments of biscuit to Clyde while Thane drank a single cup of coffee and ate two slices of toast. At seven thirty, the first faint noises beginning to come from Tommy and Kate's rooms, he kissed Mary goodbye and went out to the Ford.

The time was too early for the usual peak morning rush hour traffic and things stayed reasonable throughout his journey to work, and at exactly five minutes before eight a.m. he reached the Crime Squad compound and parked his car. Sandra Craig's white Volkswagen Golf was already there, but the vehicle lying next to the VW, an elderly red open-top MG two-seater with a faded black canvas hood, was a puzzle. Thane didn't recognise the licence plates, but that didn't matter too much – Crime Squad vehicles had their plate numbers changed at regular intervals to confuse the opposition.

But he shrugged, knowing the MG wouldn't have got into the compound without security clearance, and walked over to the headquarters building. He arrived there as most of the off-duty night shift were leaving and went upstairs, then into the duty room. It already held most of the day shift arrivals. Phil Moss, standing talking with Sandra Craig, nodded a greeting. Most of the people around were nursing mugs of tea or glancing at newspapers, and he noted Dougie Lennox gossiping to Jock Dawson. The lanky dog handler was without his dogs – Dawson didn't like them being disturbed too early in the day.

'Hello, superintendent.' There was an unmistakable Highland lilt in the voice beside him. One he remembered. 'Good to see you again, sir.'

Thane turned and looked in surprise at the young woman beaming at him. She was small and well-built, with dark eyes, raven-black hair, and an attractive, pert-nosed oval of a face.

'What brings you down here, Maggie?' he asked.

'Temporary posting, sir.' The smile stayed in place. 'Holiday relief.'

Maggie Donald was out of uniform, smartly dressed in a grey linen jump suit with a dark green silk cravat at her throat. She was a Northern Constabulary constable, although how she'd got through her force's minimum height requirements was a mystery. About a year before, as a Northern traffic officer, the same Maggie had been part of local assistance when Thane had taken a Crime Squad team north on a case which had involved murder and arson.

He understood, and it made sense. A driver for a driver. 'You're standing in for Ernie Vass?'

'Yes, sir.' Her eyes flickered across the room towards Dougie Lennox, who quickly looked away. 'I heard you had two DCs going on leave.'

'Yes. But the other relief hasn't come through.' Thane remembered something else. Up north, Lennox had made a play for Maggie Donald who at first had reacted like a hypnotised rabbit faced by a fox. But then Lennox had over-played his hand – and had ended nursing a magnificent black eye. He smiled, partly at the memory. 'Anyway, enjoy your time with us. Where will you be living?'

'I've an aunt in Glasgow.'

'Good.' He nodded. Anyone from north of the Highland Line had an aunt in Glasgow. 'Do you belong to that MG outside?'

'Yes, sir.' Her eyes showed she was pleased he'd noticed.

'Fine. For now, any problems you check with DI Moss. Remember him?' He took their temporary recruit across, turned her over to Phil Moss, and beckoned Sandra Craig aside.

'Phone Liz Rankin's home, Sandra. If she's there, tell her we're coming visiting.'

'Like now, sir?' His sergeant raised a surprised eyebrow.

'Like now,' agreed Thane.

He took a few minutes to check the overnight log to make sure that there was nothing in it from the night team that he should know about. Then he got hold of Moss and told him where he was going.

'While I'm out, Phil, keep an eye on our little Highlander,' he added.

Moss nodded. Then Thane saw that Sandra Craig was waiting, and he went over to join her.

They used Thane's Ford, but he let his sergeant take the wheel – partly so that he could think through the interview ahead. Partly, he also had to admit, because he liked to watch the confident way she drove.

Sandra Craig was wearing a freshly laundered outfit of denim trousers and a sleeveless waistcoat, teamed with a white rollneck sweater. Her feet were neat in black trainers, her burnished copper hair had been brushed until it glinted in the morning sunlight, and was held at the nape of her neck by an antique-style silver comb. She was humming one of her favourite Country and Western tunes above the steady murmur of the engine. Almost reluctantly, he broke his silence. 'What did Liz Rankin say when you told her we were coming out?'

His sergeant chuckled. 'She didn't think she could wait – she was due in at work.'

'And?'

Sandra Craig gave him a bland sideways glance. 'I said you'd be happy to come to her office, and she changed her mind.'

He gave a small, mirthless smile. As a tactic, it usually worked.

'Sir – ' his sergeant fell silent for a moment, concentrating past a clutch of three city-bound double-deck buses, packed with passengers and travelling as if tied together with string. Then

76

she slotted in ahead of the leading bus, ignoring an indignant horn blast from the driver. 'About Liz Rankin. How do we play it?'

'Strictly by ear,' admitted Thane. 'We see what happens.'

Sandra Craig digested that, nodded, and went back to her humming. This time, he recognised the tune. His sergeant always liked Dolly Parton's 'Nine to Five', and Thane had long ago decided never to ask why.

Liz Rankin had a flat in Cunard View, a modern four-storey apartment block located on the edge of Partick district, north of the river. They used the Tunnel route under the river to save time, and when they got there they left the car in a Residents Only zone. From there, they went into a building which had carpeted stair treads and polished brass name plates. Tenants would regard the thought of any outsider calling Cunard View a tenement as an act of war.

Although it was exactly that – in modern dress.

Thane and Sandra Craig headed up to the second floor landing, his sergeant's slim, younger legs getting there ahead of him, the way he'd expected. When they stopped, an oak finish front door had a brass nameplate which simply said Rankin. Edges of repaired wood along with a replacement lock told of an insurance company which, when leaned on, could still respond with tradesmen in a hurry.

Thane tried the bellpush and a buzzer sounded inside. They heard the sound of quick footsteps, then the lock clicked, the door opened, and Liz Rankin greeted them with a frosty politeness.

'Sorry about this, Miss Rankin. Not my idea,' lied Thane in a mild way which made his sergeant blink. 'This can't be helped, but it won't take long.'

'Come in.' The woman stepped back to let them enter. She closed the door firmly once they were inside, led the way through a modest, carpeted hallway which had small decorative wood carvings on the walls, and showed them into a comfortably furnished lounge. It had a large, almost floor-level picture window which gave a view across rooftops to the distant river, and beyond it to the buildings on the opposite bank.

'Quite an outlook,' said Thane.

'I pay handsomely for it in the rent, superintendent,' said Liz

77

Rankin shortly. She gestured towards armchairs around a glass-topped coffee table, where a leather briefcase lay on the glass top. The top had been wiped, but still showed small traces of grey fingerprint powder. 'Sit down, please. Let's do this as quickly as you can.'

Thane took one armchair. Sandra settled in another and brought out a notebook from her shoulderbag. Once her visitors were seated, Liz Rankin chose a chair directly opposite, with the coffee table between them.

Thane took a moment to consider the woman. This was Liz Rankin in her insurance management business mode – make-up light but effective, that short, expensively styled black hair immaculate, dressed in a tailored navy blue suit which had a mandarin-style jacket collar and a mid-calf skirt. Her black leather shoes had modest cuban heels. Her jewellery was suitably restrained – a large Rennie MacIntosh-style silver brooch pinned high on the left breast of her jacket, a watch with a thin silver bracelet worn on her left wrist, and a man's gold signet ring on her right forefinger. She sat straight-backed, knees together, skirt carefully smoothed down, hands clasped lightly on her lap.

'Well, superintendent?' She was impatient. 'I've already 'phoned to tell my office I'm delayed, but no longer than is necessary.'

'Good.' Thane gave her a small twist of a smile. 'Then let's start with more questions about yesterday.'

The woman frowned. 'I told your sergeant – '

'And now it's my turn,' murmured Thane. 'You've had time to check around after the break-in. You told Sergeant Craig that some cash and some jewellery had been taken. Anything more?'

'No.' She shook her head.

'You're sure?'

'Positive.' Liz Rankin shrugged. 'I'm just another item for the next police annual statistical report, superintendent. Things like my break-in happen several times every day, don't they? Some opportunist thief realises I'm out, takes his chance, forces my door.' She turned to Sandra Craig. 'Sergeant, didn't you say it would all have only taken minutes?'

Sandra Craig nodded. Five minutes was usually enough for a

78

straight in-and-out job. More than ten minutes meant a thief was practically stealing the wallpaper.

'Suppose this wasn't an opportunist thief.' Thane rubbed a thumb along his chin, watching the woman. 'Once he got in here, can you think of anything he might have expected to find?'

'No.' Her mouth tightened a little. He saw her hands were gripping more tightly on her lap. 'Like what, superintendent?'

Thane shrugged. 'I hoped you might have been able to tell me, Miss – Ms – ?'

'Ms is becoming unfashionable, downright dated, superintendent.' She frowned. 'I don't mind you calling me Liz.'

'Then I'll do that.' Thane shaped a smile while his grey eyes took a slow glance around the room. A small mahogany display cabinet held a few small ornaments, and he noticed a small, strangely stylised greystone figure of a squatting man who clutched his knees. Then two silver-framed photographs on the top of the cabinet caught his interest. One, a posed group, showed Liz Rankin and Muriel Baker, with a young Trudi Andrews grinning between them.

'I like your threesome photograph,' said Thane casually. 'When was it taken, Liz?'

'Four years ago.' Liz Rankin had been watching his inspection. 'We had a holiday together that summer.' Her voice thawed a little. 'We get on well together – always have, even though Trudi is so much younger.'

'Baby sister?' suggested Sandra Craig.

'Baby sister,' agreed the woman.

'And the other photograph?' It was a head and shoulders studio portrait of a strikingly handsome, dark-haired man in an airline pilot's uniform, complete with a captain's stripes. Somehow the features were familiar.

'My brother, Robin.' For a moment, Liz Rankin fingered the gold signet ring she wore. 'He died when his 'plane crashed in Africa.'

'I didn't know. I'm sorry.' Thane glanced at Sandra Craig in a way which said she should have known, should have told him. 'When did it happen?'

'Six years ago, superintendent.' The woman glanced at her watch, the message clear. 'Can we move on?'

79

'You told my sergeant how you and Trudi stopped for lunch at a canalside restaurant in Kirkintilloch – '

'But I didn't mention two clowns who tried to pick us up.' Totally composed again, Liz Rankin cut him short and gave a small, apologetic nod. 'Trudi telephoned me from home last night – after Sergeant Craig left her. We talked, she said she'd told Sergeant Craig.' She shrugged. 'There are plenty of men in this world who act like clowns, superintendent. I didn't think they mattered.'

'Tell me about these two,' said Thane grimly. 'Had you ever seen either of them before?'

'No.' She met his eyes calmly.

'You're sure?'

'Yes. Why?'

'Because I'm investigating a murder.' Deliberately, Thane made no mention of how he and Sandra had been at the restaurant or how their car tyres had been slashed. 'Then when you left, Trudi drove you back to Glasgow?'

'Old ground again, superintendent,' she said resignedly.

'All right.' Thane decided to get to what mattered. His voice took on a new edge. 'Let's talk about Sam Baker. You've said you grew to loathe him. Trudi was his secretary and came to despise him. Muriel was his wife and he seems to have put her through hell, even beaten her. He was a convicted crook, we know there's a chance he was into drugs. In short, Sam Baker was – '

'A pig,' said Liz Rankin unemotionally.

'A pig.' Thane nodded. 'Then why didn't Muriel leave him a long time ago?'

'He was her husband.' Liz Rankin drew in a deep breath and looked at Sandra Craig as if seeking support. 'Trudi and I suggested it often enough. But Muriel is one of these old-fashioned women who just accepted, stayed loyal,who wouldn't break her marriage vows.' She shrugged. 'There are still a few like that around. As a woman, sergeant, would you agree?'

'Maybe a few,' said the redhead warily. 'Not too many.'

'Sam Baker was someone very different when we first knew him,' said the dark-haired woman grimly. 'But that was – well, a long time ago.'

'And, back then, it was you and Sam Baker who were the

80

item. Yes, he eventually switched to Muriel and married her. But she only came into things later.' Pausing, Colin Thane laid his hands flat on the glass tabletop. Then, slowly and deliberately, he asked what mattered. 'Liz, did Sam Baker ever visit you here?'

'I – ' Liz Rankin's mouth fell open and she stared at him.

'Did he?' demanded Thane, iron in his voice. 'Did he visit you recently, maybe ask you to look after something for him?'

'No. That's a crazy idea.' The colour had drained from her face. Her hands gripped the front of that mandarin jacket so tightly that her knuckles showed white. 'Sam Baker wouldn't come here. I – I would have slammed the door in his face. He knew that.'

She was lying. It was there in her eyes, in the way she moistened her lips. But Colin Thane didn't want to push things too far – not yet. He needed the woman's help. 'Maybe he didn't, Liz. But I reckon that someone thought he did – and that he asked you to keep something for him.' He sat back and sighed. 'Think about it, Liz. It gives a very valid reason why there was a break-in here. Someone came looking for what Sam Baker might have left.'

'It's nonsense.' Liz Rankin spat the words like ice chips.

'Is it? A lot of people might think it could have happened.' Thane held her gaze. 'When the police told Muriel that Sam was dead, who was the first person she told? You! Then how many people did you tell?'

'I told nobody. Not in so many words. I – well, I had to cancel appointments and I had to arrange to take yesterday off.' She bit hard on her lip. 'I – yes, I think I maybe told some people that a friend's husband had died. But nothing more.'

'Then we'll leave things there – for now. But think about it. You could maybe help us in more ways than you realise.' Suddenly, without warning, Thane rose to his feet and a sur- prised Sandra Craig followed his example. 'For now, I'm fin- ished.' He looked down at Liz Rankin, who hadn't moved. 'When are you going out to Kirkintilloch again?'

'Tonight.' Looking up at him, Liz Rankin moistened her lips again. 'Trudi is picking me up after work.'

'You've a lot to talk about,' said Thane dryly. 'Any time that any of you decide there's something more I should know, get in touch. But don't leave it too long.' He paused. 'Going to work now?'

'Yes.' A bitter glimmer of a smile touched her lips. 'Thinking of offering me a lift, superintendent? Don't bother. I'd feel safer in a taxi. And you can see yourselves out.'

They did. Sandra Craig stayed ominously silent as they walked down the main stairway, and until they were on the pavement outside the block.

'Something wrong, sergeant?' he asked mildly.

'Yes – sir.' Her voice was frosty. 'Was I supposed to like the way you badgered that woman.'

'No.' Thane looked at her and sighed. 'Sandra, do you think I liked it?'

She swallowed hard. 'Then – '

'She could have had things a lot worse. I left her a with a choice, Sandra.' He looked up at the sky. The threatening rain clouds had retreated again, the sun already felt warm on his face. 'Whether she takes that choice is up to her. For now, we'll move out of sight and wait.'

They went back to the Ford and got aboard. The call-light was glowing on the radio console, but for the moment Thane ignored it while he drove the car out of the Residents Parking zone and down to the next street corner. He turned in, reversed once he was out of sight of the Cunard View building, then crawled back to the corner so that they could watch the entrance to the block.

Sandra Craig produced a fat red apple from her shoulder bag and took a first crunching bite while Thane used the radio to check on the waiting low-band call. In a few seconds Phil Moss was on the other end.

'Mostly a reminder call,' said Moss without apology. 'You're due back here for ten a.m. – will you make it?'

'Would I keep the Blessed Jimmy waiting?' Thane grinned at the microphone. 'I'll be there.' But he told Moss a relief car was needed to continue a watch on Liz Rankin. The woman's office, Rex Insurance Agencies, was in Cadogan Street, near the heart of Glasgow. 'Fix it, Phil. They either rendezvous with us there, or we'll advise by radio if anything changes.' That settled, he asked, 'Anything new at your end?'

'A Crown Office mandarin has been twittering by 'phone

about how Andy Silverhill should be handled with tender, loving care.' Moss grunted. 'Hell, from the way the bampot talked we've even got the thumbscrews ready.'

'I forgot to indent for them,' said Thane. 'Apologies to the mandarin. Maybe we'll just use batons wrapped in razor wire. So – what else?'

'The Scientific mob say they can't offer much help about Baker and his drugs habit. They managed to isolate cannabis in the blood and tissue samples from the mortuary along with traces of paracetamol – you know, ordinary painkiller. But needle marks usually mean opiates, and opiates disappear damned quickly from the human body. So that's one possible lead shot down.'

'We can't win them all,' reminded Thane.

'Why not?' complained Moss. He treated the low-band radio waves to a mild belch. 'Some other bits and pieces have come in, but they can wait.'

Thane thanked him and ended the call. The drugs angle hadn't been important, just part of the background build-up which would have to continue – and if it had failed, then at least that was one possibility less to think about.

Sandra Craig produced another apple, Thane took it, and crunched into it. Minutes crawled past. Further along the street two small and noisy boys dashed around on roller blades while a yelping mongrel dog tried to join in. Thane located a Jazz Classics programme on the Ford's factory-fitted FM radio, and for a spell, while the redhead at his side sat bored, he let the orchestral styles of King Oliver and Jelly Roll Morton fight a battle for his vote. The original 1920s shellacs were scratchy and almost primitive in their sound quality, but they were for real – and he was glad no clever-clogs record producer had so far tried to digitalise them.

'Sir .' Sandra Craig suddenly dug him in the ribs and pointed. A black taxi had just pulled in at the pavement outside the Cunard View block.

Thane killed the jazz programme, took a last bite from what was left of his apple, tossed the rest of the core into the car's rubbish bin, and then they waited. Within two minutes they saw Liz Rankin emerge from the building. She was wearing a light-weight white raincoat and carrying her briefcase. She got aboard the taxi, and the moment her door closed again it started moving. Thane already had the Ford's engine started and gently used the clutch and got it into gear.

'Playing it straight and heading for her office,' said Sandra Craig. She eyed him hopefully. 'I'd put my lunch money on it, sir.'

'No way.' While the Ford began following the black taxi travelling ahead, Thane firmly shook his head. He'd lost that kind of bet before – and, when someone else was buying, Sandra Craig's idea of lunch was awesome.

They tailed the taxi while it filtered into the heavy traffic in Dumbarton Road, where it kept on at a brisk pace. When the vehicle ahead ignored the Clydeside Expressway route, Thane relaxed and became certain in his hunch that they were heading in towards the city centre. Five minutes more, the black taxi still a comfortable few vehicles of a gap ahead, they were in sight of Central Station then followed the taxi driver's snakelike route through a jungle of one-way streets.

At last, the black taxi ahead turned into Cadogan Street, where most of the one-time old warehouses and rat's nest offices had been replaced by tall new-build high-rent structures. Then, as they followed, Thane letting the gap stay wide, a small red MG two-seater appeared close behind the Ford and Maggie Donald gave a quick half-salute through her windscreen.

Thane double-tapped his brake lights in reply. In another moment, with the MG tucked in close behind him, the taxi was slowing ahead. It stopped outside a concrete and glass office building which had a sign which said Kingsley Estates above the curve of its central entrance archway. Lower down, almost matching it in size, another sign said Rex Insurance.

He spotted an empty, metered parking bay a few yards along on the other side of the street and slotted into it. He saw the MG somehow squeeze into another space, marked Motor Cycles Only, then his attention was back with the taxi as Liz Rankin stepped out.

Then a couple of unexpected things happened. First, a figure in doorman's uniform and peaked hat dived out of the building to stop the taxi from leaving. Both the uniform and peaked cap were plain maroon. Seconds later he was followed by a burly, hurrying man who had thinning fair hair and a small bristle of a moustache. The fair-haired man, who looked around fifty and wore a dark business suit, greeted Liz Rankin with a quick hug, laughed at something she said, then kissed her on the cheek and climbed into the taxi. Thane stared on as the taxi pulled away.

The fair-haired man was one of the 'total strangers' described by Liz Rankin and Trudi Andrews as 'clowns who tried to pick us up' at the canalside restauraunt in Kirkintilloch.

So, quite simply, they had lied. About that, and about how much more?

For a moment, Colin Thane switched his attention to the doorman's lean, harsh face. He had to be in his sixties, he had thick, black framed spectacles, and there was something about the man which was strangely familiar. Yet he wasn't able to put any kind of a label on it.

Thane left it there as Liz Rankin chatted amiably with the doorman at the entrance to the building. The doorman grinned, saluted, and swung the entrance door open with an exaggerated bow. In another moment they had both gone inside.

Then the Ford's rear doors opened and Maggie Donald tumbled in behind Thane, while a pale-faced, slightly subdued DC Lennox got aboard behind Sandra Craig.

'Sorry if we're a wee bit late, sir' said the young Northern Constabulary woman apologetically. 'I met a lot of traffic.'

'Met it?' Lennox scowled at her. 'We probably created more nervous breakdowns than your average friendly armoured brigade!'

'It wasn't so bad. I'm just not too used to city streets.' Maggie Donald grinned at Sandra Craig then switched her attention back to Thane again. 'Now we're here, what do you want us to do, sir?'

'I'll show you. Look over there.' Thane turned in his seat and thumbed towards the office building. 'Both of you, work that building floor by floor, door to door. Chat up the unchattable. Use your notebooks as props. Make noises that you're a couple of market researchers conducting an opinion poll into – ' he gestured vaguely ' – well, any damned thing you want as long as you tell the same story and keep a low profile. You saw Liz Rankin, the woman who went in? You saw the fair-haired man who came out – ' he hesitated, then added ' – and the doorman?'

Lennox and Maggie Donald nodded.

'They're your targets, particularly the fair-haired man. Pick up anything you can about him.' He glanced at Sandra Craig. 'And I mean anything. Agreed, sergeant?'

'Anything.' The redhead nodded. 'Fact, gossip – whatever you two can get.'

'Then we can sort it out later,' added Thane.

He took a deep breath at the thought. Too many ragged-edged possibilities were already crowding in. God alone knew how many more could be coming the Crime Squad's way when Sir Andrew Silverhill, yesterday's *Boy's Own* hero, unloaded his worries.

That was its own reminder. Thane glanced at his wristwatch, saw he was already cutting things fine if he was to get back for Silverhill's arrival, and sent Lennox and Maggie Donald on their way. But as the pair left the car he looked at Sandra Craig then gave a fractional nod in Maggie Donald's direction. His sergeant followed them out, and spent a moment quietly talking with the younger girl.

When she returned and got back aboard the Ford she was smiling.

'Well?' demanded Thane, his mind on the last time Lennox and Maggie Donald had worked together.

'No problem, sir.' The redhead's smile widened to a grin. 'They were the only spare people that Phil Moss had left to send us. Dougie – uh – ran his hand up her leg on the way over.'

Thane scowled. 'And?'

'Maggie pulled in off the road, then told him how she'd spent part of her last leave working on her father's sheep farm. It's north of Inverness – '

'So?'

'So she explained to our Dougie that one of her jobs had been to castrate new lambs.' His sergeant fought down a giggle. 'Up there, they still do the job with their teeth – one quick bite.'

Thane winced. 'Message received?'

'And understood,' the redhead nodded solemnly. 'After that, our Dougie was one little lamb who stayed well away!'

Thane was still chuckling to himself as he drove the Ford out of Cadogan Street. Maggie Donald had a set of strong, splendidly white teeth. They also looked as though they could be splendidly sharp. Yes, the dark-haired Highland girl had worked out her own strategy of how to deal with a panting Lennox!

It was dull but still dry and just a few minutes short of ten a.m. when they reached the Crime Squad compound. and left the Ford in its bay. From there, Thane led the way into the headquarters building, where Phil Moss was already waiting for him.

'No sign of our visitor yet. He's on his way through by road from Edinburgh,' reported Moss, then thumbed towards the upper floor. 'But we've got the supporting cast – Harry Cameron and Peter Lewis.'

Cameron and Lewis were both detective chief inspectors, Cameron from Strathclyde's Fraud Squad, based in Glasgow's Govan division, Lewis from the Lothian and Borders squad, at that force's Edinburgh headquarters. Thane knew both men, but hadn't expected them together.

'They're both involved,' shrugged Moss as they started up the stairway. 'Sir Andy bases himself in Edinburgh part of the week. Then he spends the rest here in the west. For him, this business began in Strathclyde then involved Edinburgh. So everybody is interested.'

'Happy families,' grunted Thane. 'Are Cameron or Lewis saying anything?'

'Not yet.' Moss hesitated, gave a grimace of pain, then released a thundering belch which made a young orderly stare at him in open admiration. Cursing softly, Moss scowled at Thane. 'Hold on a moment, will you?'

Thane nodded, then watched as Moss fished a small, battered metal box from his jacket pocket. Opening the box, which was filled with a fine white powder, Moss took a large pinch and swallowed it. He then gave a milder belch.

The powder was industrial-strength magnesium oxide, a mineral insulation often still used for electrical power cables. Sandra Craig had persuaded Moss to try it as medication for his ulcer, citing an ancient electrician relative who swore by the tart-tasting substance. It had worked so well that a previous war between the two had become a passable truce.

'Now?' queried Thane. When Moss nodded, he asked, 'Any word back from Jack Hart?'

87

'A fax from Brussels.' Moss scowled, not totally approving of the Squad commander's regular trips to that heathen place called Europe. 'He's fine, sends good luck to us – the usual.'

'We're still using his room?'

'Maggie Fyffe has it set up for us. Best china.' When her boss was away, the commander's secretary set her own rules.

While they carried on, Moss went through some additional Sam Baker sightings that had been checked. None had mattered, except in the sheer fact that they had been eliminated.

Then it was Thane's turn to call a halt. They stood at the top of the stairway beside one of the old prison ship photographs while he gave a condensed account of his interview with Liz Rankin, and what he'd seen afterwards at Cadogan Street. After that they parted. Moss, he knew, could take much of it from there.

Thane went along to the Squad commander's borrowed office, where a distrustful Maggie Fyffe had hidden away some of Jack Hart's private treasures, including the antique police helmet and the glinting cutlass. The two Fraud Squad DCIs were already there, standing gossiping beside the electronic wall map, happily smoking cigarettes from the opened box which was lying on Hart's desk. Thane had met them before, good, solid professionals, and he shook hands with them. Harry Cameron was a bulky figure in a grey flannel suit with a small dark moustache and a technicolour taste in ties. Peter Lewis, his Edinburgh opposite number, was skin and bone by comparison with a heavily freckled face, white shirt, police club tie, and a dark blue business suit.

'Do you know what this is about yet?' asked Cameron.

Thane shook his head, and the two men exchanged a wry glance.

'This is not your lucky day, Colin,' said Lewis sadly.

'But we'll give you this for starters,' said Harry Cameron, and sucked briefly at an edge of his moustache. 'First time round, you may not believe Sir Andy's story. But you'd be wrong.'

'I go along with that,' said Lewis. 'He'll tell you about The Lazarus Widow,' said Lewis sourly. 'Lazarus, as in the Bible, right? Every time everyone hopes she's dead and finished – but no, suddenly she pops up again'

'Like now,' agreed Harry Cameron. 'The best of luck, Colin.

At the risk of sounding sanctimonious, you're going to need any luck that's going!'

4

Sir Andrew Silverhill had a reputation for total punctuality. It was exactly on ten a.m. when a green Jaguar XK120 hard top sports coupé pulled in at the Crime Squad compound with its twin exhausts burbling. The electronically operated gate opened, the Jaguar murmured through, and a uniformed man was there to wave the vehicle into a reserved parking bay near the front of the headquarters building.

'I know someone who would call that a car worth dying for,' murmured Sandra Craig. She was in the small group watching at Jack Hart's upper floor window.

'Silverhill doesn't own that beauty, Sergeant Craig. Check the personalised number plate,' said Harry Cameron. The Strathclyde officer glanced at his Lothians soulmate, Peter Lewis, and the two Fraud Squad DCIs exchanged a grimace.

'It reads DW,' grunted Lewis. 'As in Daniel Wolfson.' He nodded as he saw the light dawn in the redhead's green eyes. 'The lawyer.'

'Bill-by-the-Hour Daniel Wolfson – who doesn't give Air Miles,' grunted Cameron. He glanced at Thane. 'Did you know Wolfson was coming?'

Thane shook his head.

'Nothing we can do about it,' sighed Lewis. 'Handle him with care, Colin. Daniel Wolfson doesn't take on too much court work – he's Edinburgh based, more into general legal practice.' He scowled.' But I know a cop or two who wish they'd never met him.'

Down below, two figures had left the Jaguar. Andy Silverhill, the tweed-clad, white-haired man who emerged from the passenger side, was well in his sixties, but still the gangling, amiable figure who had once powered his victory way round an Olympic stadium – to the emotional pride of an entire nation. Emerging seconds later from the other side, the stocky, round-faced driver

89

was much younger than his passenger. He wore the black jacket and striped black trousers which were an Edinburgh law practitioner's working overalls – but in his case they were topped by a dark blue baseball cap worn backwards.

Somehow Phil Moss was out to meet them. There was a beam on his lined face as he shook hands with his hero, then he greeted Daniel Wolfson with less enthusiasm. Moss turned to Andy Silverhill again, and they spoke briefly. Then Moss left them and the visitors went in to the reception desk.

'Sergeant – ' Thane stopped the redhead as she made to leave ' – stay.' He saw her raised eyebrow. 'I want you in on this. Keep your notebook handy. Nothing verbatim, just informal notes. But we might need them.'

Another minute passed and they heard voices and footsteps. Then Maggie Fyffe ushered the new arrivals into the room and Peter Lewis began handling the introductions. But as soon as the Lothians DCI said the words 'Sir Andrew' there was an immediate protest from the former sporting legend.

'No. Just call me Andy,' pleaded Silverhill. 'Life's simpler that way. Unless – ' a wry grimace crossed his thin, raw-boned face ' – unless things get awkward. Like if you get round to thinking of arresting me, right?'

His words brought an explosive protest from his lawyer. .

'I told you, Sir Andy. Facts only – no jokes, please!' Clutching a briefcase, the baseball cap stuffed into a jacket pocket, Daniel Wolfson wasn't amused. 'No jokes, no misunderstandings. Police don't always appreciate a sense of humour.'

The introductions completed, Andy Silverhill and his solicitor sat at one side of a table which had been placed under the electronic wall map of Scotland. Thane and the two Fraud Squad DCIs settled opposite and, helped by Sandra Craig, Maggie Fyffe offered round coffee and biscuits before she left. Quietly, Thane's sergeant eased into the armchair behind the absent Jack Hart's desk, her notebook ready.

'Can I presume we're not being taped?' queried Wolfson.

'*Aide mémoire* notes only,' promised Thane. 'But I – uh – didn't know Sir Andy would be legally represented, Mr Wolfson.'

'Sir Andy didn't know either,' said Wolfson grimly. 'Then he told me that he was going to do this alone, and I said only over my dead body – '

'Which could be arranged,' scowled Silverhill. 'Look, Daniel – '

His solicitor ignored him. 'There are two things to be understood, superintendent. First, that my client volunteered to come here today. Second, that any information he gives is not to be incorporated in any statement – ' he saw Andy Silverhill's expression and added ' – at least, not at this stage. I'm here as an observer, nothing more. I promise I'll say as little as possible. Agreed?'

Thane nodded. 'So who begins?'

'We do, I suppose,' said Harry Cameron. The Strathclyde Fraud Squad chief raised an eyebrow at his opposite number. 'You or me, Peter?'

'Be my guest,' nodded Lewis. He gave a small, neutral smile. 'Mr Wolfson, I'll only kick in the reminder that we haven't given Superintendent Thane any real outline on this. That was deliberate. We reckon it better he hears the story direct from Sir – uh – Sir Andy.' He helped himself to another chocolate biscuit from Maggie Fyffe's secret hoard, and sat back. 'Over to you, Harry.'

'So now we start.' Cameron gave a small sigh. 'For both Strathclyde force and Lothians, this case goes back about eighteen months. That's when Sir Andrew – ' he heard a warning sniff and corrected himself ' – Sir Andy first came to see Peter Lewis in Edinburgh. I got involved pretty well straight away. As soon as we heard his story, we knew what had happened. He'd tangled with the Lazarus Widow – and we weren't surprised when our inquiries didn't get far.' He paused and rubbed his chin, and turned his faintly embarrassed attention directly to Thane. 'Look, Colin, eventually the whole matter died down and was more or less forgotten. Until now – then, first, I heard on the grapevine about your murder. Next, a Records photograph of Sam Baker landed on my desk, along with a background fax about him. That was when my memory went click, and a few things came together!'

'So he told me,' said Peter Lewis. The Lothians detective gave his colleague a sympathetic grimace. 'I gulped a few times, I checked my own files, then I charged out to see Sir Andy – '

'And here we are together,' said Daniel Wolfson gloomily. The solicitor moved uncomfortably in his seat. 'In a nutshell, Superintendent Thane, my client identifies the late Samuel Baker as someone known to him as a Sam Fraser. Fraser was a front man

91

in a highly professional gang of swindlers who came close to destroying my client and badly damaging several charities. It's – well – ah – '

'Embarrassing?' mildly suggested Sandra Craig from the background and drew glares.

'A nice understatement, sergeant,' agreed Andy Silverhill sarcastically. He combed a hand unhappily through his white hair. 'I came within an inch of being ruined and probably imprisoned. This bunch thought they were going to get away with a haul of – well, it could have been at least half a million pounds sterling.' He looked down at the table. 'All because I behaved like a damned fool – '

'But in fact, thanks to my client's subsequent actions, no charity funds were actually lost,' squeaked his lawyer in a quick protest. 'Naturally, if I'd known anything about it at the time—'

'Daniel, shut up,' said Andy Silverhill fiercely. 'This is about me. I'll tell it.'

Daniel Wolfson subsided, muttering under his breath.

'Like I said, I behaved like a damned fool.' Silverhill took a deep breath. 'Thane, let's begin with me. I saw a day coming when the natural process of just getting older would put me out of athletics. So I prepared for the future, I built a nice little business career for myself – and yes, I'll admit that being an Olympic gold certainly helped. Then six years ago we were bought out, and I could have retired. But instead I agreed to chair a fund-raising operation run by a group of small medical charities – none of them very rich or fashionable, but all needing money.' He gave a wry smile. 'You know the definition of a chair? Something usually thick and wooden, that people sit on. But I tried not to play it that way.'

Instead, Andy Silverhill had poured his energy into his new role. In two years, he doubled the amount of money raised for the charity group.

'How much do you know about fund-raising, Thane?' he asked.

Thane shook his head. 'Not a lot. Organising fetes and sports events, local flag days, that kind of thing – '

'And worthy ladies baking cakes and running jumble sales?' Andy Silverhill pursed his lips. 'Let's be honest. Yes, we need the worthy ladies. Among other things, what they do is good public relations. But in revenue terms, that's usually talking petty cash – and the National Lottery has become our deadly enemy, in that area.

'The real prize up for grabs? That's when some rich old dear with only her cat for company dies alone, worth millions – and her will leaves most of it to charity. We're talking legacies.'

'Even today?' Thane showed his surprise.

'Particularly today.' Silverhill reached for his coffee cup, found it empty, and paused long enough to coax a fresh half-cup from the pot on the table. He took a sip from the cup. 'Ask the Lifeboats people. They keep adding new lifeboats to their fleet. Yet at today's values, it can cost well over a million sterling to buy a new long-range lifeboat – plus another £140,000 for the damned engines!'

'Simple modern – ah – economics,' said Daniel Wolfson. Clearing his throat, the Edinburgh solicitor made an almost apologetic gesture. 'I've seen all the relevant accounts. In the charities world, things began to go sour for many groups a little more than three years ago. Sir Andrew's medical charities group took a major fall in the value of their fund-raising income.'

Which was exactly when their research bills had unexpectedly soared.

Faced with a major problem, the medical charities group had searched for any possible economies while the situation steadily worsened.

'Then it happened,' said Andy Silverhill wryly. 'I received a letter – posted in Switzerland, marked personal. I've brought the original.' He glanced at his solicitor. 'Show him, Daniel.'

Daniel Wolfson nodded, opened his briefcase, took out a slim cardboard file, and slid a letter, a single sheet of expensive quality notepaper, across the table. The embossed address at the top was a simple fax number, the letter was dated almost two years back, and the notepaper still held the faint scent of a Givenchy perfume.

'Dear Sir Andrew,' began the typed letter. 'You are someone I have admired since your Olympic years, someone I known can be trusted – '

Thane saw that both DCIs were watching him. Harry Cameron gave a lopsided grin, nodded, and thumbed towards another briefcase lying beside him. They had their own copies.

He read on.

Helena Bosso, the writer, claimed to be the widow of a Nigerian Army lieutenant colonel who had been governor of Kano Province. Her husband, she said, had been killed in an air accident caused by sabotage.

'I have recently been contacted by other senior army officers and my late husband's legal representatives. Unknown to me and using a fictitious name, my late husband had accumulated secret funds totalling $ US 19.5 million. The bulk of this amount has been willed to me as his widow, and I now seek to overcome Nigerian government exchange controls in order that this money can be disbursed in accordance with his wishes. For this, an outside foreign banking connection is required.

'It has been resolved that an amount equal to 25% of whatever money is freed through your help will be paid to reimburse your charities group for the use of bank accounts. Five per cent will be used for facilities fees. Five per cent will be used to pay various international expenses and as my husband's widow I will receive the remaining 65%. Absolute secrecy is obviously essential.'

If Andy Silverhill wanted more details, all he had to do was send a fax to the number on the letterhead. He had nothing to lose, and he did.

Back came another letter from Helena Bosso, with the same perfumed paper and one-line fax address. To carry out the electronic transfer of funds from Nigeria to Andy Silverhill's bank, the next stage was a simple matter of faxing a signed sample of his charities group notepaper and its bank account details. Once this was done, then information about the next stage would be given. But absolute secrecy remained esssential.

'I didn't know it then,' said Andy Silverhill simply, 'but I was being set up for an advance fee fraud.'

'And – ' from her isolation at the desk, Sandra Craig made a gulping noise ' – you mean you went along with things?'

'I thought there was maybe a risk, but that it could be worth taking, sergeant.' Andy Silverhill rose from his chair, made a long-legged progression over to the window, and sadly considered the view beyond the glass – an uninspiring mix of an overhead stretch of motorway and some air freight storage warehouses. 'So I kept my mouth shut, yes – and like they asked, I

94

didn't consult anyone.' He didn't look round. 'When I ran my own business, I often had to gamble. Ever heard of a putter-out? Go back to sailing ship days, and putter-outs were people who invested money in a ship setting off on a trading expedition. They received a high rate of interest if the ship ever returned home. If the ship simply disappeared, that was their hard luck.

'There are still putter-outs around today. I tried it in business a few times – and mostly, it worked.'

Andy Silverhill's charities group badly wanted new money. The temptation was strong – and becoming stronger as needs grew.

So there were more faxes to Switzerland and reply letters. Andy Silverhill was being careful – until the day a postal package arrived from Geneva. Inside was a return British Airways first class air ticket to Lagos booked for flights out on the following Monday, the return flight coupons open-ended and undated. With the ticket came a simple invitation on that perfumed notepaper. 'Come and hear for yourself!'

On the Monday, he left Glasgow Airport on the connecting flight to London. At Heathrow, he was in the International Departures lounge waiting for the Lagos flight to be called when a well dressed man with a Scottish accent came over and introduced himself as 'Sam Fraser, a friend of Helena Bosso, sent along to act as your guide.'

'Sam Fraser' and Andy Silverhill had neighbouring seats on the long flight out, and his fellow traveller used a lot of that time to explain that the one-time Olympics hero had been carefully selected by the widow's advisors as 'a man of proven honour and integrity'. When the aircraft touched down at Lagos it was Sam Fraser who smoothed the path through customs and immigration with a practised insertion of bribes into passports and travel documents.

They parted in the main passenger concourse area – where Andy Silverhill had been handed over to a large, sharp-suited European who claimed to be an army major. The major had a chauffeur-driven limousine waiting, and they travelled on a brief drive within the airport perimeter which stopped beside a small twin-engined aircraft.

As soon as Andy Silverhill and the European major were aboard, the aircraft took off. There was time for drinks served by a Nigerian steward in army uniform, then after a flight of less than an hour they landed at what was obviously a military airport. Silverhill's major was saluted by a uniformed sergeant, and a military jeep took them to a small building at the far side of the airfield.

Where a beaming Nigerian in full general's uniform was waiting, with the news that the widowed Helena Bosso had also arrived and would see him. A tall, dignified and middle-aged African woman joined them. She spoke English with an American accent, she used the same Givenchy perfume that scented her notepaper. While the general pushed the hard sell profit side of their proposals, she used the gentle approach. Whatever they had intended between them, they put in a performance which was so slick it left Andy Silverhill desperately worried.

Then Helena Bosso departed. As soon as he could, still being pressured to supply the information which would give access to the charity bank accounts, Andy Silverhill also managed to leave. The same aircraft took him back to Lagos, where Sam Fraser was awaiting his return and took him along to the hotel where they had been booked in for the night.

'By then, I'd decided that all I wanted was to get home – and do it in one piece,' said Andy Silverhill with a shamefaced grin. 'I sneaked out of the hotel around dawn the next morning, I took a taxi to the airport, then I bribed my way onto the next flight to London.' He spread his hands in a gesture of surrender. 'So I was an idiot. But – '

'But no banking information was revealed,' emphasised Daniel Wolfson again.

The Edinburgh solicitor paused while he returned the widow's letter to his file. 'Any expenses incurrred were met by my client. Once he had taken more time to think it over, he reported the entire matter to the police. There has been no further contact of any kind from these people.'

'You were damned lucky to get out in one piece,' mused Peter Lewis. The freckled Edinburgh DCI shook his head. 'If you'd given those banking details – ' he glanced at his Strathclyde counterpart.

'They'd use a few simple, unchallenged electronic transactions to empty those bank accounts overnight,' said DCI Harry Cameron. 'You wouldn't have known until it was all over.' He grinned, scratched an edge of his small moustache, then turned to Thane. 'And forget the money – it never existed. The widow – let's call her the Lazarus Widow – was in it up to her neck. There are half a dozen international gangs working the same racket, sending out letters as if they were soap coupons.'

'What about the army side of it?' puzzled Sandra Craig.

'We ran some Interpol checks.' Cameron shook his head. 'The whole Nigerian episode was a fake. Rented actors, hired uniforms, a backwoods airport – it has happened before, sergeant. Set in different parts of the world. It will happen again.'

The sky was clearing outside. A bright gleam of sunlight swept into the room and seemed to act like a cue for the veteran athlete. He glanced at his companion, who nodded agreement.

'That's the story, folks.' Andy Silverhill rose to his feet. 'I need to leave now.' An almost boyish grin back on his face, the white-haired sportsman rose to his feet with Wolfson following his example. 'I'm due to chair a charities meeting back in Edinburgh.' The grin broadened and he surprised them with a wink. 'You know, things are genuinely beginning to look better! Remember I told you about how we need a supply of nice old ladies wanting to give money to charity? Well, we've found one, and she's talking well into six figures!'

'Good luck with her,' said Thane.

They shook hands and Thane told Sandra Craig to see the two men out of the building. Once they'd gone, he sighed and turned again to his two Fraud Squad visitors.

'At least now you know,' said Harry Cameron. Opening his briefcase, he dumped a cardboard folder on the table beside him. 'That's a copy of everything we've got, and there's not a lot of it.' He thumbed in the direction taken by their visitor and his lawyer. 'There goes an idiot who must have kept his brains in his legs. He was damned lucky nothing much happened to him.'

'Meaning?'

As if they were taking it turn about, Peter Lewis answered. 'We've authentic stories of businessmen being kidnapped, beaten up, then held to ransom. There are several murders in Russia and at least a couple in South America – all starting off when what began as an advance payment fraud went wrong.'

'Plagiarism,' said Thane sourly. 'Get back to our Lazarus Widow – who first gave her that tag?'

'I'd like to say it was some clever cop,' shrugged Cameron. 'But it wasn't. Someone on their side is a joker with a sense of humour. Every now and again, just when Interpol are getting word of another successful fraud, they also get a greetings card. All it says is "The Lazarus Widow sends her love." Like they were running a damned franchising operation!'

The rasp of a powerful engine starting up reached them from outside, and they reached the window in time to see Daniel Wolfson's green Jaguar XK growl out of its parking slot. As the compound's security gate opened, Sir Andy Silverhill waved a farewell from the passenger window – then those twin exhausts bellowed and the car had roared away.

'Any help we can give, let us know,' volunteered Peter Lewis. 'But we're leaving too. There's a new fly fishing tackle shop in Glasgow I want to check out. Then – ' he gave a mock bow towards Cameron ' – then Strathclyde is buying me lunch.'

'Which Strathclyde will then charge to the Scottish Crime Squad,' murmured Cameron. 'Forget your canteen or the local greasy spoon, superintendent – sir! Where can you recommend that's clean, good, and expensive?'

Grinning the two DCIs made to leave. Thane let them almost reach the door before he heaved a handy telephone directory in their general direction.

He cursed as he missed.

After they'd gone, Colin Thane collected the advance fee frauds file, went through to spend a few moments talking with Maggie Fyffe, then went to his own room. When he passed Phil Moss's cubbyhole office on the way, he could hear Moss busy on the telephone, but when he looked in Moss waved a greeting which translated that everything remained under control – more or less.

There were no fresh messages lying on Thane's desk and he still had the best part of an hour to spare before he was due to visit the Riverman. Taking off his jacket and settling behind his desk, he opened the file, and began reading.

The first few pages came down to an illustration of just how many innocents existed in even the hi-tech electronic world of e-mail and the Internet. One item was an up-to-date Interpol briefing which simply stated that international fraud gangs were currently operating attempted scams on a world-wide basis running into multi-million dollar frauds.

Every week, hundreds of carefully tailored letters were being despatched to potential victims In Britain alone, the Foreign Office admitted that it could have papered whole walls in its building with queries from businesses who had received advance fee appeals.

The Foreign Office had reached the stage of having a pro forma letter for replies to their queries.

'No response should be made. Any letters or faxes should immediately be sent to the nearest police Fraud Squad.' Then came a section which Sir Andy Silverhill could now approve. 'Some businesses have been approached to travel out to other – mainly Third World – countries with the lure of business contracts. Anyone who responds could be placing themselves in danger.'

Neither Interpol nor the Foreign Office could be certain how many firms had fallen for the advance fee sales pitch – or how much they'd lost in the process. Usually the victims just wanted to lie low and lick their financial wounds. But the known list was long enough and included some prominent names. When it came to commercial contracts, a suggested bargain deal for some twenty million dollars of surplus military aero engines had apparently been taken up by six different companies at the same time.

The next group of papers in the folder dealt with Andy Silverhill's case, and Thane couldn't fault the way the Strathclyde and Lothian Fraud teams had investigated what they had. The Swiss fax number was a rented service which had suddenly shut down. The air tickets had been bought in Geneva for cash and their trail ended there. Sam Baker, travelling as Fraser, had apparently used a false passport. There had never been a Lieutenant Colonel Bosso, killed or otherwise. But his so-called widow remarkably matched the description of a woman who had several convictions in South Africa for bank fraud offences.

If Sir Andy had been selected because of the possible financial weakness that had overtaken his charities group, the two Scottish fraud teams had been unable to find out how that confidential background information had been discovered.

99

Though, mused Thane, there was still a fundamental truth in the suggestion that the Olympic veteran had always kept his brains in his legs. He sighed, then turned another clipped together section of pages.

One page was an official statement from the Central Bank of Nigeria, warning that neither the Bank nor Nigeria's Federal Government could be held responsible for 'bogus and shady deals transacted with criminal intentions'. It talked of 'the basic gullibility or greed' of victims. The Nigerian statement was attached to half a dozen similar warnings from the Middle East, Central America and the Far East.

Then Thane could hear footsteps and voices coming along the corridor towards his office. He closed the file and pushed it to one side as the room was invaded by a thoughtful looking Phil Moss, followed by one triumphant detective chief inspector in the shape of Tina Redder, and finally by stony-faced Sandra Craig.

'No guarantees, Colin. But I think I can hand you a present,' declared Tina Redder. She perched on the edge of Thane's desk, those famed nylon-clad legs swinging confidently. 'Still interested in where Sam Baker could have had his hideaway?'

'That could be an understatement.' Thane sensed that whatever he was going to be told, Phil Moss already knew – and didn't seemed totally convinced. 'Try me.'

'You mean in front of witnesses?' Tina Redder gave a wink of mock delight. 'Careful, superintendent – I could have you for sexual harassment, and that wife of yours would give you hell!' The Broomstick Lady swung round on the desk to properly face him. 'Colin, you've a map of Glasgow taped up on the duty room notice board and pins on it marking every known sighting of Baker in the week or so before he vanished. Right?'

He nodded. It had been Phil Moss's idea, with Sandra Craig delegated to keep the marked locations up to date. Most were in a patch of the city centre not far from St George's Cross, an area where old tenements were overshadowed by new high-rise business and commercial buildings – and where every part of Glasgow's bustling ethnic mix seemed to have established some kind of mini-market toehold.

'Right.' Tina Redder tapped Thane's desk-top with a demanding forefinger. 'Then listen. I caught that forensic mention of paracetamol in Baker's blood and tissue samples.' She sighed. 'All right, I run the Squad's drugs team. But didn't paracetamol ring any bells? Why would some people use paracetamol?'

'Pain relief for headaches?'

'Try again,' she invited.

Sandra Craig showed her strong white teeth in sudden understanding. 'Bash?'

'Bash. Yes, correct!' Tina Redder was sarcastically delighted. 'The Baby Sergeant strikes again. Well done!'

'We've been sending her to night classes,' murmured Moss, giving the redhead a warning glance which damped down her reaction.

'Bash – ' a memory of a recent drugs lecture came back into Thane's mind ' – that's street talk for a mix of heroin and paracetamol. Injected, it acts like a home-made depth charge.' The rest of it returned. Bash had been among the unpublicised reasons why an outwardly idiotic set of rules governing paracetamol tablets sold to the public without prescription had been suddenly introduced.

'There's one particularly nasty side-effect.' Tina Redder took over, sure of where she stood. 'Bash can cause gross and sometimes rapid liver damage. I 'phoned Doc Williams and checked. He says Baker's liver showed gross damage, and that will be in his final report.' She paused for triumphant effect. 'So then I thought again about Bash, and I took another look at your sightings map. There are a scatter of drug dealers in that area, yes. But when we're talking Bash, the one you want has to be Wee Willie Colston.'

'Nice catch, Tina.' Thane closed his eyes for a moment, then nodded. 'Where do we find him?'

'Willie? I checked with my people.' She came down off the desk, now totally businesslike, as if someone had thrown a switch. 'Between now and twelve noon most days, he hangs around a betting shop over at Bellside Avenue. He's there now.'

'Gritters Racing,' said Sandra Craig softly. 'My girls know it.'

Thane knew what that meant. His sergeant had her own private circle of women informants. Bag-ladies, prostitutes, homeless drunks, drug addicts or just ordinary female casualties of the system, they trusted the redhead. She had already tried them about Sam Baker and had drawn a blank. But now—

'There's a local school located just across the road from the betting shop,' said Tina Redder. 'One of Wee Willie's kids goes there, so he takes care not to be anywhere around when the classes break for lunch.' She shrugged. 'No need anyway – there's a story that he franchised the school off to a couple of sixteen-year-olds who are on probation for armed robbery.'

'Is Willie a friend?' asked Moss sardonically.

'I know him,' she corrected grimly. 'We've tried, but we've never been able to nail him. He's difficult. One smell of cop and he runs – and whatever you've got in mind, take along back-up. Wee Willie always carries heavy insurance.' She glanced at her wristwatch. 'What do you want to do, Colin?'

Thane looked across at Moss. 'Anything else in the frame for us?'

Moss considered and shrugged. 'Nothing that can't wait.'

'Then we'll pick him up,' decided Thane. 'Tina, what else do you know about the place?'

She told them.

They set off five minutes later, a three-vehicle convoy with no drama of sirens or flashing lights, simply travelling at a moderate pace under blue sky, sunlight, a gently gusting wind, and occasional drifting cloud. The first vehicle was Sandra Craig's white VW Golf. She was driving, with Thane beside her in the front passenger seat, Phil Moss in the rear. Close behind the Golf came the Land Rover dog van, carrying Jock Dawson and his two dogs. The rear car was a Rover saloon carrying two detective constables who were newly back in from another fruitless Sam Baker follow-up, grabbed as they headed for a canteen coffee break.

That made six Crime Squad officers in all. Tina Redder hadn't wanted to contribute any of her drugs team to take any active part in the operation, for very good reasons. The drugs side of the Scottish Crime Squad's activities was mushrooming, and most of the men and women in the Broomstick Lady's team were working from deep cover which had sometimes taken months to achieve.

Even in the face of a murder, it would have been wrong to 'burn out' one of these undercover officers. Their unsuspected

102

existence was the reason why the Crime Squad could claim such a run of successes against a string of tartan drug barons.

'The woman is good,' mused Phil Moss. 'Take last week.' He chuckled, ignoring a caustic sniff from Sandra Craig. 'She gets a tip about a coach bringing an amateur football team back from Paris. There was heroin with a £200,000 street value among the dirty strips in the baggage hold.'

'I heard,' muttered the redhead, snatching a noisy gearchange in a way that underlined her irritation. 'In fact, she made damned sure everybody heard!'

'Ease back,' warned Thane. 'Understood, Sandra?'

'Sir.' The redhead scowled but subsided.

'I've a problem.' Moss leaned forward, looking puzzled, his voice suddenly confidential. 'Is it true a certain lady DCI's favourite hobby is mud-wrestling?'

Sandra Craig's hands quivered on the steering wheel, the car lurched a little. Then it steadied, and she hooted with laughter.

It was thirty minutes before noon when the little Crime Squad convoy reached the start of Bellside Avenue and pulled in. Ahead, the avenue ran straight in a slight downhill slope until it reached a curve. On one side was a line of two-storey brick and concrete tenements. They were fronted by what a well meaning architect had intended should be garden space. But time had changed that into a strip of overgrown waste ground which held the occasional abandoned car, a couple of demolished bus shelters, and scattered mounds of thankfully unidentifiable rubbish. The other side of the avenue held the local school and a playground area next to a railway station and its fenced-off track.

Bellside Avenue was a layercake sample of city life. Some of its families lived an honest, hard-working, reasonably comfortable existence. Too many others, Thane knew, were either unemployed or unemployable – some into the third generation, some still struggling, others already given up. For them, the highlight item in any week was cashing a Benefits giro order. Down there, despite New Whatever politics, poverty meant that almost half of all school children qualified for free school meals and – with the figures still rising – around sixty per cent received welfare clothing and footwear grants.

Put together, it made Bellside Avenue a good location for any betting operation.

Gritters Racing sat across from the school, just on the curve, at one end of a block of four flat-roofed single-storey shops. Thane lifted the compact but powerful Japanese binoculars which Sandra Craig kept in the VW's glove compartment, fine-tuned the focus to suit his eyes, and studied the block for a moment.

From right to left, the four shops were exactly as Tina Redder had described. First was Gritters Racing, by far the largest, with a bright paint job covering its glass windows and a neon tube sign which no planning committee had probably even heard about. Second in line was a mini-market grocery store with a delivery van parked outside it. Then came a Chinese fast-food carry-out restaurant and finally – inevitably – that other necessity of Glasgow housing scheme life, a video rental store with a notice advertising a twenty-four hour delivery and collection service.

None of the shops looked busy, but there were several cars and some motor cycles parked outside the strip. Satisfied, Thane put the binoculars away again, lowered his passenger window, signalled, and all three vehicles started moving. They had talked it through before they left, everyone knew what to do.

First the VW murmured to a halt outside the bookmaker's door, the target for Thane, Moss and Sandra Craig. Moments later the Land Rover dog van quietly stopped at the kerb not far behind, their mobile reserve. Then the Rover with the two detective constables bumped its way down a small lane that led to the rear of the block, where Gritters Racing had a fire escape back door.

In the VW Golf, one hand ready on the car's door handle, Colin Thane counted fifteen seconds under his breath. Then he got out, followed closely by Sandra Craig and conscious of Phil Moss climbing out at the rear. As they reached the bookmaker's door it opened and two elderly men ambled out. The first, needing a shave and without teeth, smiled at Sandra and held the door open while Thane thanked him.

Then the three Crime Squad officers had walked into a noisy, brightly lit world which could have belonged to another planet. There had to be at least fifty people inside Gritters, where the decor was gloss paint and threadbare tartan carpeting and the atmosphere was a noisy, rancid blend of stale cigarette smoke, staler human sweat, and an overlay of cheap disinfectant. Banks

104

of TV monitor screens were filled with horse and dog betting details. There was film of recorded Australian horse racing with a noisy commentary. One solitary screen, devoted to stock exchange prices, was being ignored, and a half-size snooker table was being used as a seat by several punters while they listened to either the low background music or a 'blower' ExTel audio forecasts line.

Gritters' punters were a mixture. There were talkative pensioners, and a couple of young mothers rocked prams as they eyed odds. A heavily pregnant woman was using a hand-held calculator. Someone had a small, yelping mongrel dog on a leash. A wooden shelf for writing betting slips ran along two walls, and an entire corner was taken up by an office partition which had two small windows, one for taking in betting slips, the other for paying out. A sign which said Fire Door pointed beyond them.

Someone shoved past Thane, heading for the pay-out window. A man in bus driver's uniform finished drinking a can of beer and abandoned the empty can beside others on a shelf. Another pregnant woman had propped her back against the wall and simply scowled.

'To your right.' Sandra Craig made it a nudge and a murmur.

He made it a glance. Wee Willie Colston, small, sleek, and dapper, exactly as described by Tina Redder, was lounging near to the pay-out window. The only man in the room with a collar and tie, he wore an expensively designed leather jacket, pink trousers which would have been more at home in the Florida Keys, and a yachting cap with Captain in gold lettering on its peak. Arms folded, surveying the scene with a smirk on his round face, he had his hands stuffed deep in his trouser pockets.

'Got him,' Thane murmured. He took another quick glance around the room 'Where's Phil?'

'Putting on a bet,' said his sergeant with near incredulity.

Phil Moss was doing exactly that, handing over a betting slip and stake money, having the line stamped, making solemn discussion with the counter clerk about paying betting tax. Overall, their arrival in Gritters seemed to have been ignored.

But Wee Willie Colston always had back-up. Thane took a new, careful look around, realising that a thin scatter of men located around the dealer had their eyes on the people in the

105

room and not on the betting screens. All were in their twenties, casually dressed, with close cropped hair and an assortment of small battle scars.

'I count five,' said a sudden hiss of a voice in Thane's ear. 'Low-grade neds. But watch it, boss.'

A thin, unshaven scarecrow of a man who smelled of spilled beer and now carried the small mongrel dog, had already moved away. But Thane had just had time enough to realise he knew the man in his normal, cleaned-up state. A detective constable on Tina Redder's team, and it made sense that he didn't want to get involved any further.

A cheer came from one group, groans from others, as an Australian race film finished and the result flashed on screen. As it faded, a list of odds being offered for players competing in an Anglo-Irish golf tournament flashed up. A few of the crowd in the betting shop began to leave, their share of the action over, their money finished for the day, one at least probably on his way to find a car worth breaking into and a radio worth stealing. Thane remembered what a resolutely bright-eyed Salvation Army woman had once told him in another area like Bellside. Faced with what they had, the more politically correct called theft part of the redistribution of wealth.

He pretended an interest on the lists of odds while he marked the men who were Colston's minders. One with a blue short-sleeved shirt and a dragon tattoo had a bulge in his hip pocket which had to be a cosh. Another, younger and with a deep scar across his nose, very plainly had a knife strapped low down under his right trouser leg. All had the obligatory knuckle-duster-sized gold sovereign rings – then Moss had eased back beside him again. Thane raised a questioning eyebrow.

'I know. Seen them.' Moss had a hard glint in his eyes. 'When?'

The decision was taken for them as the front door flew open, a woman making a frantic entrance.

'Cops, Willie!' Her warning was a shrill scream 'Get out!'

For perhaps three seconds the inside of the betting shop suddenly froze into a total silence, only the broadcast voices of the race tipsters still unchecked. Then, just as suddenly, all hell broke loose with a chorus of shouts and screams. People were scattering towards the front door, which was still swinging.

Others were rushing towards the rear fire door, throwing it open, trying to escape.

Willie Colston's minders were protectively closing in around him, but the small figure in the gold lettered Captain cap didn't move, briefly scanning the confusion all around him. Then he saw Thane and stared.

'Everybody out!' yelled the little man. 'Go! Go! Go!'

Except that the people swarming out of the main door were tumbling back in again while Jock Dawson and his dogs made a noisy entrance – and the others who had begun pouring out of the fire door were also falling back, herded by the two shouting, baton-waving detective constables.

Wee Willie Colston was retreating through the chaos towards the betting office area as Colin Thane shoved through the confusion towards him. One of Colston's minders suddenly blocked Thane's path, swinging a short length of metal pipe. It wasted seconds. Thane ducked and weaved, got in close, and slammed a knee hard into the man's crotch in a way that made him scream. Someone else took the man's place, waving a knife, then yelped and went down as Phil Moss used a snooker cue in a club-like blow which snapped a collarbone.

A confusion of things were happening. For some reason, Sandra Craig had handcuffed one of the pram-pushing mothers to the rails of the betting shop's pay-out window. The giant mass of tan-and-black fur and muscle which was Rajah, the German shepherd, was all white fangs and fury as he kept two more of Colston's minders cowering against a wall. Goldie the labrador, had her teeth bared in a total warning as she joined in. An old woman cursed as she tried to club Moss down with her zimmer frame, the bookmaker's staff were involved in a fierce struggle with a couple of opportunists who had made a dive over the counter for the betting shop's cash drawer, and Sandra Craig had the bulky figure of a six-foot man in overalls against a wall, rhythmically slamming his head against it.

For a heart-stopping moment, Wee Willie Colston seemed to have vanished. Then Thane dived forward, past the struggle at the cash drawer, and headed straight for what had been like a large noticeboard covered in postcards and pin-ups of footballers and race horses. Except that now it was ripped open. Behind it, there was space and what looked like a narrow shelved

107

cupboard with a door lying open at the far side. He looked round, saw Moss trying to reach him, and the only other friendly face in sight was Tina Redder's undercover man, sitting dazed on the floor with blood pouring from a cut on his forehead

'Phil, over here!' Thane pointed at the gap and charged through. A moment later he was out the other side of the cupboard space and into the next-door minimarket He knocked over a piled display of tinned fruits, heard a woman shopper scream, ran past an open-mouthed shop assistant, then saw where a shopping trolley had been used like a battering ram to smash open another disguised gap on the other side of the store. Another, braver, shop assistant, a dark-skinned girl holding a meat cleaver, made to stop him reaching the gap.

'Police!' yelled Thane.

She hesitated, then Moss was also pelting in from the betting shop escape route. Police whistles were blowing. The girl jumped back, still keeping the glinting cleaver handy, and the two detectives charged into the new gap, through another cupboard, then out through a beaded curtain, out into the Chinese carry-out – and into a scene of panicking customers and frightened staff.

One of Wee Willie Colston's minders, the man with the scarred nose and dragon tattoo, had made it this far. Howling defiance, trapped by a deep fry unit, he picked up a glass display cabinet, heaved, and sent it smashing down beside Thane. Then he looked round for something else to use – and screamed as one of the white-coated kitchen staff tossed a ladle filled with smoking hot cooking oil straight into his face.

And once again there was another newly broken hole in the wall on the far side – a hole that led straight into the rear of the video rental shop at the far end of the block. Except that the street door was lying open, the middle-aged woman behind the rental counter pointing speechlessly.

Thane reached the door and looked out. Willie Colston was running hard along the road, heading past the school playground, still not far away, the sun winking on the sharp steel of a hobby knife brandished in his right hand. The menace was enough to send a postman diving clear from his path.

'He's mine, boss,' said Jock Dawson laconically, appearing beside Thane. The dog handler had reached the video shop by

Thane's route, enthusiastically followed by both dogs. He took a moment to brush some of the fragments of plaster debris from his overalls, then asked, 'How do you want him? Nipped or chewed?'

'Whatever.' There were still occasional shouts and screams coming from along the little line of shops, some people were scurrying away, and Thane stared at the unexpected sight of two more Crime Squad cars lying outside the betting shop. Exactly when Beauty and the Beast's Audi coupé and Maggie Donald's little MG had both arrived, he didn't know. But both were lying empty and he caught a glimpse of the Beast towering over two prisoners whom he had by the scruff of their necks. That could wait. He nodded towards the fleeing Colston. 'Take him.'

'Sir.' Jock Dawson stooped and clapped both dogs lightly on their excited, quivering flanks, and pointed. 'Rajah, Goldie – go!'

Two four-legged thunderbolts, one a hairy, heavy black and tan, the other slim and young and with fur as golden as her name, raced off in pursuit of the man in the hat that said Captain. As they neared their quarry, Jock Dawson gave a single sharp-noted whistle.

It was all the instruction the two dogs needed. This was a game they'd learned from puppyhood, a game they knew usually ended with a reward, one with variations they'd worked out for themselves. Rajah was the brawn, siege-dog size, his age showing from the first grey hairs around his muzzle. Goldie was the brains, multi-purpose trained, as expert at sniffing out explosives as finding drugs or bodies. And their game, even with the threat of that glinting knife, was something to be enjoyed.

Wee Willie Colston was taken like an errant sheep. Still working without orders, only exchanging an occasional glance one to the other, the two dogs raced towards him, then separated, Rajah reducing his pace to a steady trot. His tongue showed large and pink, those massive teeth were bared in a white-fanged grin. Goldie, darting ahead then weaving back, began a routine of barking and snapping.

'Bastards!' The curse came from Colston like a keening rage. Still running, but stumbling and breathless, he was past the school and its playing fields and at the edge of a grassy slope which led down to the railway station. 'Get away, damn you!'

That was when Goldie suddenly dived for the man's legs then, as Colston made to take a despairing swing with the knife, Rajah took a single, pouncing leap. The full weight of the giant German shepherd took the drug dealer in the back, those massive jaws clamped like a vice on his knife arm. Wee Willie Colston screamed, then tripped as Goldie nipped an ankle. He fell head-long, vanished from sight down the slope with a mysterious crash from below, then both dogs pranced clear.

'What the hell was that, then?' asked a puzzled Jock Dawson.

Then he and Thane ran to investigate. They stopped at the edge of the slope, looked down, and Dawson gave a grin of near disbelief. The railway station was at the foot of the slope. Wee Willie Colston had lost his knife in the tumble, his hat had rolled onto the nearby railway line, and he was lying half-in and half-out of a smashed railside plastic container bin.

'Get the knife, bag it as posible evidence, then bring him back,' ordered Thane. He allowed himself a small chuckle. 'And stand the dogs a bone each, on me. In fact, you can have one too, Jock.'

'Thank you, sir,' said Dawson gravely. 'But I'll settle for a dram.'

Thane was almost back at the shops again when Sandra Craig walked towards him. She was someone he'd wanted to see.

'How did they get here, sergeant?' he asked, nodding towards the two recently arrived Crime Squad cars.

'The Broomstick – ' she saw a warning glint in Thane's eyes and quickly corrected herself ' – DCI Redder chased them out when they returned to base. She said you could use them.'

'Be glad,' suggested Thane. Then he frowned. 'You grabbed one of those women who had a baby and a pram. Why?'

'That's how Colston was moving his drugs, sir.' Pleased with herself, she raked the fingers of both hands through that copper-red hair and chuckled. 'I got lucky and spotted it happening. The way they work it, a buyer pays one of Colston's minders, another minder gets what's wanted – '

'From the pram?' Thane blinked.

'Fixes on Wheels. Stowed under the baby. That pram is carrying a stop-me-and-buy-one load of heroin and cannabis,' she declared cheerfully. 'Any problems, and it's easy enough to get a pram clear.'

Thane nodded. Not many cops would want to think of arresting a mother and baby, most would simply chase them on their way. No wonder Wee Willie Colston had had a good run for his money.

They stayed outside the block until they reached the betting shop entrance. Inside, it was like a battlefield clear-up station with his reinforcements lining up prisoners, taking names and addresses, keeping a selection who included Colston's battered minders, then sending the others on their way. Phil Moss was over beside the pay-out window, talking with the undercover cop who was holding a wadded handkerchief to his injured forehead.

'All right?' asked Thane quietly.

'Fine' murmured the injured man. He grimaced. 'Getting hit by a cop gives me a good alibi with the locals.' He gave the slightest of winks to Moss. 'My ma always said I'd a thick skull, inspector.'

'You, Phil?' asked Thane.

'Nobody was exchanging visiting cards, were they?' said Moss defensively. He scowled at his victim.' I owe you a pint. Now get lost.'

The plain clothes man departed, making suitable protesting noises about police brutality. As he did, a carload of local uniform men pulled up outside the betting shop, closely followed by an ambulance.

'We've a woman having a baby,' complained Moss. 'And the ned who got stir-fried at the Chinese needs burns treatment.' The small, scrawny detective tapped Thane's arm and winked. 'But come and see what's in the back lane!'

Thane followed him over to the rear fire-door, looked out, and gave a soft whistle. Parked outside was a dark blue Transit van which had a distinct dent in its front bodywork.

'Whose?' he asked.

'Colston's,' said Moss dryly. 'Call it a bonus.'

They went out to the front door again, getting there more or less as Jock Dawson and his dogs arrived with their prisoner. Grubby, dishevelled, and without his Captain's cap, Colston didn't look particularly impressive. But he made an attempt at a show of aggression.

'What the hell is going on, then?' he demanded, glaring at Thane. 'You're the boss of this bunch, right? I've been attacked,

I've been savaged by your damned dogs, I've friends who've been injured – '

'And now you're under arrest,' said Thane unemotionally.

'What charge?' scowled Colston.

'To start with, vandalising railway property.' Thane's face was empty of expression. 'Then a few other things. Maybe a couple involving the Transit round the back.' He saw a sudden uncertainty on the man's face. 'Or maybe something about a murder.'

'Murder?' Colston's courage crumbled and he swallowed hard. 'Now stop it right there, mister – '

'Shut up, wee man,' said Phil Moss softly.

'Now wait, you – ' Colston took a half-step away, as if ready to run. Both dogs began to growl.

'I said shut up.' Phil Moss gripped him by the shoulder, half-spun him round, and slapped him once, lightly, across the jaw. 'You, wee man, will behave. We're Scottish Crime Squad. You call me Detective Inspector Moss, or Sir. I'm only nice to people at the weekends, and this is only Wednesday!' He indicated Thane. 'He's a detective superintendent. He's never nice to anyone, any time. It's against his religion. Understand?'

They turned Colston over to Jock Dawson again, and he was led back out of the betting shop. Once he'd gone, Thane glanced at his wristwatch and swore under his breath.

'Thinking of the Riverman?' guessed Moss. 'Get there the same day you arranged, and he'll be happy enough.' He wiped the back of one sleeve across his nose, considered the result with mild interest, then faced Thane again. 'Go and see him now. I'll tidy up this shambles.'

'It would help, Phil.' Thane saw Moss scowl towards the betting shop pay-out window. 'Something wrong over there?'

'That horse I put money on.' Moss gave a small, peeved belch. 'It came in first, at thirty to one – and some idiot arrests Gritters' cashier.'

'Life's full of problems,' sympathised Thane.

He saw Sandra Craig, signalled her towards their car, then on an impulse went into the Chinese carry-out – this time by the orthodox front door. When he came out, he was carrying two newspaper-wrapped parcels of their A47 speciality – king prawns with stir-fried rice.

On the way to the car, he passed Dawson's dogs. Their tails

112

wagged furiously as they played together, each pulling at an end of what little now remained of Wee Willie Colston's yachting cap.

When they saw him, they stopped for a moment and sat watching him.

Thane remembered an earnest animal pyschologist who had lectured him long about how animals didn't possess a sense of humour. Not for the first time, he decided the man had been an idiot.

Otherwise, why were both Rajah and Goldie grinning from ear to ear?

There is nothing easy about the business of trying to drive both quickly and safely through traffic while eating a Chinese carry-out which happens to be balanced on your lap – particularly when you are plain naturally hungry. But Detective Sergeant Sandra Craig managed the task with the combined aid of resolute determination plus Country and Westerns oldies like 'Rhinestone Cowboy' and 'A Boy Named Sue' coming from her personal transistor radio, which was propped on the Golf's dashboard.

They drove into the parking area beside the Humane Society boathouse at one fifteen, left the car, and started down towards the riverside. There was a cool, gusting wind. Despite the blue sky, the Clyde was dull grey in colour and mood and Thane saw his sergeant give a small, involuntary shiver.

'Cold?' he asked.

'No, sir.' She pointed ahead. 'That.'

There had been no need to worry about being late for their appointment with the Riverman. He had been on a call-out, now he was on his way home again, rowing upstream in his gondolier style towards the boathouse jetty, and they could see a limp body draped lifeless at the stern of his broad-beamed wooden boat. On the shore side of the jetty a black mortuary van had parked, two attendants and a police constable at ease against its front.

'Your Riverman has a hell of a job,' said Sandra Craig quietly.

'They're not always dead,' reminded Thane. 'Every time he rescues a live one – '

She nodded. They stood by the footpath railing while the rowing boat bumped the jetty. Then, as the mortuary van attendants went forward with a folded metal trolley and a black body bag, the Riverman tied his boat to a mooring ring, then waved towards Thane.

'Give me five minutes, Colin,' he hailed and gestured at his clothing. 'I need a shower and a change.'

'God.' Sandra Craig realised what he meant and grimaced.

They waited, watching the skimming seabirds and the oddments of flotsam which bobbed past on the current. As soon as the Humane Society officer had disappeared into the boathouse the mortuary van's crew set about their task with a practised skill, shifting the recovered body from the boat into the black bag, then smoothly loading it aboard their van. Then, as they drove away, the constable who remained came over, gave Thane a small smile of recognition and saluted.

'I'm leaving too, sir,' he reported. 'I'll come back later to pick up details. That's – uh – unless you need me for anything?'

'No. Go ahead,' Thane told him, then thumbed in the direction taken by the mortuary van. 'What was it this time?'

'A seaman who fell overboard from his ship. The propellor got him, then his body jammed against the rudder.' The constable grimaced. 'Pretty messy.'

He left them and they stayed waiting by the rail while a fish that could have been a large sea trout twice jumped and splashed out in mid-river. At last, the Riverman emerged from the boathouse, tucking the tails of a clean shirt into the waistband of fresh trousers, his hair still damp and smelling of shampoo.

'Sorry to keep you,' the Humane Society officer apologised, then glanced towards his moored boat. 'Well, I'm clean – but she'll need to be hosed and scrubbed before she goes out again.' He shaped one of his wry, gap-toothed, almost boyish grins. 'Still, that can wait. We'll use one of the spare – there's something I've got to do, and now.'

He beckoned, and they followed him along the jetty to a smaller, narrower boat. It swayed a little as Sandra Craig got aboard, then rocked more alarmingly as Thane climbed in and settled at the stern. The Riverman chuckled, quickly cast off the line securing it to the jetty, stepped aboard, then took up his familiar position, standing and facing forward as he rowed.

'We can talk while I'm doing this,' he suggested, then glanced back at the redhead. 'Tell me again how you feel about bodies, sergeant.'

'I prefer them warm,' she said flatly.

'So do I. Very much.' He was already rowing hard, the boat cutting through the river water. 'Your boss will have told you why you're here.' He glanced back again and shrugged. 'But there are bodies and bodies. Remember the flood waters we had a few months back? When the water receded, they found a dead man caught in branches six feet up a tree – but drowned.'

Thane glanced at his sergeant and nodded confirmation. At first, a certain police sub-division had been ready to assume they had been handed a murder.

'Then there's the other kind.' The Riverman paused, peered ahead, brought the bow of his boat round a little, and kept her moving. 'We had a show-off drunk make a very professional looking dive into the Clyde off a bridge parapet one night. He didn't surface again – and thank God a sergeant who knew better stopped a young cop from going in to rescue him. Because there was deep, soft mud below the water where the drunk went in.

'When they sent down divers, only his legs were still showing. The rest of him had gone into the mud like an arrow.'

Sandra Craig sighed. 'You're trying to tell me that a river can be unpredictable?'

'No, that I don't give guarantees.'

The Riverman stopped rowing, brought the oars inboard, and lifted a boathook. For a few seconds the boat drifted on, the river water chuckling against her bow. Then, using a single thrust of the boathook, he gaffed a small, almost awash home-made raft. The raft was constructed from broken pieces of white polystyrene which had been crudely lashed together. In the middle, some child had tied on a small, very battered rag doll. A new upward swing of the boathook brought the dripping raft over into the boat.

'Job done. Kids play with rafts, kids fall off rafts, kids drown. Call me a professional spoilsport.' The Humane Society officer picked up the oars again. Two powerful strokes brought the boat's head round, bow pointing towards its home jetty again. For the return, he settled into a steady but slower pace. 'Now, to why you're here?'

Thane nodded. 'Our body maybe came out of a car.'

'I heard.' The Riverman put in another powerful stroke. 'Professor MacMaster called me last night.' He gave a mild smile at Thane's surprise. 'When there's a problem, Johnny MacMaster is always ready to help me, just the way I'm always ready to help him.'

'Does it make a difference?' asked Sandra Craig carefully. 'The car thing, I mean?'

'Not as long as I know.' He rowed on for another short spell. 'I've got this database, girl. I've fed it all I know about this river – from my records, from the records every Riverman has kept. Lives saved, lives lost. And a tidal river is a lot trickier than the open sea. We're talking weather and temperature, we're talking currents and tides, storm drains and bridge pillars, river bed conditions, and a whole lot more.' He glanced back again, past her, towards Thane. 'And one other thing. Colin – I've told you often enough, right?'

'Bodies,' nodded Thane.

'Bodies.' The Humane Society officer rested on his oars for a moment. 'Ideally, I should know sex, weight – like was the victim fat or thin – clothing, last meals. Then – ' he thumbed at the recovered raft ' – hand me that old doll, will you?'

Sandra Craig freed it from the raft and passed it over.

'Rough illustration. 'The man held the doll out between finger and thumb. 'Someone falls into the river. Watch.' He let the doll fall. It splashed into the water, floated for few seconds, then began to settle. Slowly at first, then more quickly, sinking, swirling, it disappeared from sight. 'That's what happens, girl. When people go under, once they stop struggling, they simply sink to the bottom. Then – well, they don't do much drifting around. Mostly, they lie where they sink. That's until corruption and decay and body gases brings them floating up again, to where the tides and the currents are waiting.'

Her face pale, the redhead made a sudden gagging noise and clapped a hand over her mouth.

'Sorry.' The Riverman was genuinely apologetic. 'To me, it's

116

shop talk. I – uh – keep forgetting about other people. We'll get back.'

He bent to the oars again and said nothing more until he had tied up at the boathouse jetty and had helped his passengers ashore.

He beckoned, and they followed him deep into the shade of the boathouse and into the rear of the building, to an area where a group of wooden packing cases sat along a wall already partly filled with some of his pieces of welded metal artwork. In front was the office area – a large, badly scarred wooden desk, a couple of old filing cabinets, a crammed bookcase, and what Thane mentally dubbed as an all-singing, all-dancing personal computer set-up. The printer screen was on, showing a chart of a long section of riverside.

'Sit down,' he invited, clearing more pieces of artwork from a couple of spare chairs. Once they had settled, he took his own seat in front of the screen.

'Here we go.' He smiled sympathetically at Sandra Craig. 'There are a few other ingredients in the recipe I haven't mentioned. For instance, if the drowning is on the north of the river, then the body maybe takes a few days longer to surface than it would on the south side. That's because the north side gets less sunlight, so the water temperature can be a degree or two cooler. Then, along with currents and other factors, your surfacing body will drift down with the outgoing tide for six hours, then go back the same way with the incoming tide. Anyway – ' he began tapping the keyboard ' – I've already fed in all relevant detail.'

The computer screen began to quiver and change. The river chart vanished, then a new, enlarged section took its place. One point on the north shore was marked cursor-style.

'I make it there,' said the Riverman, sitting back. 'Finnieston Quay, not far from the Moat Hotel – which has a damned good restaurant.' He grinned. 'A restaurant where a certain detective superintendent I know owes me dinner once this is over.' He tapped the pointer on the screen. 'Get a diver down exactly there, and there's a good chance he'll land on the roof of the car you're talking about. Does that help?'

They waited while the Riverman printed off two copies of the chart section. Then, after Thane had thanked him again, they said goodbye and left.

117

Somehow, it was no particular surprise to find Tank Grant waiting in the parking area, his thick-set figure lounging against the Golf's front.

'So you're back again, Mr Thane.' The burly self-appointed vigilante leader nodded and scratched the stubble on his chin. For a moment, he ran an appreciative eye over Sandra Craig. 'Who's this?'

'His sergeant,' said the redhead curtly. 'Why?'

'Just curious.' Grant chuckled. 'A sergeant? We'd nothing like you when I was in the army.' Still grinning, he faced Thane. 'We've had it dull here, superintendent. Total Dullsville. The bampots who tried to hassle the Riverman just haven't been back.'

'Have you found out anything more about them?'

'Nothing.' The man shook his head.

Thane sensed more.' But?'

'Their interest is this character Baker, the floater, right?' Tank Grant fished cigarettes out of the top pocket of his football shirt, fed one between his lips, and lit it with a match which he struck with his thumbnail. 'Now it seems they weren't the only ones. There was money flashin' around.' He frowned a warning. 'I'm talking heavies, Mr Thane. Heavies with guns – and not necessarily local boys just trying to make good.'

'But armed?' asked Thane sharply.

'That's how I've heard it.' Grant took another pull on his cigarette. 'Which is not my scene as you know, Mr Thane. Guns I don't like too much – and I'm not joining any queue to get a bullet in the back of my head!'

Thane pursed his lips. 'Tank, this one matters. – '

'Sorry, no.' Grant shook his head. 'I'm a family man, Mr Thane. I've a wife and two kids. They happen to be all that matters to me. So don't ask. Fair?'

'Fair,' admitted Thane.

For someone like Tank Grant, there was no other reply.

5

The green call button was flashing when Thane and Sandra Craig returned to the white Golf, and as soon as they were aboard he answered on low-band.

The message that came left him with a suspicion of a grin. He had wanted to have Wee Willie Colston put on ice, well away from general sight – and Phil Moss had decided that Colston being found vandalising railway property meant he could be offered as a prisoner to British Transport Police. The BTP bar officer had been happy to oblige. The fact that the drugs dealer had crashed into the station platform bin and trashed it while being chewed by an on-duty police dog was, everybody agreed, incidental.

Leaving Colston to worry in isolation behind railway police bars would do no harm at all until they were ready for him.

Thane had something else to arrange. He radioed that he wanted his Squad team gathered for a conference meeting at four p.m. When he had finished, Sandra Craig started the car and they drove out of the parking lot, giving him one last brief glimpse of Tank Grant still standing where they'd left him. Hands stuffed in his trouser pockets, the thick-set man was frowning as he watched them leave. But it was probably the first time that Tank had ever voluntarily helped law and order in any way, and the shock would take time to wear off.

Thane took a fresh glance at Sandra Craig as their car joined the main traffic flow again. There, at least, Tank Grant had been right. His sergeant was unusually quiet and her face was distinctly pale.

'Strathclyde headquarters next,' he ordered. 'But we'll make a diversion.'

They parked the car near to the Baton Bar, a small public house almost hidden in a side street off Woodlands Road, close to the city centre. Among its near neighbours was the cherished bronze statue devoted to the memory of Lobey Dosser, Glasgow's fictional comic-strip cowboy sheriff, riding on his two-legged horse El Fideldo. The statue was maintained by public subscription, and Lobey Dosser had several hundred fund-raising, card-carrying deputy sheriffs. They included a small army of cops, with Thane among them.

When they walked into the Baton, it was quiet. The owner, a retired detective inspector, saw them come in, and bustled out from behind his counter to install them at a corner table. The man looked at Sandra Craig for a moment. Then, without saying a word, he went off. When he returned, he laid two large brandies in front of them, then left again.

'Medicinal,' said Thane, taking a modest swallow from his glass.

The redhead nodded, took a large gulp from her brandy, then fought down a gasp as the spirit hit home. She took a few moments to recover and some of her colour began returning.

'I'm still not much good around a dead body,' she confessed sadly. 'I'm sorry.'

'Don't let it worry you. In time, you'll get used to them.' Silently, Thane hoped that if she ever did then it wouldn't change her too much. He sipped his brandy. 'For now, I'm more interested in why Liz Rankin will be visiting Muriel Baker at Kirkintilloch tonight.'

'What's wrong with friendship, sir?' The redhead frowned at him over the rim of her glass.

'Nothing is wrong with friendship, sergeant,' said Thane patiently. 'But I've a feeling that Trudi Andrews will be there too. When that little coven get together, I wouldn't mind being a fly on the wall.'

'Except we're low on that kind of miracle.' She understood. 'But as second best, maybe we could pay a visit?'

Thane nodded. 'That's one thought I have. I want to hear from Liz and Trudi why they both lied to us. Would working for a couple of hours tonight cause damage to your social life, sergeant?' A Royal Navy lieutenant commander who carried a bright-burning torch for the redhead was currently commanding a fleet minesweeper out in the Persian Gulf. But Sandra Craig always had a stable of other eager candidates available. 'I mean serious damage?'

'Not so you'd notice, sir,' she said demurely and smiled, the way he had hoped she would. 'Anyway, my mother always says make them suffer a little.'

He laughed, told her to finish her drink, and after that they left.

Third largest in the UK after the London Met. and Manchester, larger than either in terms of ground area covered, Strathclyde Police have well over seven thousand officers on strength who are assisted by another two thousand or so civilians ranging from traffic wardens to canteen waitresses. Force headquarters is in Pitt Street, in the heart of Glasgow, and amounts to a single, remarkably ugly brick building which covers an entire city block. It is several storeys high above ground, has basement levels and is complete with floor after floor of underground parking space.

Even so, no matter how it is expanded, Strathclyde headquarters alway seems to be in danger of bursting at the seams. Several specialist departments had been shipped out to other satellite locations. A genuine cop in a genuine uniform was a rare sight among the clerks and typists who paraded the Pitt Street corridors or jammed its elevators. Prophets of doom were ready to forecast that headquarters would eventually become just another business-style call centre, with an executive suite for Chief Constable and senior management located like cherries on the top.

And there were already half-joking threats of pinning a notice on the front door, directing would-be customers to where the nearest real police station was located.

There were no vacant spaces available in any of the underground parking levels, it was even worse outside, and Sandra Craig finally abandoned the Golf under a No Waiting sign outside the headquarters block. By the time they had walked round to the main door and into the building, Thane had already divided out the visits they had to make.

His own first call was Scenes of Crime. The duty staffer was a young, blond-bearded civilian named Harvey Brown – who was good at his job and knew it. No, he admitted it was still too soon for any forensic report on the blue Transit found behind the Gritters Racing to have been completed.

121

'But we can give you a reasonable run on some other items,' said the staffer, using a small blue pocket comb to scratch at the edges of his beard. 'The late Sam Baker's home at Kirkintilloch either had a visitor his wife didn't know about or one she didn't want to talk about – we found rogue traces of an outsider's prints in three different locations in the house. There were also matching prints of the same outsider found in their garage.' He paused, putting the comb away. 'But none of them were good enough to give us any kind of a match. Incidentally, there was a smudged couple of fingerprints on that hobby knife used to slash your tyres out there. But the same story – not enough to give a clear reading.'

Thane nodded. But half a result was always better than none. 'How about Lizbeth Rankin's flat at Cunard View?'

'The break-in incident?' Brown used a computer, tutted his way through several key-strokes, then grimaced when its monitor screen steadied. 'Here we are superintendent. Yes, a real live break-in, but your bad guy wore gloves. Apart from that, this Rankin woman keeps a tidy house – too damned tidy from our viewpoint!'

Criminal Records and Modus Operandi came next. To get there, Thane had to walk down two floors of the building, then navigate his way past a maze of administration corridors.

When Thane went into the Records section, Steve Christie, its second in command, looked up from his desk. A bald, lanky, middle-aged DCI with rimless spectacles and a tendency to frown, Christie greeted him mildly.

'I can guess what you're hoping for, and you're not going to get much, superintendent,' he said sadly. 'These head-and-shoulders drawings the Riverman made of the men who threatened him are damned good. But we've got a few hundred similar faces on file.

'We're still working at it, but tell him he's welcome to come in and have a look for himself.'

'They were using an old Peugeot station wagon,' suggested Thane.

'Sorry. Means nothing.' Christie took off his spectacles and polished the lenses with his handkerchief. 'But we might have something for you about this character Willie Colston we've heard you picked up. You're looking for possible links to Sam Baker?'

'Whatever you've got,' agreed Thane hopefully.

'Colston was in Barlinnie Prison at the same time as Baker.' Christie gave an owl-like blink and replaced his spectacles. 'They were on different landings, but they'd probably meet. And Colston was suspected of supplying drugs to prisoners, but was never actually caught at it.'

It was the kind of lead Thane needed and a lot might depend on how far he could play it.

For good relations sake, he had to talk football with Christie for a few moments. The bald DCI was a Motherwell supporter, an endangered species, a fact which accounted for much of his frowning view of life. Then Thane set off again through the endless maze of headquarters corridors. He was heading for the Forensic Laboratory, but at a coffee-break time, which meant tides of typing pool girls in summer dresses were crowding every corner.

The laboratory was guarded by a female dragon who seemed to have held that job for ever. But she used her internal 'phone, then nodded him through into the main laboratory area with its clinically clean benches and desks, a place where white-coated staff were busy around magic-shop electronics and space age equipment. Thane walked through, exchanging nods with some of the technicians. At the rear was a glass-partitioned private office which Matt Amos, the Forensic Services director, viewed as his second home.

'Hey there, Colin! Slumming?' Amos, a slim, bearded anarchist of a man who who always wore technicolour bow ties, beckoned him in, and raised a surprised eyebrow. 'So where's your little copper-knob, Attila the Hen?'

'Working for her keep.' Thane grinned. 'What's happening with you, Matt?'

'I've a wife who is making me do gardening things, and my golf has gone to hell. I need more time off,' complained Amos. 'But does that kind of trivia matter to the mandarins up in ivory tower land? Does it hell! Sit somewhere, will you?'

Thane cleared a corner of a chair by moving a small mass of reports, then settled on its edge while Amos scowled and shuffled his way through the pile of papers on his desk. Patience paid when dealing with the Strathclyde Forensic chief, who survived his unending battles with 'ivory tower land' by the pure, unmatched quality of his forensic skills – and, in the background, the total loyalty of his staff.

Amos shuffled his papers a second time, swearing under his breath. Then he gave up, walked to his office doorway, and gave a yell. 'Anna – I need you! Get up off your backside and over here! Now!'

Amused heads looked up from around the benches as a petite, raven-haired Chinese girl wearing a white laboratory jacket over a short-length blue silk dress made a calm, unhurried way towards them holding a couple of report sheets in one hand. Anna Huang, Hong Kong Chinese by birth, reared in Canada, finishing a doctorate course at Glasgow University, was more than capable of coping with Matt Amos and his ways.

'Yes, oh master?' she asked acidly, joining them, giving Thane a smile in the process. 'Is there a problem?'

'Yes. Him.' Amos thumbed towards Thane. 'We've something for him, but I can't find the stuff!'

'Because you gave me the reports to check,' she reminded with a sigh. She indicated the papers in her hand. 'These. Did you forget, beloved master?'

'He's getting poor at remembering things,' suggested Thane.

'I'd say that beloved master is getting poor at most things, superintendent.' Anna Huang gave a wicked grin. 'That's the difference between animals and people. There's a stage where you can shoot a failing animal as a kindness. But what about people?'

'Confucius-style chat I can do without,' grumbled Amos. He appealed to Thane. 'Is Attila the Hen any worse?'

'Probably,' said Thane stonily. 'But when we see the early signs of trouble we throw her back into her cage.'

'That I'll believe,' chuckled Anna Huang. She glanced at the report sheets in her hands, then wrinkled her nose in apology. 'Well, we tried, superintendent. But we haven't won prizes – except maybe for that cleaning tag on Baker's jacket. The printing on it was almost totally faded out by immersion. But we tried chemical separation, then computer enhancing, and that worked.

The tag carried a coded marker number, from a dry cleaning firm down in Ayr.'

'There's more,' said Matt Amos smugly, back in his chair, hands clasped behind his head. 'Go on, tell our wooden-top friend.'

'There were some small, unusual stains – not much more than specks – still visible on the front of the the the jacket,' said Anna Huang carefully. 'At an educated guess, it was like the cloth had been spattered with drops of some powerful solvent.'

'The same kind of industrial solvent that left the stain on the Kirkintilloch garage floor,' added Amos. He lightly fingered the edges of his bow tie and beamed. 'Strong stuff, that solvent. I'd maybe use it to de-wax machinery, but not much else. Helpful, Colin?'

'Worth knowing,' corrected Thane. He paused. 'Scenes of Crime have some off-cuts of thick waxed paper that might tie in.'

'We'll get hold of them and look.' Matt Amos scratched his chin. 'You know about your man injecting Bash. Apart from that, I'd try this dry cleaning shop in Ayr. They might remember what kind of a state the jacket was in before they treated it.' He glanced at Anna Huang. 'That's our lot, isn't it?'

She nodded. 'Except – '

'I haven't forgotten.' Amos pursed his lips. 'Colin, you can do Anna a favour? She is one of a squad of Chinese girls studying at the University. One of them is getting engaged to another student, a lad from Liverpool. They're planning a party to celebrate. But – uh – none of them is exactly flush with cash.' He paused and tried a beaming smile. 'Now, I heard this Baker thing started rolling after you and Customs cracked down on a liquor-smuggling team. True?'

'True.' Thane raised an eyebrow, with a feeling he knew what was coming. 'So?'

'Someone in Customs told me that there are liquor stores over in Lanarkshire where you go in, you lay a single £5 note on the counter, and simply say you want the usual. What you get is a litre bottle of whisky, a litre bottle of vodka and a litre bottle of gin – the bargain of the millennium, forget the century.' Amos sighed. 'He just didn't say which stores.'

'That's a pity,' said Colin Thane mildly. 'I've heard it too. Sorry I can't help.'

Amos and the girl exchanged a glance and a sigh as Thane smiled and went on his way.

The way they'd arranged, Sandra Craig was waiting for Thane at the top of the headquarters entrance steps in Pitt Street. She wasn't alone, standing talking with two men who were full-time Police Federation officials. He had to lever her away from whatever was going on, then back out towards where they'd abandoned the VW Golf. There was a slight drizzle of rain in the air and, inevitably, the car had acquired a parking ticket. Equally inevitably, she left it to Thane to remove the ticket from her windscreen.

'So what was going on back there?' he asked, shoving the ticket in his pocket to sort out later. 'Has the Federation found another windmill to tilt at?'

'There's a sergeant getting a raw deal from Discipline Branch.' The redhead unlocked the car. Then, when they were aboard and ready leave, she frowned. 'Sir, if you have any problems with me being the Squad's delegate, I'd really rather know.'

'Would I dare?' He chuckled and shook his head. 'You know the saying. "Better the devil you know –" Head back to base, Sandra. They're waiting on us.'

Sandra Craig started her car and began driving in the direction of the Kingston Bridge and the M8. Once she had settled into the traffic flow, the rain just enough to need an occasional sweep of the wiper blades, Thane gave her a quick rundown on how he'd got on. There was enough in it to make her frown a couple of times, then it was her turn.

'The underwater unit are on their way to Finnieston Quay now. They'll search for Baker's car where the Riverman suggested – in fact, they're ready to take bets he'll have it right.' She grimaced a little. 'At least they know Baker isn't inside it.'

'You mean you don't fancy the job, sergeant?' he asked maliciously, and drew a glare.

Sandra Craig had been busy in other areas. While Wee Willie Colston had been put on hold, the others arrested in the Gritters raid would appear at the local Divisional court the next day on charges of assault and – in a couple of cases, including the pram woman – additional charges of handling controlled drugs. Some had already been identified as being wanted for other outstanding warrants.

'I got hold of Chief Inspector Arnott out at Kirkintilloch. He knows you may be out to see Muriel Baker sometime tonight.' She made a smart heel-and-toe drop-down gear change, rocketed the Golf in a swish of tyres past a chauffeur-driven Rolls-Royce which had been hogging the middle of the wet road, and exchanged gestures with the chauffeur in a way that needed no translation. 'As far as I can check, there's nothing new in from either Fraud Squad team and everything else is on hold until you say different.'

Thane hoped it would stay that way. But he had a growing feeling it probably wouldn't.

Somehow, Sandra Craig had also managed to raid the headquarters canteen and had escaped with an emergency ration brown paper bag crammed with four bananas, some chocolate biscuits, and a wedge of slightly tired looking cherry cake. Thane helped himself to a banana, heard her humming as she chewed some of the cake, and smiled to himself.

It didn't take much to make Attila the Hen feel happy again. Even in rain!

They reached the Crime Squad compound with several minutes in hand, parked the Golf in its slot, and then parted. Inside the building, Maggie Fyffe had temporarily abandoned her role as Squad commander's personal secretary and was standing in at the reception desk, and spared a quick smile when she saw Thane.

'I passsed most of the calls for you through to Phil Moss,' reported the middle-aged brunette. 'But Commander Hart phoned again from Brussels, wanting a word. The latest is that Our Leader will now be stuck there until tomorrow, so it stays your show until he gets back.' She shrugged. 'There's nothing much in his diary, I've cancelled some appointments I know don't matter. Meantime he says you've not to start any wars. I told him you got along all right with our Sir Andy Silverhill.'

'And he said?'

'A simple thank God, and he'll call again later.' She thumbed towards the stairs. 'Phil Moss has your troops in the main duty room. But before you think of going up there, Mary called. I told her you'd call back, and she's at home.'

Thane nodded. On Wednesdays, his wife spent only mornings at the medical centre. He pulled over a reception desk 'phone, tapped for an outside line, then called his home number. Mary answered on the third ring.

'Me,' he told her. 'Can you feed me if I make it home for a couple of hours then disappear again?'

'I think I can cope,' said Mary wryly.

But there was something in her voice. Thane asked, 'Have we a problem?'

'You tell me,' she answered. 'Tommy is home from school with a black eye, Kate is going ballistic, but they won't tell me what happened. They say they'll sort it out on their own.'

Thane sighed. 'Keep them tied down for now. I'll be home in an hour or so.'

He hung up and grimaced to Maggie Fyffe.

'The peasants revolting again?' she asked sympathetically.

'They'll survive,' he said flatly, then headed upstairs.

With one absence – and a couple of unexpected additions – there was a full team turn-out waiting when Thane walked into the duty room. A semi-circle of chairs had been drawn up in the sunlight pouring in through one of the windows and their other Maggie – Maggie Donald – was briskly dispensing coffee from a large metal pot into large stoneware mugs with a smile on her pert young face. The reason might be the way in which Dougie Lennox was keeping his distance from her. In fact, the baby-faced detective constable seemed to be wary of every woman in the room.

Which, surprisingly, included DCI Tina Redder. The Broom-stick Lady had brought along Francey Dunbar, a slim detective inspector in his late twenties who had jet black hair and a straggle of bandit moustache and who walked with a limp and the aid of a black ebony cane with a silver knob. The limp was a permanent souvenir of a crash in which another Crime Squad man had been killed.

'Mind if we sit in?' asked Tina Redder. 'There's a chance I could give some input – '

'Or maybe even learn something,' said Sandra Craig sweetly

from a few paces away, where she had been talking wih Phil Moss.

'You're welcome, Tina.' Thane treated his sergeant to a warning glare, then looked around. 'Where's Jock Dawson?' The dog handler was the absentee.

'Kennel time,' shrugged Phil Moss 'He says he'll be around when he's needed.'

Thane drew a deep, patient breath and let it out slowly. It was all spelled out in Dog Branch agreements. Police dogs and handlers were rostered for a standard seven hour shift – plus what was known as the kennel hour, when each dog had to be groomed and whatever else was needed. Even detective superintendents could envy some Dog Branch agreements.

Most police dogs lived at home with their owners, as part of the family. If a dog handler ended carrying his dog around in his own car, he could charge mileage. He could charge valeting the vehicle – and if he decided he needed a second vehicle to transport his police dog around, then there were even interest-free car purchase loans available. But not a penny of it was grudged when one of those same dogs was equally ready to face a gun or knives at a simple command.

'Then let's get to it.' Thane looked around as they settled in chairs. Beauty and the Beast were nearest the window, Beauty at her china-doll best, the Beast, needing a shave, looking more than ever like a gorilla in disguise. Whatever their appearance, Beauty could be as hard as any cut diamond and Thane had seen the massive Beast weep tears at the sight of a murdered child. Discounting Tina Redder and Francey Dunbar, adding Jock Dawson, he had a team of seven at his immediate disposal – a reasonable number by normal Crime Squad standards, with others available if he had to haul them off other investigations.

For now, at least, they should be enough. He found a chair for himself, sat astride it saddle-style resting his elbows against its wooden back, and gave them a reasonably friendly scowl.

'To date, we haven't exactly covered ourselves in glory – agreed? So let's try again. I'll start at the top, then everybody tries to fill gaps!'

Thane gave his briefing carefully, yet concisely. Now and again Phil Moss would add a seasoning of additional fact. Tina

Redder chipped in that while Willie Colston supplied Bash, he was also a source of the equally infamous Jelly Joints – blended temazepam and cannabis, too often a housewife's favourite against despair and depression.

Thane thanked her, knowing that handing over Colston had already cost the DCI. Real success in a drugs operation came from undamaged contacts, from an ability to trace back to a known dealer's supply sources. Every time a local dealer was put away there was a queue of other criminals eager for the job. But hitting at the international links lurking deep in every background was what really counted.

'And we can really rattle Wee Willie's cage,' mused Francey Dunbar, gently stroking the silver knob on his ebony cane. 'He certainly caught us wrong-footed with the baby in the pram trick.'

'We had a lucky break.' Moss gave a vicious belch, then glanced at Thane. 'We still leave him in his cell until tomorrow?'

'Why not?' asked Thane gravely. 'Call it thinking time.'

'And a good night's sleep, poor soul,' agreed Moss with appropriate solemnity.

Next on the list came Muriel Baker and her friends. With nothing new relating to Sam Baker's widow or the Kirkintilloch inquiries, the more immediate target had become Liz Rankin, with her flat at Cunard View and her office located at Cadogan Street.

Where there had been richer pickings. Neighbours in her Cunard View block of flats claimed to have heard the sounds of late-night visitors, from footsteps to her door opening and closing. One couple had twice heard a man's voice raised in an argument. Scenes of Crime, checking the flat after Liz Rankin's burglary report, agreed that there seemed to have been a genuine break-in – but they had been unable to find any backing, unsmudged fingerprint evidence.

The Cadogan Street office scene had been for Dougie Lennox and Maggie Donald. The building's main tenant was Kingsley Estates, a land management and factoring service with responsibilities covering everything from farms and forestries to housing estates and industrial sites. While Kingsley Estates were sole occupants of the two top floors in the Cadogan Street building, part of the two lower floors were on a long-term sub-let to Rex

Insurance Agencies, an outside company which handled general home and life insurance and also had a specialised interest in pensions investments.

'They've about thirty of a staff and this Liz Rankin manages the pensions investment side, sir,' reported Maggie Donald, the soft Highland lilt strong in her voice. 'She's been with Rex Agencies since – '

'Since her teens,' agreed Thane. 'That part we know. Move on, Maggie.'

'Sir.' Maggie Donald flushed, but ignored a small snigger from Dougie Lennox. 'She may be one of the bosses, but she's still well enough liked. No particular hang-ups that anyone knows about.' Pausing, their temporary recruit glanced at a page of her notebook. 'The fair-haired man you saw her meet is Adam Oliver, who is manager – '

'Chief executive,' corrected Dougie Lennox cheerfully.

' – chief executive of Kingsley Estates.' She took the new correction with something close to a snap, and her flush deepened. 'Cadogan Street is their head office, and they've around forty employees. The Rankin woman and Oliver, have been seen together on dates. She has told colleagues there's nothing serious in it, but they don't believe it.'

'Why should they?' grinned Lennox. He leaned forward in his chair and took over. 'For the record, boss, Kingsley Estates came to Cadogan Street about three years ago and rented their spare space to Rex Agencies soon afterwards. Rex Agencies moved from their last address because they needed more room.' He beamed at Thane. 'End of story.'

'What about the doorman?' reminded Thane coldly.

'I – uh – ' the baby-faced detective constable hesitated and gave a quick, hopeful glance at Maggie Donald.

'Tam Reynolds, sir.' She picked it up seamlessly. 'Moved into the job soon after Kingsley Estates arrived in Cadogan Street. Not particularly liked and enjoys making important noises, spends most of his time running after Oliver.'

'Always keep the boss happy,' grunted Moss. 'Empires are built that way.'

Thane let it pass. 'Have we anything on Oliver or Reynolds?'

The dark-haired girl shook her head. 'I checked with Records. Nothing on file, boss.'

Which left the third and youngest member of Muriel Baker's small coven. Trudi Andrews, with her razor-cut brunette hair and streaked highlights, was still a relative unknown. Beauty and the Beast had put in some work on her, and had come across one surprise. Kingsley Homes, the estate agencies chain, which employed the late Sam Baker's one-time secretary was a solely owned subsidiary of Kingsley Estates.

'These bloody women!' Thane made it a groan. 'Does Trudi work in any regular way with her Glasgow office or with Adam Oliver?'

'None that we know about, boss,' declared Beauty.

The Beast gave a deep grunt of agreement.

'We have to follow up that Ayr cleaner's tag on Baker's jacket,' Thane told them. 'But we do it quietly. We want to establish things like when the jacket was put in for cleaning, what if anything they remember about the customer, when it was collected after cleaning.'

'Before we finish with Trudi Andrews, what about the mystery boyfriend?' asked Moss.

'Anyway, his name is Gary Shaw,' Beauty chipped in, 'his day job is managing a travel agency in Irvine. The other hat he wears is as a freelance poet. He does a weekly poetry column for one of the dailies and sometimes he gives readings in pubs. That's how he met Trudi, by all accounts.'

'I know his kind.' Tina Redder laughed, a sound like a fractured bell. 'They're usually harmless. If he tripped over a murder, he'd apologise and keep walking.'

There were a scatter of areas to mop up – or pursue. Thane parcelled them out among his team, saw most of them leave, thanked Tina Redder again, then was heading out of the duty room when Phil Moss returned from wherever he'd been.

'It's your lucky day!' A vinegar grin crossed his lined face. 'We've had a call from the Underwater Section. Twenty minutes ago they put two scuba divers into the river at Finnieston Quay, where the Riverman suggested.' Moss happily smacked his thin hands together. 'Ten minutes, and one of them was walking on the roof of Sam Baker's Nissan.'

'Good.' Thane allowed himself a lopsided smile. 'They're sure?'

Moss nodded.' Licence plate checks out. Boot lid and driver's door had burst open. There's a mobile crane getting ready to haul the thing out. Do we go?'

'Yes.' This was something Thane didn't want to miss.

Half an hour later, they were standing on a sunlit Clydeside quay almost under the shadow of one of Glasgow's newest and largest hotels. A guest looking out of many of its bedroom windows could have been tempted to flick a cigarette end across the quayside below and into the river.

Further along, beside the hotel car park, a heavy recovery truck was in position on the quayside, close to the edge. The truck's extended crane boom reached out with a thick wire cable hanging from it into the water, where an Underwater Search launch waited with its engine barely murmuring. One diver was visible beside the launch and a steady plume of air bubbles marked where another was working under the surface.

'No mystery about this one, Mr Thane,' said the bear-like police inspector standing beside them.

Ben Isson ran Strathclyde's Underwater police squad. One of Isson's favourite training routines for new recruits was to have them march into the river on one shore and keep going until they marched out on the opposite bank. Whatever he said always mattered.

'Tell,' invited Thane.

'The way the Nissan is lying on the bottom, she was deliberately dumped. She's still in gear, the key is in the ignition. For the driver, it was a point and jump job.'

Isson shrugged. 'Late at night, this side of the car park, there would be no witnesses. And it is reasonably deep water – in the old days, trans-Atlantic liners could berth along here.'

'What about the way your lads found the boot lid and driver's door lying open?' Phil Moss gave a questioning frown.

'That happens. When a car hits water, there's impact accompanied by a surge of air displacement. I've seen them come up with every door open, plus bonnet and boot.' Isson stopped as someone waved from the launch. 'They're ready to lift. Okay?'

Thane nodded and Isson signalled the recovery truck. The truck engine began throbbing, the winch drum began turning, and that thick wire cable quickly lost its slack. More and more dripping wet cable came out of the water, a first glimmer of metallic paint became visible then, finally, the Nissan's roof broke surface.

Five minutes later, Sam Baker's powder blue coupé was back on the quayside, paintwork covered in river mud and slime, water still pouring from its doors and boot. Respecting the finders' rights, Thane and Moss allowed Isson and his crew of divers to make a brief first inspection.

'Things are the way you'd expect after being under water, superintendent,' reported Isson after only a brief delay. 'But no more bodies.' He wiped his mud-covered hands on the chest of his scuba suit. 'Did you expect any, sir?'

'No. And it's not a disappointment. I've problems enough.' Thane thanked the man, then turned to Moss. 'Phil – '

'I know,' said Moss resignedly. 'I wrap things up here.' He gave a half-strangled belch. 'You want the car to be delivered straight for full forensic examination, and when you say examination – '

'I mean I want it totalled,' agreed Thane. 'Say we'll want their report by morning.' He glanced at his watch. 'I'm heading home. For once, I'll maybe make it on time.'

'Enjoy your meal,' scowled Moss. 'Don't even think of me.'

'But I will,' promised Thane. 'I'll ask Mary for a doggy bag!'

Even if some cloud was beginning to push in, the evening was still dry when Colin Thane reached home. The time was a little before five p.m., and a woman further along the street was cutting her grass with a badly silenced petrol mower. Some children were massacring each other with toy guns in a game of what looked like cowboys versus spacemen. When Thane stopped the Crime Squad Ford in his narrow driveway and climbed out, he could also hear Clyde barking somewhere indoors. But there was no sign of Tommy or Kate.

That was never good.

He found Mary in the kitchen, and she gave him an ominously quick kiss then went back to setting the table for their meal.

'Kids upstairs?' he asked.

She nodded and glared at the ceiling. 'I'm thinking of murdering them.'

134

'Want me to talk with them?'

'I've a better priority,' she said grimly. 'I need a drink.'

Thane poured measures of whisky into two glasses, left the drinks neat, and brought them over. After a few sips, he asked, 'Have they said anything more?'

'No.' Mary finished her drink in a single gulp and set down the glass. 'All I'm told is to leave them alone – that they'll handle it.' She shrugged. 'Usual routine, all right? After we've eaten, I'll try Tommy, you tackle Kate. It usually works better that way.'

The meal wasn't quite ready and there was time to go into the front room and watch part of the local TV news bullletin. Except that at about halfway through he heard the telephone ringing. It was answered, then Mary stuck her head round the doorway.

'For you,' she said. 'Jack Hart.'

Thane went through and took the call. Wherever the Crime Squad commander might be, he could hear laughter and music in the background.

'Heavy weather, these conferences,' said a solemn Hart over the line from Brussels. 'Maggie Fyffe says that you know I can't make it back until tomorrow. But my nose is still troubling me. You're happy about what happened with our Sir Andy?'

'You'd have been proud of me,' said Thane sardonically. 'I said Please and Thank You at all the right places.'

'That makes a change.' Jack Hart gave a relieved chuckle. 'And the rest of it?'

'Nothing that can't wait until you get back,' reported Thane unemotionally. He heard another burst of laughter at the Brussels end of the line. 'Enjoy your evening.'

'Well, of course, it's another work session. Remember, until I return you've full authority. Any decisions you take, I'll back.' The Squad commander made a quick, throat-clearing noise. 'I – uh – I called Gloria.'

'She'd be glad to hear from you.' Thane grinned at the mouthpiece. Jack Hart's wife wasn't the kind of woman he'd ever want to cross.

'Uh – yes, she was. Good night,' said Hart, and hung up.

As the TV news bulletin finished, Thane heard Tommy and Kate being called down for their meal – and when he went through and saw them, it was hard to keep a totally straight face. Tommy had a scowl, a half-inch cut on his lower lip which still oozed blood, and the makings of a prize-winning black eye. Kate was unmarked, but she was fussing around her brother as if he had been in mortal combat. In between times, Thane could almost feel the anger coming from her in waves.

Sensibly, Clyde had disappeared from sight.

The meal began with a creamed vegetable soup, then came a home-made lasagne with a thick, lightly crisped Gloucester cheese topping which was one of their children's favourites. But it was still a meal eaten in what was close to a sullen silence, and at the finish Thane had had enough.

'You.' He pointed at Kate then thumbed at the door. 'Now.'

She got up, said nothing, dabbed at her mouth with a tissue, then followed him through to the front room. Once they were in, Thane closed the door behind them.

'Do we shout at each other standing up or sitting down?' he asked gravely.

The start of a grin showed at the corners of her mouth and she settled into the nearest armchair. Thane chose the one opposite. At last he gave in and broke the silence.

'So what's going on?'

'Nothing.' His daughter shrugged. 'Nothing. It's like we told mum – nothing that Tommy and I can't sort out.'

Thane sighed. 'Wrong answer, Kate. I'm a cop, remember?'

'Are we likely to forget, dad?' she said bleakly.

He winced. It was always there in the background. Police families lost out easily. On the one hand, wife and family were expected to be shining lights in their community. On the other hand, if anything did go wrong the verdict was that they should have known better. He'd known cops who loved the job yet still eventually resigned because family pressures became too much.

'Will I try again?' he asked quietly.

A small devil of amusement showed in her eyes. 'Aren't you supposed to caution me first, dad? Can't I ask for a lawyer or a 'phone call or something?'

'Give over.' Thane rubbed his hands across his face and sighed. 'Who's involved in it, Kate? You or Tommy?'

Her mouth tightened for moment. 'It started with me, then Tommy got dragged into things. But it's like I said – we can sort it out.'

'If you can't, you'll tell us?'

136

She nodded.

'Until then, you stop taking it out on your ancient parents. Agreed?'

'Agreed.' She surprised him by crossing over and touching his shoulder. 'Thanks, dad.'

'Get lost!' He grinned a little and considered his daughter carefully. 'For now, tell your brother it's time he learned the best way to block a punch. You get your own punch in first!'

Five minutes later he heard them both leaving the house. They were taking Clyde for a walk on his leash, and they were laughing. When he went through to the kitchen to help Mary clear up, she gave a slightly happier smile which said all that was needed.

As they'd arranged, Sandra Craig parked her white Golf outside Thane's home at nine p.m. By then the night had become bright with moonlight in a velvet sky which twinkled with stars. When his sergeant came into the house, she received her usual welcome from dog and children, while Mary inspected her visitor with more interest than usual.

Detective Sergeant Craig had set aside her usual working denim outfit. In its place, she was wearing a short-length sleeveless linen shift dress patterned in cream and brown. The shift had a scooped neckline, she had tied a long fine chain of antique silver around the waist, and she had brown calf leather cuban heeled shoes. A cream wool jacket was slung loosely over her shoulders, and her hair had been brushed until it shone like spun copper.

'Like the outfit,' murmured Mary enviously 'Going on to a date, Sandra?'

'A late invitation to an airport party.' Sandra was cautious. 'It starts at midnight. A bunch of brand new Fleet Air Arm pilots want to celebrate.'

'That could be wild,' said Mary with a wistful note of envy. 'Enjoy.' Then she smiled at Thane, who was approaching. 'Whatever happens, get there. And I want to hear about it – but don't tell him!'

Minutes later, Detective Sergeant Sandra Craig was in the front passenger seat of the Ford when Thane set off. As they turned towards the motorway junction, Thane felt his nostrils twitch and fought down a grin in the darkness of the car's interior. Sandra was trying out a new perfume, one that had to be expensive – and the kind that probably came with a built-in man-killing guarantee!

It was a quiet time on the route to Kirkintilloch, still too early for travellers off on an evening out. Most of the time Thane drove in silence, once again going over in his mind what had to be dealt with when he met up with Muriel Baker and her friends. Then, with the lights of Kirkintilloch on the skyline ahead, he flicked on the car's FM set, punched one of the buttons, and they travelled the rest of the way listening to one of Radio Clyde's quieter jazz programmes.

Kirkintilloch itself seemed deserted as they travelled through its streets. They halted briefly at a road junction by a traffic signal which had no other traffic to control. Then it was down into Legion Grove, past a parked unlit police car – local police, fulfilling their promise to maintain a token presence for a day or so – and on to the small grey stone villa halfway down the Grove's length.

'Well, now,' murmured Sandra Craig as they slowed to a stop. 'What have we got?'

Now they weren't alone any more. Two cars were already parked and empty outside the house. Trudi Andrews' red Renault four-door saloon was lying nose to tail with a large white Mercedes-Benz saloon. As the Ford became third in the line under a solitary streetlamp, Sandra Craig was already radioing in for a PNC vehicle check and seconds later the reply came back as a soft murmur over a speaker.

'Andrew Oliver?' asked Thane.

She nodded.

'Good.' Thane had the feeling another piece might be about to fall into place.

'Let's go meet him.' He reached for his door handle, then stopped for a moment. 'Sandra, we watch our backs. Understand?'

'Sir.' She climbed out, carefully smoothed down the front of her shift dress, and was ready.

They walked the gravel path to the front door, seeing lights behind closed curtains in the front room and hearing muffled

138

voices. But the conversation ended on the ring when Thane pressed the bellpush. A few more moments, then a quick, low murmur of voices began and ended inside. They heard soft footsteps, then an outside light came on above their heads and there was a click as the front door was unlocked and swung open.

'Superintendent Thane – Sergeant!' Muriel Baker looked out at them, an oddly wary expression on her thin face, and moistened her lips. 'We – I've got visitors. In fact, we talked about you, Mr Thane, only minutes ago.' She frowned. 'It's late. Why are you here?'

'We've recovered your husband's car from the river,' Thane told her.' I thought you'd want to know – and I'm sorry, but we've more questions to ask.'

Baker's widow drew a deep breath, then nodded. 'Come in. I don't mind an audience.'

Thane and Sandra Craig went in and waited in the small, drab hallway while Muriel Baker closed the door again.

It might be less than twenty-four hours since they'd last seen Sam Baker's widow, but in that time the woman had already acquired a new poise and there was a degree of fresh confidence behind that cautious smile. Her mousey hair was still worn in that thick French pleat, but now with a broad ribbon of white lace woven through it. The black wool sweater and shapeless grey skirt of yesterday had gone, and in their place Muriel Baker wore a blue cotton dress that looked brand new and shrieked Designer Label. She wore lipstick, and she had a single string of pearls around her neck.

'How have things been?' asked Sandra Craig mildly.

'No problems, sergeant.' Baker's widow led them over to the door to her front room, opened it, and beckoned them through. 'You know Liz and Trudi, of course – '

There were four people seated in the softly lit room, and there were drinks lying on a small table to one side. Trudi Andrews and Liz Rankin shared a couch, the younger woman wearing tailored, tan coloured trousers and a dark, embroidered top, Liz Rankin in a russet brown knitted suit with a scooped neckline, and their welcome was restrained. The two men with them were already on their feet, expressions hard to read, while Thane, recognising them both, kept his own face impassive.

139

'Detective Superintendent Thane, Detective Sergeant Craig, this is Adam Oliver – ' Muriel Baker dealt with introductions without fuss or emotion ' – Adam gave Liz a lift out here tonight. And Gary Shaw – Gary came out with Trudi.'

Thane shook hands with the two men. The chief executive of Kingsley Estates was dressed in a white rollneck sweater, dark corduroy trousers and a lightweight blue blazer. Beside him, Gary Shaw, looked much less assured. When he managed a nervous smile, it revealed that one of his front teeth was badly chipped.

'Why don't we all sit down,' suggested the widow quickly. 'Adam, if you can pull in a couple of extra chairs – '

Adam Oliver dragged over two chairs then perched himself on the edge of the couch beside Liz Rankin, while Muriel Baker settled in one of the additional chairs and Sandra Craig took the other.

'Superintendent – ' the widow gestured towards the remaining chair.

'I've been driving. I'm happy to stand.' Colin Thane went back to the door and leaned against it. 'I'm glad all of you are here. As meetings go, this one is overdue.'

'I don't understand, Superintendent.' Liz Rankin frowned and used one hand to brush back a loose strand of her long, jet-black hair. 'What do you mean, overdue?'

Thane smiled then looked at the men opposite him. 'Tell me something. Did you both enjoy your meal at the Lock Gate yesterday?'

Any movement in the room seemed to freeze to a dramatic halt. Gary Shaw visibly swallowed, Oliver glanced towards Liz Rankin and Trudi Andrews, and both women simply stared.

'What do you mean?' Shaw began a weak bluster. 'What meal?'

'I think he knows,' said Trudi Andrews wryly. She turned towards Thane, and the room lighting caught the blonde highlights in her razor-cut hair. 'So we were wasting our time?'

'With the story about the strangers who tried to pick you up?' Thane nodded towards Sandra Craig. 'I've a sergeant who has to be fed at regular intervals. We decided to take a meal break – but our table was on the outside.'

'Damn,' said Adam Oliver softly. Then he smiled. 'You know,

140

superintendent, if you'd come along about half an hour earlier you'd have arrived in time to hear us telling Muriel – and apologising for what we did.'

'It's true.' Baker's widow nodded. 'They have. I'm still trying to understand why they did it.'

'We told you,' said Gary Shaw and gestured with his long, thin hands. 'There wasn't any real need, for a start. What difference did it make? Who wants to tell the police anything they don't need to know?'

'It was my idea,' admitted Oliver. He paused for a moment, sucking at an edge of that toothbrush bristle of moustache. 'The girls suggested we both travel out here yesterday and separately from them – that we might be needed to help. So we did.'

'Why separately?'

'Personal reasons.' The man angrily slammed one fist into the palm of his other hand. 'We were there, but we weren't needed. End. Damn it, Liz and I try to keep a low profile about what we do together. We've enough problems with office gossip.'

'And you two?' Thane raised an eyebrow towards Gary Shaw and Trudi Andrews.

Shaw shrugged. 'We just did. It didn't matter to me one way or the other – or to Trudi. We didn't see how it could make any difference to Muriel to go along with what Adam and Liz wanted.'

'Mrs Baker?' Sandra Craig leaned forward in her chair and looked directly at the widow. 'Would it have made a difference?'

The woman shook her head. 'If I'd known about that or the other things – no.'

'You still wouldn't have minded?' suggested Thane. His voice hardened. 'Let's talk about those "other things". Suppose we do that, starting with you, Muriel. Are there any changes yet in what you've told me?'

'No.' Bitterly, she shook her head. 'If Sam ever did sneak back here – '

'She said no already,' cut in Trudi Andrews fiercely. 'Leave her alone!'

'We want to do that,' said Thane.

Sandra Craig nodded grimly. 'But we're not exactly being helped, are we?'

That silenced the little group around them.

'These other things,' persisted Thane. 'Were they why our car tyres were slashed at the restaurant car park?'

He met blank, puzzled stares. So blank that they had to be genuine.

'What do you know about a blue Transit van?'

Muriel Baker pursed her lips. 'The local police asked about a blue van seen around here.' She shook her head. 'No, I can't help.'

There were other questions which Thane and his sergeant tried around. None brought any kind of answer that mattered and, while Adam Oliver had lapsed into a resigned patience, it was different with Shaw. The younger man had moved nearer to Trudi Andrews.

'How much longer does this go on?' he complained. 'I've had enough of it!'

'Gary and Adam came out to help,' reminded the young brunette fiercely.

'And that's what we're asking you to do, Mr Shaw,' soothed Thane. His attention had strayed. Liz Rankin had got to her feet and had gone over to the window. She had opened a small gap in the closed, faded velvet curtains and was looking out.

Shaw's sallow face darkened. 'Then why do I get the feeling that I need a lawyer?'

'Because of some questions?' Thane shook his head. 'I wouldn't say so.'

'You're helping us, maybe we're helping you,' suggested Sandra Craig. 'You can write one of your poems about it all.'

For a moment Shaw stared at her, then he moistened his lips. 'Who told you I write poetry?'

'We know a few things about most people, Mr Shaw.' Thane gave a scowl towards his red-haired sergeant, wishing that she had kept her mouth shut.

Liz Rankin looked round from the window, a hand resting above the neckline of her dress. 'Muriel, maybe you'd like to pour another round of drinks. I – I'd like a private word with Superintendent Thane.' She looked at him. 'Please?'

Thane nodded. While the others sat in temporary silence and Muriel Baker moved to refill the glasses, he followed Liz Rankin

142

out of the room. The raven-haired woman led the way out into the hall, closed the room door firmly, then faced him.

'This morning you asked if Sam Baker ever came to my flat,' she said quietly. 'I'll give you my answer now. Yes, he did. At one time, years ago, often. Too often. More often than I ever wanted, once I discovered what he was really like. So I threw him out – for my sake as well as for Muriel's.'

'But Muriel didn't know?' guessed Thane.

'Still doesn't.' The woman looked at him earnestly. 'Does she have to now?'

'Maybe not. I can't promise,' said Thane carefully.

'I'll settle for that.' Liz Rankin chewed her lower lip for a moment. 'We're talking years back now. And after he came out of jail, he'd come round only occasionally, usually half-drunk – and I would try not to let him in over the doorstep. There was nothing else to it.'

Thane nodded. 'But?'

'Less than a month ago, just before he disappeared, he appeared on the doorstep three times in one week. He said he needed my help.' She shook her head. 'I refused, point blank.'

'What kind of help?' asked Thane.

'To look after a package for him,' said Liz Rankin simply. 'He said he had to hide it, that it was worth a lot of money. But I still said no – and threw him out.' She pursed her lips. 'Look, superintendent, after they married I was – well, briefly involved with him. But that was years ago, and Muriel was always my friend. I – I just don't want to have to tell her, particularly now. But, my God, she's well rid of him.'

'Tell me about Adam Oliver.' Thane nodded towards the room door. 'How does he fit in?'

'Adam?' Her expression lightened. 'I told you about my brother Robin, who was killed in an air crash. He and Adam were pilots together, friends. Afterwards – well, after a spell Adam got in touch with me again. Now we are close.' She paused. 'Very close, superintendent.'

'One question,' said Thane slowly, choosing his words carefully. 'Did Baker say what was in the package he wanted you to hide, or why it was important?'

'No.' She shook her head. 'The last time he came, I took a saw-edged bread knife to the door with me.' She gave a tight, almost hysterical giggle. 'I threatened to cut his throat if he came back again. And – well, I didn't see him again.'

When they went back into the room Muriel Baker had finished topping up the drinks glasses. She went through the motions of offering Thane and his sergeant a drink, but didn't seem disappointed when they refused.

He had a few more questions to ask, none of them important, most bringing answers he had expected. Then he signalled to Sandra Craig and they left.

Muriel Baker saw them out. The ribbon decorated French pleat in her mousey hair swung against her shoulders as she walked ahead of them through the little hall. But Thane's last impression was something very different.

As they left the room he had casually glanced back to say goodbye. In that moment, he met Adam Oliver's gaze. The man's cold blue eyes had acquired a hard, merciless quality. Then, just as suddenly, that look had gone and the one-time flier was smiling towards Liz Rankin.

But that moment was something Thane knew he shouldn't forget.

Night had acquired a chill September edge as they walked back towards Thane's Ford and Sandra Craig, shivering in that lightweight shift dress, burrowed deeper into her wool jacket.

Thane had the Ford's heater churning as soon as they were driving out of Kirkintilloch. As they travelled, partly to sort the story in his own mind, he told his sergeant the details of Liz Rankin's story.

'So it looks like Sam Baker really had come up with something,' said the redhead softly.' And he was becoming scared.'

'But he wasn't rushing to get to us with it.' Thane slowed at a junction near a busy hotel bar-lounge with bright neon signs and a full car park.

'Suppose he was hoping for a way to play both ends against the middle?'

As they got under way again, Sandra Craig frowned in the faint glow of the car's instrument lights. 'If he was fool enough – '

His sergeant left it there as they heard Thane's call-sign

coming over the low-band speaker. She used the handset to answer, listened, then swore under her breath.

'Repeat please,' she asked, and switched the message to the centrally mounted speaker.

Thane listened as the calmly detached voice of the Squad's night team supervisor repeated the message. Shots had been fired from a car, aimed at a house in Bellside Avenue, Glasgow. The house was occupied by the family of a William Colston, presently in police custody. No injuries had been reported.

'Tell them we're on our way,' said Thane grimly. He heard Sandra Craig sigh as she once more reached for the handset . 'We'll look, we'll see. Fair?'

'Fair,' said the redhead resignedly.

Then Thane had the Ford's accelerator pedal on the floorboard and their speed began climbing while their blue lights began flashing and their siren cut in with its screaming wail. Despite having to fight a way through the dregs of traffic exiting after two separate floodlit league football matches, they still managed to reach Glasgow and Bellside Avenue within the half hour.

Wee Willie Colston's home was easy to spot. Incident tape barriers sealing off part of the roadway outside the three storey tenement block, second because of the total lack of any sign of life, from house lights to spectators, for some distance around.

Bellside's residents had long adopted their own the Three Wise Monkeys philosophy of see no evil, hear no evil, speak no evil. Translated, it amounted to 'They're polis. Keep your mouth shut.'

Thane pulled in at the end of the line of other police vehicles. One, he was glad to see, was a Crime Squad car with its two night shift crew already heading towards his Ford. Climbing out into the chill night, his sergeant at his heels, he met the pair halfway.

'Anybody hurt?' It was the thing that mattered most.

'No sir.' The night man who answered, a stolid Edinburgh sergeant not noted for imagination, shook his head. 'It was a drive-by, usual style. Stick a gun out of the car window and spray as you go past. Colston's house is first floor, the front windows were shot out by an automatic weapon – 9 mm, and they've collected eight cartridge cases so far.'

'Witnesses?'

'None, sir.' The night team sergeant paused, he and his companion both eyeing Sandra Craig's party-going outfit with surprised interest.

'That's about it, sir. Scenes of Crime are around somewhere.' Nudged by his companion, the Edinburgh sergeant glanced over his shoulder and sighed. 'And here's the local DI – keeps asking what the hell is going on.'

The local divisional DI was a Campbell, horse-faced, and awkward enough, like most Campbells, to demand a sight of the new arrivals' warrant cards before he talked sense.

'Sir.' Campbell's long face grew longer. 'I heard you're already holding Willie Colston in custody. Maybe I should have a word with him – wherever he is.'

'Sorry.' Thane shook his head. 'He's our prisoner. Right now, I don't want him meeting anyone. Even his family.'

'But – ' Campbell flushed. ' – but – '

'Sorry.' Thane cut him short. 'Later. It stays that way unless you want to make an official written request – from your Chief Constable to our Squad commander.' He said a quick mental prayer. Jack Hart would go berserk if that happened. 'We're probably only talking a day or so.'

'Then we'll just wait, sir.' The mention of his Chief Constable had been more than enough for Campbell. He offered a quick token to sooth any ruffled feathers.

'Uh – our Scenes of Crime people think the weapon was probably a Uzi machine pistol. Though where the hell the drive-by team got their hands on one – '

'Liverpool,' said Sandra Craig mildly. 'There's a Yardie team down there who'll do a rental deal.' She smiled at Campbell's surprise. 'There was a fax about them a couple of weeks back.'

'Right.' The divisional man nodded his thanks and looked at the redhead again. 'Oblige me, sergeant. Can I see your warrant card again?' When Sandra Craig fished it out, he took a second quick glance under the streetlighting, then nodded. 'Thanks. I – uh – just wanted to check on your name.' Another nod, this time towards Thane, and he had departed.

'Fan club material?' asked Thane dryly.

'I never date cops,' said his sergeant coldly, and took a quick, sad glance at her wristwatch.

'Wise, sergeant. Very wise.' Thane turned back to the two Crime Squad men.

'Hang about, see this out. Don't stand too hard on Campbell's toes. But tell – no, ask the Transport Police to make sure that there's no way Willie Colston can hear about this shooting until we're ready. Looks like his would-be successors were sending a message to him. He's finished, in a few days his business will belong to someone else. It will be as if Willie never existed.' He beckoned. 'Sergeant, come on. Or do you want to damage the morale of the Fleet Air Arm?'

'Ready when you are, boss,' grinned Detective Sergeant Sandra Craig and they headed back to the Crime Squad Ford.

Thane resisted the temptation to use siren or lights on the drive from Bellside across the city to his home. But he couldn't have been accused of wasting time, and even Sandra Craig sat very quiet most of the way. They arrived at Thane's home at eleven fifty and within seconds she had tumbled out of the Ford and was heading for where her white Golf lay waiting.

'Sergeant – ' Thane hailed her as she opened the driver's door ' – enjoy your evening. But usual start time tomorrow.' He grinned. 'Well, give or take a little, all right?'

'Sir.' Then she was aboard and the Golf was rocketing on its way towards the airport party.

Shaking his head, Thane got out and walked towards his front door. Mary opened it as he arrived.

'You got her back in time?' she chuckled her surprise. 'How?'

'Desperation,' said Thane woodenly. 'Women terrify me.'

'Do they?' asked Mary in a murmur, and hauled him into the lobby. 'That's interesting, officer. Tell me more – the kids are asleep.'

And she very quietly closed the front door.

6

Thursday morning brought a grey drizzle of a dawn and Colin Thane, needing an early start, had set his alarm for six a.m.

While Mary groaned and burrowed deeper under the sheets, he forced himself out of bed,showered, shaved, teamed a blue shirt and a knitted blue tie with his Donegal tweed suit, then went downstairs. By then Mary was already there, wandering around in her dressing gown, fresh toast made and coffee ready to pour.

'You didn't have to get up,' he protested, while a bleary-eyed boxer dog glared at them both from his basket.

'Why alter the servile habits of a lifetime?' His wife yawned, swallowed some coffee from her cup, and rested her elbows on the kitchen table. 'Good luck with your day. I'll maybe go back to bed again.'

Ten minutes later Thane had left home and was on his way to work. The roads, wet with overnight rain, were still building their early-start traffic, and he made good time. It was barely seven a.m. when he drove the Ford into the Crime Squad compound. At that hour, the headquarters building was almost deserted and he surprised the night duty team, who were mostly killing time until their dayshift replacements arriving. The upper floor area was deserted, but when Thane went into his office a larger than usual batch of faxes and report sheets was waiting on his desk, all held down by an old brass ashtray filled with paperclips.

Until Commander Hart returned from Brussels, the extra paperwork went with his being second-in-command. Thane sorted his way through the overnights, some of them reports on overnight inquiries from his own team. A couple of them he folded carefully and put in an inside pocket. Then he turned to the rest, which covered everything from a major art robbery in Edinburgh to a warning from the Royal Canadian Mounted Police that a man on an incoming flight from Toronto to Glasgow was wanted for murder. He scribbled notes on some, initialled the rest, and dumped everything on Sandra Craig's desk for whenever she arrived.

Finished, he was ready to leave when Maggie Donald surprised him by coming into his office. The Northern Constabulary girl was wearing chinos and a bright red football top, and had the bright-eyed chirpiness that went with a good night's sleep.

'Good morning, sir.' She gave a broad smile. 'Making an early start?'

'Good guess, Maggie,' he said sourly. 'And what the hell are you doing in at this time?'

'Sandra – uh – I mean Detective Sergeant Craig asked me to cover for her,' explained their temporary recruit. 'Just until she arrives.'

'Whenever that might be.' Thane sighed his acceptance. 'Here's a starter for you. Yesterday, you ran a check on Adam Oliver. Oliver had a friend named Robin Rankin – Liz Rankin's brother. She says that Robin died in a 'plane crash a few years back.'

Maggie Donald beamed. 'You want that checked, sir?'

'Yes.' Thane decided there were mornings when he hated all bright-eyed people. 'But quietly.'

'Quietly it is, sir,' promised the dark-haired young policewoman. She grinned. 'Did you know that the expectant mother who was at Gritters has had a baby boy? Both well!'

'Hooray,' said Thane absently. 'Warn Records.'

He left her. In another couple of minutes he was back in his car, heading for Glasgow and the British Transport Police base.

He arrived there around eight a.m., left the Ford in the Police Only parking area at the rear and went into a modern building where the view was out towards part of Strathclyde University campus. Phil Moss was already established in the railway police canteen, drinking tea and eating an egg and fried bread sandwich.

'You're living dangerously,' warned Thane sourly. 'You've been warned often enough. Fries knock hell out of ulcers.'

'It's my flaming ulcer, not yours.' Moss gave a derisive snort. 'So mind your own damned business – sir.' He set down the newspaper he was reading, a late edition which had an inside page lead story on the Bellside Avenue drive-by shooting. 'Have you heard about the Gritters Racing baby?' He grinned when Thane nodded. 'The mother says I was kind to her. So she wants to name the child Phil, after me!'

'Which is a hell of a way to start any child's life,' said Thane sarcastically. He nodded at the newspaper. 'Colston still hasn't heard about the shooting?'

'That's guaranteed,' said Moss.

'Good.' When Colin Thane had arranged that Wee Willie

149

Colston should be isolated overnight, that had only been intended to help increase the little drug dealer's worries before being questioned. Now it could be even more important. If Colston had heard of the drive-by shooting at his home, any attempt at questioning him would have been a waste of time. Thane picked up Moss's newspaper and tucked it in a pocket. 'Let's rattle our Wee Willie's cage.'

They went through to one of the BTP's basement interview rooms, spartan clean and furnished with a basic table and chairs. As soon as the two detectives were seated behind the table, Colston was escorted in by two large uniformed railway constables. One constable had a thick black beard, both had military service ribbons on their tunics, and the little drugs dealer was dwarfed betwen them.

'Prisoner, halt!' bellowed the bearded constable. 'William Colston as you asked, Superintendent Thane!'

The constables came to attention with a thunderous crash of boots, and Colston visibly quivered while the bearded constable gave Thane a flicker of a wink.

'Sit, you,' snapped Moss.

Unshaven, still dishevelled after his night in a railway police cell, Wee Willie Colston was propelled into a chair on the other side of the table. His soft leather jacket was crumpled, the pink trousers and his shirt were stained and creased. On top of it all, the little man seemed to have physically shrunk since the loss of his Captain yachting cap.

'Sleep well?' asked Thane stonily.

'Sleep? Me? No chance of that from these railway bastards,' complained Colston unhappily.

'I'm afraid there was a wee problem, superintendent.' The black bearded constable made an apologetic throat clearing noise. 'We arrested two vanloads of football drunks around the railway stations last night – all trying to get home after the matches in town. So our cells were full, and the damned fools kept up a sing-song until God knows when this morning.'

'What kind of sing-song?' queried Moss, poker-faced.

'Off-key and obscene – the usual tribal stuff, inspector. Not the kind to win prizes at a Gaelic Mod.' The constable tweaked his beard and indicated Colston. 'The prisoner did – uh – complain.'

'Noted,' murmured Thane. 'Thank you, officers. We'll see him alone.'

'Sir!' Two sets of railway police boots crashed to attention again. Then the constables marched out, the interview room door slamming again as they left.

'When does somebody tell me what the hell is going on?' Wee Willie Colston glared across the table towards Thane. 'Look, Mister – '

'You address him as Detective Superintendent,' corrected Moss stonily. 'Get it right, wee man.'

'Listen, are you pair deaf or something?' snarled Colston his face flushing. 'I asked what the hell is going on! Since I was brought here, it's been like I was in solitary! I haven't as much as heard a radio, the only other people in the world seem to have been football drunks or woodentop railway cops!' Fury boiling over, he slammed a fist on the table. 'I don't care who the hell you two are, pal! I want a lawyer, and I want him now!'

'Shut up, listen, and learn,' ordered Moss. 'Colston, right now, you're in trouble all the way up to your neck. It could get better, it could get even worse.' The scrawny detective inspector had cut himself shaving, and the wound was bleeding again. Little drops of blood were joining the traces of bacon grease spotting his shirt and tie. Dabbing at the cut with a grey-white rag of handkerchief, Moss wasn't happy. 'Which way it goes is going to depend on you.'

'You can't – ' Willie Colston stopped, swallowed, then moistened his lips and waited.

'Don't expect any "good guy – bad guy" routine from us, Colston.' Colin Thane's grey eyes were cold and diamond hard as he considered their prisoner. 'People like you, dealing in drugs, crawl out from under stones.' He stabbed a warning finger across the table. 'Wee Willie Colston is finished, wiped out. We've already got you more ways than we'll ever need. I'm simply going to spell out how much prison time you could be facing – then we'll talk. You understand?'

'Do I have a choice?' For a moment, Colston clung to a fading remnant of a sneer. Then that vanished as Phil Moss released a thunderous warning belch. He moistened his lips. 'All right, I'll listen.'

'We'll start with the obvious – your Gritters drugs operation

151

is wiped out.' Sitting back, Thane loosened his tie then, reaching into his jacket pocket, he brought out the two message slips left for him by Tina Redder. 'Most of the punters we picked up yesterday are queuing to tell us anything that gets them off the hook. We've got you on possession of drugs, we've got you on supply of drugs.' He allowed himself a small, lopsided smile and pushed the first of the two pieces of paper towards the man. 'We can even forecast who's likely to take up your sales territory. The overnight betting is that it goes to someone you maybe know – '

Wee Willie Colston stared at the name on the slip of paper. 'Benjie Lewin – ' he swore in bitter, tight-lipped disbelief ' – that bampot? But – '

'You know how it goes,' mused Thane, with a brief, mental thanks to that unshaven, undercover detective constable on Tina Redder's team. 'When one of your kind goes down, the big boss suppliers down south have the next candidate already lined up and waiting.' He shrugged at the shaken figure in front of them. 'Maybe you've thought of yourself as a big-time drugs baron, Colston. You're not. To them, you're a corner shop operation and nothing more.'

'And now you're going down, wee man.' Moss's voice was like acid. 'You've a schoolboy son who matters to you, right?' He gave a mock sigh. 'As of now, we can put you away for life, Willie.'

'With luck, you might be out on licence for his twenty-first birthday party,' consoled Thane. 'But don't count on that.'

'Keep the boy out of this,' muttered the little man, his plump face paling. 'My family aren't involved.'

'Probably not. But we're checking.' Thane reached for the second message slip and fingered it. 'Let's get back to you. You can be charged with offences involving a total of three controlled drugs – heroin, cannabis and temazepam. Agreed?'

Colston gave a sullen shrug, but said nothing. In the silence, they heard a vehicle engine start out in the yard. A horn blasted, someone shouted, then the noise ended.

'Phil – ' Thane pushed the slip of paper towards Moss. 'Tell him.'

'This is a list of penalties for proven drugs offences.' Moss tapped the sheet in front of him. 'Controlled drugs are either

152

Class A, Class B or Class C. There are separate penalties for possession and actual supply.'

'I'd heard,' muttered Colston sarcastically.

Moss shrugged. 'No harm in reminding you, is there? Heroin comes under Class A. Possession of a Class A substance can mean up to seven years imprisonment or a fine, or both. If we're talking Class A supply, then we're looking at possible life imprisonment.' He paused, moved a finger down the list, then stopped and looked up. 'Then there's cannabis, Willie – number two on your list. Cannabis is a Class B substance. Possession, up to five years imprisonment or a fine. Supplying cannabis? Up to fourteen years imprisonment.' He gave a wolfish grin and tapped the list again. 'And guess what? Here's your number three – temazepam. It's in Group C, small time, but still up to two years or a fine for possession, and up to five years for supply.'

Thane took the list from Moss, folded the sheet, and silently returned it to his pocket. As a tariff, it was one of society's weapons in the fight against drugs.

Class A drugs ranged from heroin to cocaine, from pethidine to diconal, and took in both LSD and Ecstasy plus half a dozen others. Class B, home of cannabis and cannabis resin, also included codeine and amphetamines on its list. Leaving Class C as a catch-all selection of controlled drugs from temazepam and diazepam, temgesic and duromine. Some could be legally pre-scribed for medical purposes. In the wrong hands, all could kill.

'Could we do a deal?' asked Colston suddenly, earnestly.

'You know the rules,' said Thane softly. He kept his face impassive and avoided looking at Moss. 'No deals. But there are maybe different ways of looking at things.'

'Right.'

The little man nodded eagerly. 'You're interested in Sammy Baker?'

Moss gave a quick warning rumble. 'You were formally cau-tioned yesterday. That caution still applies. You understand that, Colston?'

'Would I forget?' Colston's sudden eagerness was almost pathetic. 'Look, about Sammy and me – well, we did prison time together, right? He picked up a drugs habit – nothing big, but he came to me for what he wanted. We – well, we became what you could call friendly. Once we were both outside again we stayed in touch.'

'Meaning that any drugs he used, you still supplied?' asked Moss.

'Yes. He was into a heroin mix, but he kept a grip on things.' Colston brushed that aside. 'The way we got along together, I scratched his back, he scratched mine – he brought me duty-free booze, that kind of thing.' He turned hopefully to Thane. 'But I can tell you that Sammy was scared out of his mind the last few times I saw him!'

Thane raised an eyebrow. 'Why?'

Colston shrugged. 'All he'd say was that he'd discovered something which could get him off the hook with the law, yet could also be worth a lot of money – if he managed to stay alive long enough to collect it.'

'What kind of something?'

'If I knew, I'd tell you.' The little man shrugged uneasily and stuffed his hands into the pockets of his leather jacket. 'That time Sammy didn't make too much sense – he'd been drinking.'

'We need everything he said.' Phil Moss released a low rumble of a belch. 'Anything he told you, anything you remember. Then we decide whether it makes sense. So try, man. For your own sake.'

'Mostly, he rambled on about some widow – she was the one who mattered.' Colston scowled in concentration. 'The way he went on, it was like she came out of the Bible.'

'The Lazarus Widow?' suggested Thane.

'That's her.' Colston gave a surprised nod. 'Good guess!'

'Bloody hell,' said Phil Moss softly. 'What about this Widow?'

'Uh – like it was like some kind of a joke. That she had been hauled out of the grave and was going back to work again.' Nervously, Colston combed his fingers through his greasy hair. 'Look, if I'm helping, you won't forget?'

'We won't,' assured Thane.

Then, between them, Thane and Moss took Wee Willie Colston over the same ground again. There was still nothing more he could tell them.

But it was very different when they moved on from there. Yes, he had been out at Kirkintilloch several times with his blue

154

Transit van, watching around Sam Baker's home in the days after Baker had vanished. Yes, he had seen the gathering at Kirkintilloch after Baker's body had been recovered. Curious about what was happening, he had followed Trudi Andrews and Liz Rankin when they had driven to the Lock Gate Restaurant – and he had seen Thane and Sandra Craig arrive in their cars a little later.

'Then you slashed our tyres.' Thane pursed his lips. 'Why?'

'Well, you were cops, right?' Colston made a vague, comically apologetic gesture with his hands. 'There was nobody around to see me do it. So why not?' He sat back with a hopeful sigh. 'I could use a cup of tea and a fag, Mr Thane.'

'We're not finished,' said Thane curtly. 'Forget Kirkintilloch. Did you know that Baker kept another place here, in the city?'

'Yes.' Colston gave a wary nod.

'Where?' Thane leaned forward grimly. 'And don't even think of messing me about.'

'House C12 at Halloran Flats. It's a tower block south of the river, near Shawlands.' Colston said it in a rush, then a wisp of bleak humour showed in the man's eyes. 'The name on the door is Riley – Betty Riley, a Life-Begins-at-Forty blonde. It's her house, but Sam had what you could call an arrangement. She was his bidie-in – you know, live-in comforts.'

'Have you been near her?'

The man shook his head vehemently. 'Over there, I'm out of my territory, Mr Thane. Hell, I'd sooner stick my head in a lion's mouth!'

And this time they believed him. They got to their feet and headed for the door.

'Mr Thane – ' Wee Willie Colston made it a plea ' – what am I looking at?'

'Now?' Thane shrugged. 'Maybe ten years – we'll tell the court you helped. Keep your nose really clean inside, and you could be out in under four.' He took Moss's newspaper and tossed it on the table. 'Here. Compliments of the Crime Squad. We'll be back.'

He followed Moss out of the room and past the two railway constables waiting outside, then they walked through the corridors of the Transport Police station and out at the main exit. The

155

drizzle of rain had become a downpour, and a swarm of students were scurrrying through it between two of the nearest University campus buildings.

'Do you think he'll enjoy my newspaper?' queried Moss, turning up his jacket collar against the rain.

'Not too much.' Thane gave an unsympathetic grin. 'But there's always the comic strips.'

But there was little humour in his heart as they hurried through the rain to their car. If Colston was right, if the Lazarus Widow was being resurrected again, it meant that one more target was being lured into danger.

Sir Andy Silverhill had been lucky and had got out. The next time, things would not necessarily end in the same way.

Thirty-five minutes later, the rain ended and blue sky overhead again, they were standing outside the high rise block named Halloran Flats. A bleak and time-weathered fifteen-storey tower of pre-cast concrete and steel-framed windows, it sat on a drab surround of broken cobbles and large vandalised pieces of anonymous sculptures which represented local authority culture. Some of the windows above them displayed small, flowering windowboxes – brave attempts by a few tenants to add their individual colour.

'Damn the politicians who build monstrosities like this,' muttered Moss. 'They should be made to live in the bloody things!'

'Are you talking about our leaders who we know and trust?' queried Thane dryly.

'I'd exterminate the lot – and their planners.' Moss paused then gave a grunt and pointed.

Sandra Craig's white VW Golf had just pulled off the main road outside the high rise block and was coming along the approach driveway towards them. The back-up Thane had requested by radio had arrived. In another few moments, the Golf had parked and his detective sergeant emerged pale and tired-eyed from the driver's side. The redhead had brought Dougie Lennox as her passenger, and the baby-faced DC stayed a warily diplomatic pace behind her as they walked over.

'A good time last night, sergeant?' asked Thane, keeping a straight face.

'Yes, sir.' Sandra Craig managed a wan nod.

'What time did your party finish?' queried Moss gravely.

'Late.' She was neat in an outfit of leather waistcoat, green shirt-blouse and slate-grey corduroy trousers. But she looked exhausted. She hadn't spent much time on her hair, and she still showed traces of the previous night's make-up. Thane would have wagered money that for once she didn't care. 'Very late.'

'Did the navy fly-boys survive?' asked Phil Moss with a cackle.

'They all seemed in perfect working order, inspector.' She swung round at the sound of a giggle from Dougie Lennox. 'Something amusing you, detective constable?'

'No, sarge.' Sometimes even Lennox had some sense.

Thane took a few moments to brief his new arrivals. Then they headed into Halloran Flats, where the lobby smelled of damp and worse and where the communal noticeboard was covered in inked graffiti which included comments on the sexual needs of its tenants. But high rise blocks came worse than Halloran Flats. For a start, two out of the three elevators were actually working. Then when one elevator's door opened the elderly woman with a shopping bag who emerged offered them a friendly smile and a nod.

It wasn't always that way when strangers visited tower blocks.

'Dougie – ' Thane kept the elevator door open with one arm ' – stay with the cars, keep an ear to the radio, let me know if anyone starts screaming for us.'

Lennox nodded and ambled off. Stepping into the elevator, Thane beckoned Moss and Sandra Craig aboard, then punched the button for Floor Twelve. They had a rumbling ride upwards. Then, after a creaking halt, the door slid open again, and they stepped out into territory where all trace of damp and smells had been left behind. An air conditioning unit purred nearby, the cream paint on the walls was unmarked, and there was even a narrow runner of turkey red carpet across the landing's concrete.

'C12 – ' Moss pointed to a door to his right ' – that one.'

It was a heavy oak door, varnished, and not the type that normally came standard in high rises. The name 'Riley' was on a cottage-style ceramic nameplate above the handle, and an expensive security door lock had been fitted below it.

Thane pressed the doorbell, heard chimes inside, waited, and tried again.

157

He peered at the area around the keyhole, but to the naked eye there was no sign of any attempt to force the lock. Then he looked up as he heard a shuffle of feet coming along the landing.

'Can I help you, mister?' asked a woman.

She came nearer, carpet slippers on her feet, a mildly interested but slightly wary expression on her face. In her early sixties, her greying hair in pink plastic curlers, she was dressed in a dark two-piece outfit and a white lace blouse.

'We're looking for Betty Riley,' said Thane.

'That's her door.' The woman kept the same wary expression on her face.

'I'm Sheila Taylor, along in D12. Uh – are you friends or maybe relatives?'

'Police.' Thane showed his warrant card.

'Can't your people get their act more together?' She sighed in exasperation. 'She's dead. You didn't know?'

'No. We didn't. I'm sorry, Mrs Taylor.' Sandra Craig was first to answer and managed an apologetic smile. 'We're – well, from a different department.'

'It's Miss Taylor, not Mrs,' corrrected the woman firmly. 'I'm not married, and none the worse for it.'

'Miss Taylor.' Sandra tried again. 'When did it happen?'

'About two weeks ago. Eleven nights back, if you want it exact.' The grey-haired woman allowed herself the luxury of a small shudder at the thought. 'Your people say it would be sometime after midnight, though her body wasn't found until the next morning.' She sighed. 'Blonde Betty – that's what we called her, poor soul. It looks like she went up to the fifteenth floor laundry area. Then – well, just walked over the edge.'

'Suicide?' asked Moss.

'What else?' She gave him a small, interested smile, the kind of smile Moss always drew from women her age, then smoothed her plastic curlers. 'Fifteen floors is a long way to fall – and she lands on top of one of those stone statue things down there.' With an earnest horror, she turned to Thane. 'Dear Lord, it was messy! They needed a brush and shovel, and then they had to hose the place down!'

'Eleven nights ago.' Thane calculated back. It meant that Betty Riley had come off the fifteenth floor of Halloran Flats within a day of Sam Baker being killed. 'Mrs Taylor, we've a photograph we'd like you to look at.'

Sandra Craig silently produced a passport size head and shoulders photograph of Baker and the woman's eyes widened.

'You know him?' asked Thane.

'He was Blonde Betty's fancy man,' declared Sheila Taylor. 'Don't ask me about him – he's always been a mystery. He can be here for a few days, then vanish for weeks – just as he likes, nobody even knows his name. But he paid her bills – and I should have been so lucky!'

'And he hasn't been seen since this happened?' asked Thane.

'No.' She shook her head. 'So he has a shock coming when he does turn up – if ever.' Then, as Sandra put the photograph away again, the woman frowned. 'If you want a look inside her flat, the beat policeman left me a key.'

The grey-haired woman went away and was back in less than three minutes. But in that time she had removed the plastic curlers and brushed her hair, had achieved a fast make-over job with powder and lipstick, and had swopped her slippers for a pair of smart, low-heeled shoes. She also had the Riley door key in one hand.

'How many people have borrowed it?' asked Sandra Craig.

'Nobody.' The woman shook her head. 'I'm just doing an obligement for the police – there's no one else, no relative, no other friend. But if anyone has a good reason, I go along with them and stay with them.' She turned the key, and the heavy lock clicked open. 'If there had been anyone troublesome, I'd have chased them – I keep a nice big hammer behind my door!'

'Don't overdo the bravery bit,' murmured Sandra. 'We can't afford the medals.'

Sheila Taylor laughed, then pushed the flat's door open and waved them on. Thane was first, stepped into the lobby of Sam Baker's hideaway, and found he was walking on thick, wall-to-wall wool carpeting. A series of small African wooden carvings of animals ran along one wall and were faced by an ornate brass-framed mirror. Apartment C12 might only amount to an ordinary high rise three-room flat with kitchen and bathroom. But it was furnished and fitted in luxury style – the total opposite of the Kirkintilloch house – and lacked for nothing.

They saw things like a wide-screen digital TV and entertainment console, a fully stocked bar, and a leather upholstered lounge suite. The dining room was furnished in a bleached lime, the kitchen was a dazzle of electrical appliances, and the bathroom had Italian tiles with full-length mirrors. In the bedroom, where there was a king-sized bed with a bright froth of quilts and covers, one wall was lined with built-in wardrobes with a dresssing table in the middle.

'That was Betty Riley.' The grey-haired neighbour pointed to a framed studio portrait on a night table beside the bed. 'Maybe she'd been around the block a few times, but she was still good looking.'

Thane nodded. The photograph showed a generously built blonde with back-combed hair and a laugh on her lips. At very least, Betty Riley had been in her mid-forties. But she didn't look potential suicide material.

'She moved in here about five years ago,' volunteered her neighbour.

'And the partner?'

'Him?' The woman shrugged. 'He appeared about three years ago. Never talked to anyone. I'd a notion he sometimes thumped Betty – but she never complained.' She looked around. 'Well, that was her business, I suppose.'

Thane said nothing. But there was one thing very wrong about the inside of Flat C12. Yes, there were photographs of Betty Riley. The wardrobes and drawers were filled with her clothing. But it was as if a determined effort had been made to wipe out even a memory of Sam Baker. There were empty hanger gaps in one wardrobe and some had areas of half-empty drawer space. From ties and shirts through to shoes and suits, there was not a single item of male clothing to be seen.

It was the same story everywhere. There was not a photograph of Sam Baker, not as much as a letter, not even a receipted bill to tell anyone that he had existed.

So what had happened?

Moss and Sandra Craig were continuing a methodical search through the flat, with the escorting Sheila Taylor never far away. Thane left them, went back out into the landing, and walked the two remaining floors to the high-rise roof area.

Out in the open, the sun was bright and the wind came in

small gusts. He walked across to the low iron guardrail which edged the roof, then looked over. Fifteen floors was a long way down to the cobbles and slabs at ground level, with the stone sculptures seemingly shrunk to toy size. Someone had told him once how many inches the average high rise was built to flex and sway in bad weather. He felt strangely glad that he couldn't remember . . . and the world seemed cold despite the sunlight.

'Some view,' mused Phil Moss, suddenly joining him. The small, whipcord thin inspector pointed out across the city skyline to a patch of blue water with a background of mountains. 'That has to be Loch Lomond, which makes those hills fifty miles away.' He turned, slouching against the guardrail, sunlight emphasising the lines on his thin face. 'So, back to the old classic. Did she fall or was she pushed? My money says pushed.'

'And the flat cleaned out at the same time.' Thane nodded. He didn't blame the police team who had followed up the initial reports. Male or female, middle-aged jumpers weren't unusual wherever there were high rises, and the local divisional officers hadn't know the Sam Baker background. He took a deep breath, pushing out of his mind how Betty Riley's body would have been smashed up at the end of that fall. 'The first part's easy enough, Phil. Whoever killed Baker would get his house keys when they emptied his pockets.'

'So they get in, surprise the Riley woman, and take their time about the rest.' Moss grunted his agreement. 'But why clear out all his stuff?' He frowned, then answered his own question. 'To avoid complications if the Lazarus Widow is back in business again?'

It had to be that way. Thane stayed on the roof a few minutes longer, thinking ahead, occasionally bouncing an idea against Moss's built-in cynicism, assembling his thoughts.

'Let's move back in,' said Moss, shivering in the wind. 'Then do you want me to hang on?'

'For now.' Thane nodded. 'I'll leave you Sandra and Lennox for company.'

'And there's a likely double act!' Moss gave a high-altitude belch. 'But send us food. Leave Baby Sergeant hungry for too long and she'll be measuring young Lennox for a microwave.'

'And what would be wrong with that?' queried Thane.

161

Except that the Crime Squad inventory even had to account for problem DCs like Lennox – they left the roof, and a little later he rode one of the elevators down to the ground floor.

It was around ten thirty by the time Colin Thane returned the Ford to his slot at the Crime Squad headquarters parking lot. He had started to walk away from the car when he heard his name called, looked round, and saw the sergeant in charge of the Squad transport pool signalling him. Nobody quarrelled with the transport pool sergeant, not if they wanted to ensure a supply of reliable wheels. Thane went over.

'Something to show you, sir,' said the transport sergeant briskly. 'Scenes of Crime and a couple of Traffic mechanics were here for a spell. They worked on that car we hauled out of the Clyde yesterday.'

'Are they finished?'

'Finished and gone.' The man nodded. 'Like to see it?'

Thane followed him across to a large anonymous shed set at the rear of the parking area. It was a place used for everything from holding – and sometimes hiding – damaged Squad cars to garage storing other vehicles seized during an investigation. The transport sergeant opened the front door then snapped on the white neon tube overhead lights as they entered.

Spluttering to life, the neon tubes shone down on what had started off as Sammy Baker's powder blue Nisssan coupé. The car sat in the middle of a cleared area, a residual drip of river damp still staining the shed's concrete floor, and obviously the visitors had spent a busy morning. Jacked up, wheels removed, doors and bodywork stripped down, the Nissan was reduced to a skeleton with even its seats and carpets set in a neat row to one side.

'No drugs, no weapons, nothing else that seemed to matter, sir,' said the tranport sergeant. He paused and frowned. 'Except they couldn't understand this. It was hidden under the rear seat squab.'

Still wrapped in torn plastic sheeting, blackened by damp but obviously originally grey, a tight roll of heavy waxed wrapping paper had been left in front of the Nissan. It was about a yard long and as thick as a man's arm. Puzzled, Thane squatted down to look more closely. The waxed paper still had droplets of river water clinging to it where they had leeched in through the plastic.

'Anything special about it, sir?' asked the transport sergeant. 'If there's any risk of it exploding or anything, I want it out of my shed. Like now!'

'Don't ask me.' Thane reached a hand under the plastic sheeting and felt the heavy waxed surface, remembering the off-cuts of waxed paper he'd found in Baker's garage. 'But we'll look after it. Send the roll up to my office – ' he corrected himself ' – no, to the duty room. We'll take it from there.'

Leaving the man eyeing him still suspiciously, Thane left the shed, walked over to the headquarters building, and went straight upstairs. In the main duty room the only occupants were Maggie Donald, who was talking earnestly on a telephone, and Jock Dawson, who had a pen clasped in one large fist and who was writing with intense concentration. Aware of his priorities, the dog handler was filling in an overtime sheet before clipping it to his Gritters report. The report was almost an equal priority. Every time any police dog saw bite-sized action, no matter how justified, there had to be a report.

'Any problems?' asked Thane.

'None, sir.' Dawson gave one of his lazy grins. 'The dogs are fine. A wee bit excitement never does them any harm, and I always make sure their shots are kept up to date. We can't be too careful. God knows where some of those two-legged vermin they chase have come from!'

'Amen,' agreed Thane, then left him. Maggie Donald had just finished her 'phone call, and the dark-haired Northern girl looked pleased with herself.

'So tell me,' invited Thane resignedly. 'What is it?'

'Adam Oliver and Liz Rankin's brother Robin, sir – ' she took a quick, double-checking glance at her notebook ' – it's like she said. Oliver and her brother flew together as captain and first officer for almost three years. I checked with the British Airline Pilots Association – '

'The plumbers' union,' nodded Thane impatiently. 'Go on.'

'They split when Adam Oliver took a well-paid long-haul job on the Hong Kong route,' reported Maggie Donald. 'Only two months after that, Rankin was killed in an air accident in Egypt.

163

But – ' she looked pleased with herself ' – when Oliver and Rankin were flying together they worked for a tourist charter airline based at Larnaca.' She beamed at Thane. 'Larnaca, Cyprus!'

'So?' Thane raised a questioning eyebrow.

'The Lazarus in the Bible, raised by Jesus from the dead, has his tomb at Larnaca, sir,' she said patiently. Turning, she picked up a slim opened book. 'I remembered that from the Bible Class when I was at school in Inverness. And it's listed here, in the official Cyprus for tourists guidebook. Suppose that was where Adam Oliver got the notion of inventing the Lazarus Widow – ?'

Thane was staring at the guidebook. On one page there was a photograph of a three tiered abbey church, described as sheltering the site of Lazarus's tomb. On the opposite page – he stared at the other illustration, a photograph of a strange little Cypriot carved stone statuette, identical to the one in Liz Rankin's home.

'Sir?' she asked.

'Bless you for a dark-haired little witch, Maggie,' he said softly. 'Well done – but keep this to yourself until we're ready for it!'

He went through to his office, glanced at the few messages waiting on his desk, then sat down and pulled the telephone nearer. His first call had to be to F Division, which had Halloran Flats inside its territory. It took a few minutes of mutual diplomacy to persuade the F Division duty uniformed superintendent to send his Scenes of Crime team back to the Flats again – with no guarantee there would be any new result.

Next Colin Thane dialled the City Mortuary. For once, his luck was in – the mortuary's schedules showed that Doc Williams had carried out the post mortem on Betty Riley – and at that moment the police surgeon was in the building, working in one of the autopsy suites.

Thane was asked to hold. Then, another voice came on the line which made made him sigh. But Fred, everyone's favourite mortuary attendant, was in good spirits.

'Doctor Williams is closing up a customer,' said the man. 'He'll be with you in a couple of minutes.' Then Fred chuckled. 'Mr Thane, I've got a good one for you. Uh – have you heard about the Aberdonian who found a pair of unused corn plasters?'

164

Thane counted to five. 'Yes,' he said stonily.' He thought about it, then he went out and bought a new pair of tight shoes.'

'Oh.' The mortuary attendant didn't hide his disappointment. 'Well, hold on – '

Another minute passed, then Doc Williams came on the line.

'Whatever it is, keep it short, 'Colin,' he warned. 'I'm due on the first tee at Hilton Park in half an hour, and I'm christening a new carbon shaft driver. So – go. I'm counting!'

'You did a p.m. on a woman about ten days ago. A blonde, name of Betty Riley.' Thane kept it as brief as he could. 'Remember her?'

'Could I forget?' The police surgeon sighed. 'If women who even think of jumping off high flats roofs' could see the results – '

'Who says she jumped?' asked Thane bluntly.

'I – ' Doc Williams stopped and swore under his breath. 'You're saying different?'

'I think so.' Thane waited.

'Thrown?' the police surgeon groaned. 'Look, Colin, she fell fifteen storeys, then a stone statue practically harpooned her – hell, it was difficult enough just putting the bits together again!'

'Can you say she wasn't shoved?'

'No. Any more than I can say she wasn't fired from a gun on the moon!' Doc Williams clacked his teeth a few times. 'I'll run more tests, we might come up with something. I suppose this means I have to forget about Hilton Park?'

'There'll be another day,' soothed Thane. He hung up and returned to the duty room.

For the next half hour he was busy juggling priorities as, among other things, Beauty and the Beast reported in. They were still in Ayr. Staff at the dry cleaning shop where Sam Baker's jacket had been brought in, express cleaned, then collected again next day could remember it well enough. The jacket had been badly smeared by green seacoast rock slime – and its owner was equally remembered for his abusive language.

Then Beauty and the Beast also had contributions to make to the overall picture that was gradually coming together – an often frustrating process, when it was still too early to know what mattered and what didn't.

There was more local background on Trudi Andrews. The young brunette with the streaked highlights was a sparkling success as a Kingsley Homes sales negotiator. There was gossip that Adam Oliver, as boss of the parent Kingsley Estates Management, had originally offered her the job. But she now more than held the job by her own efforts.

Things were very different when it came to Gary Shaw. His background vague, the poetry-writing travel agent was a loner who lived in a tumbledown cottage a few miles outside Glasgow. Neighbours knew his name but little more. None of his colleagues in the travel shop where he worked could have called him a friend. But wherever Trudi Andrews went, Gary Shaw was also likely to be around.

Which left Adam Oliver. Maggie Donald had put together a snapshot outline of what they had to date on the former airline captain. Eventually, he appeared to have left the aviation world against a background of unpaid debts in three African countries. Then there had been a blank period of over a year before he had arrived in Scotland to buy his way in as executive director of the Kingsley Estates land management company – and to pick up his relationship with Liz Rankin.

'People who've worked with him say he's efficient, sir.' Maggie Donald hesitated. 'But I wouldn't say they particularly trust him.'

Thane shrugged . . . That was probably rated as one sure way to identify a successful businessman for the second millennium.

'How did he meet up with our travel agent poet?' he wondered.

'Probably through Liz and Trudi being friends, sir.' Maggie Donald frowned. 'But we don't really know for sure. DCI Redder said she'd put some of her people to work checking any possible airline link from the past, but they haven't come back to us yet.'

Photocopies of the drawings of the two men who had threatened the Riverman continued to be circulated with several forces, but so far without result. Thane ordered the Special Search request to be repeated in case some CID team had missed it first time. Then the telephone in his room was ringing and he was being shouted through by a stray constable who had answered. Matt Amos, the Scientific Bureau director, was at the other end of the line.

'I'm working through a list, and it's your turn,' said Amos

166

breezily. 'Remember those off-cuts of waxed paper from Kirkintilloch?'

'I do,' said Thane woodenly. 'But I thought you'd forgotten.'

'We've been busy,' protested Amos.

'Understaffed, underpaid, under-appreciated,' countered Thane. 'Hum the tune, Matt. I know the words. Except now we've come up with a full roll of the same waxed paper. It was found when Baker's car was stripped down.'

'Then listen,' urged the bearded bureau director. 'Remember that even after his jacket had been commercially dry-cleaned we still found specks of a strong industrial solvent on the cloth. That same solvent was powerful enough to break up the concrete floor in his garage – and when we ran some tests, it took the same strength of solvent to de-wax that paper.' Matt Amos paused, obviously thinking. 'Colin, maybe we should take a look at that roll.'

'How soon could you do it?'

'Let's see now.' Amos whistled tunelessly through his teeth for a moment. 'I've a small quantity of similar strength solvent in the laboratory's stock – not a lot, but enough. The quickest way would be to send Anna Huang out to your place with a sampling flask – if you needed, we could do full laboratory tests later.' His voice became reproachfully sanctimonious. 'You know, our Anna is still trying to find a cheap supply of liquor for that wedding party – '

'Is she?' parried Thane.

'Damn you,' sighed Amos. 'I'll send her out anyway. But you're knocking hell out of police race relations policies.' The line went dead.

Ten minutes later a fax message came in from Strathclyde's ballistics team.

Bullets and cartridge cases recovered from the drive-by shooting over at Bellside had been identified as being from a 9 mm Uzi pistol. Ballistics can prove the weapon has a known history – used twice in the previous year, first in a Midlands bank shooting then in a murder attempt on a Belfast politician.

Which made it from the rent-a-gun world, which could mean Liverpool. The going rate for Uzi rentals was around £25 a day if returned wihout being fired, doubling to £50 a day if fired.

Jock Dawson wandered around handing out mugs of frighteningly strong coffee, his personal answer to Squad canteen's brew. Thane tasted a hint of cognac in his and knew it came from the medicinal brandy the dog handler somehow obtained for the first aid kit for his charges. More 'phone calls came and went, and suddenly the duty room began filling with people. That included Beauty and the Beast arriving back from Ayr, then hard on their heels Phil Moss returned with Sandra and Lennox.

'We left when Scenes of Crime arrived,' reported Moss, sitting on the edge of Thane's desk with his feet dangling. 'But we gave Flat C12 another going over.' He glanced at Sandra Craig, who was perched beside him. The redhead, now more back to her usual self, was demolishing her way through an apple. 'Show him what you got, Sandra.'

'These, sir.' Thane's sergeant reached into her handbag, brought out a slim wad of US dollar bills secured by two yellow elastic bands, and slapped it down in front of him. 'Two thousand dollars, pinned behind one of the bedroom drawers.'

'Emergency grab-and-run money – the same way he had some stashed away in Kirkintilloch.' Thane combed a hand through his thick dark hair and considered the find. A mere two thousand dollars fell far short of a motive for murder. The people behind the Lazarus Widow scam were searching for something more.

'There's more. Dougie Lennox hadn't much to do, so I put him to work door-knocking up and down the block.' Moss bared his yellowed teeth, pleased at the result. 'He found three tenants who remembered one of the elevators being operated very late on the night that the Riley woman died.

'How late?'

'Around three a.m. – and being used several times. Then they also think they heard a van leaving. One tenant was as mad as hell. She had a baby who kept waking up.'

Several times – an elevator going up and down long after midnight and the sound of a van fitted with the fact of what had been removed from Flat C12 that night. The night when a woman had fallen those fifteen cruel storeys to her death.

'Lennox took statements?'

Moss nodded.

Thane's telephone began ringing again.

'Yes?' He answered it impatiently.

'In one of our happier moods, are we?' asked the Riverman mildly, his voice crackling just a little over the line. Crackling meant a local call. Long distance now gave the clearest in-the-next-room type conversations.

'Sorry.' Thane grimaced an apology at the mouthpiece. 'I'm having a busy time.'

'Me too.' The Riverman left it at that, in a way that meant a further increase to his personal body count. 'But I finally got round to hosing out the boat I used when I recovered Baker's body. The jet washed a wee surprise out from under the stern sheets.'

'Hold on.' Thane slapped a hand over the telephone mouth-piece and glared at Moss and Sandra Craig, who had gone into a muttered discussion. 'Give me some hush, will you?' As they went silent, he lifted his hand from the mouthpiece. 'So – what kind of surprise?'

'The cap from a ballpoint pen stamped National Trust for Scotland. I'd take an oath it wasn't there before I rowed in with Baker's body. So – '

'So it could have fallen out of one of his pockets?'

'Give the man a prize,' declared the Riverman cheerfully.

Thane promised to have the pen top collected, then hung up.

Anna Huang arrived half an hour later, driving an old red Saab station wagon which she parked in the yard. When the Hong Kong Chinese doctorate student came into the building, carrying a large and stoppered stainless steel flask and a small airline flight bag, she was met by an almost drooling Dougie Lennox. Taking the flask from their visitor, Lennox grinned like a bemused Cheshire cat as he made sure she went ahead of him up the stairs to the duty room.

'Thanks for coming, Anna,' said Thane when she arrived there. For once he had a certain sympathy for the baby-faced DC. Normally, Anna Huang wore a baggy white laboratory coat like it was a uniform. But the coat had been left behind. She was dressed in a cream linen skirt and jacket, the skirt slashed to mid-thigh, the jacket short-sleeved and with a mandarin collar. Turning to Lennox, he gestured towards a table where the roll of waxed paper lay waiting on a piece of old canvas provided by the transport sergeant. 'Over there, Dougie.'

Lennox set the flask down beside the waxed roll then, while an audience gradually built, Anna Huang got to work. Stripping off her linen jacket to reveal a thin sleeveless blouse, she handed the jacket to a wide-eyed Lennox, then opened the flight bag and took from it a thick plastic apron and a pair of elbow-length rubber gloves.

'The substance I'm using is highly volatile, superintendent.' She smiled apologetically. 'I need some windows open, otherwise some of us might feel very ill.'

By the time two of the duty room's large windows had been swung open Anna Huang was wearing the apron and rubber gloves and had pulled on a pair of protective goggles. Carefully, she opened the stoppered flask and produced a thick but fine-haired laboratory pastry brush. Then, dipping the brush into the flask, she brought it out with a transparent, watery fluid dribbling from its bristles.

The first brushstroke over the waxed paper brought a quick bubbling reaction and a thin, rising cloud of pale smoke. After a few more brushstrokes, a pungent odour had begun filling the duty room and a pool of dissolving wax was forming on the sheet of canvas protecting the table top.

'It's working.' Anna Huang smiled at Thane, then gave a quick, warning shake of her head as Sandra Craig moved nearer. 'No, not too close, sergeant. Please! Even casual contact with this stuff can cause skin damage.'

They waited. More brush strokes followed, the odour caught at throats and left some of her audience with watering eyes, and the pool of dissolving wax grew under the roll. Finally she stopped, resealed the flask, then took two thin, long-jawed tweezers from the flight bag.

'Now – ' her goggle-protected almond eyes smiled at Thane ' – let's see if the hunch I think we both may have is right, superintendent!'

Using the tweezers, the young doctorate student carefully gripped both ends of the waxed paper. For a moment, nothing happened – then the roll was splitting like a layered onion, winding back under her steady continuing pressure.

'What's that in there?' Phil Moss peered and swallowed.

Then he forgot the warnings and took a long step forward,

staring. Sandwiched between the layers of paper, a thin coating of US dollar bills lay in the sunlight coming from the windows.

'Real?' asked Colin Thane quietly.

'Real.' Moss had something close to disbelief in his voice. 'Or real enough.'

Silently, Anna Huang used the forceps to unwind another short length of the de-waxed paper. Then the wax began to stick again, but not before several more banknotes had been revealed.

'And what the hell have we got going on here?' boomed a familiar voice, then Jack Hart pushed his way through to the front. The newly returned Squad commander stopped at the table, stared, and swore. 'No! I don't damned believe it!'

'Believe what, sir?' asked Thane woodenly.

'This stuff – ' Hart gestured blindly ' – and my damned Brussels conference! We had one whole lecture yesterday on how to beat what our European friends call the blue paper scam.' He scratched his head of sparse, iron-grey hair. 'Which was the first time I'd even heard about it. Then I come back here and walk into this – this grey paper version!' The newly returned Squad commander gave up.' All right, everybody give over – and out! Our thanks to our visiting expert. We'll leave it to the Scientific Bureau to finish this part.' The Squad commander scowled at Thane. 'In my office, superintendent. When you're clear.'

Hart left. Thane waited to see Anna Huang on her way. When the slim-hipped Hong Kong Chinese girl departed with her magic flask of solvent, her flight bag, and the carefully re-wrapped roll of waxed paper, she was under the close escort of Dougie Lennox.

Once Anna Huang had gone, Thane went through to Jack Hart's office.

On the way he passed Maggie Fyffe, and the Squad commander's middle-aged personal secretary quickly shoved a slim, gift-wrapped package in a drawer and turned to examining a large box of Belgian chocolates.

'Think of the calories,' murmured Thane. 'And what's in the package?'

'Mind your own damned business,' grinned Maggie Fyffe. 'Except I'd like to know how he knew my size!' She nodded towards Hart's door. 'You've to go in.'

171

Thane went through, to find Jack Hart standing beside his desk and removing the price tag from an even larger box of Belgian chocolates. Another gift-wrapped package protruded from his opened briefcase.

'Gloria's loot?' asked Thane dryly.

'What else?' Hart cheerfully ripped away the last of the price tag, and glanced at his wrist watch. 'Right. Whatever has been happening, tell me over lunch. I'm paying.'

Jack Hart's official car was a black Jaguar with a veteran sergeant as driver, and the sergeant had the car moving as soon as his passengers had settled in the rear seat. He had obviously been instructed in advance about their destination.

'It's an out-of-town golfing inn I know. Food's good, and the place is quiet enough so we can talk,' volunteered Hart. 'Before you ask, Brussels was hell. Full of our new European alleged friends, God help us. What we got were some ideas about inter-force co-operation that probably won't happen, and a general consensus that the bad guys are getting cleverer – the usual.' He leaned back against the Jaguar's leather upholstery. 'The waxed paper trick surprised you?'

Ruefully, Thane nodded.

'Like I said, it's maybe new enough here, but not inter-nationally.' Hart grimaced. 'The thing is straight out of the Lazarus Widow stable, and known as the wax paper laundering scam. It works like this – you're an importer, you're bringing in say – machinery from abroad. For protection, your imported machinery is always delivered wrapped in waxed paper, right?'

'So you're offered ready-wrapped money?' Thane envied the way the Jaguar barely noticed a sudden road pothole it had to go through.

'You think,' said Hart sourly. 'There's a Far East gang who specialise in producing these waxed paper money rolls, except only a few have money all the way through. In others, it runs out almost straight away. Then they use the old story about some redundant dictator who has to get his money out to the West.' He scowled as a local police traffic car dared to tuck in at their tail, then grunted as the Jaguar was recognised, and the patrol car vanished. 'Anyway, the Fraud team invest seed corn money for their waxed paper to be used on particular consignment – '

172

'And surprise their pigeon with a demonstration of the hidden money?'

Hart nodded. 'Then here's the twist – they say the money should be in every third shipment's wrappings, and the deal is one in which they're having to trust the buyer to play it straight. So they sell the solvent at prices like it was liquid gold, and the warning that using any other chemical could destroy the bills.'

'And it works?'

'Trust me, I've been to Brussels,' said Hart sarcastically. 'One Scandinavian forked out fifty thousand Canadian dollars for ten litres of solvent. He got two thousand dollars out of the wrappings on his first shipment, and no more after that – then discovered the solvent was low grade paint stripper!'

It made sense. The roll of waxed paper hidden in Sam Baker's car had been worth a small and untraceable fortune, enough of a bait to attract others like him – including Wee Willie Colston – who might know about its existence.

But not enough, surely, to influence the other things that really mattered – like leaving Sam Baker inside that car in the Clyde, or heaving Betty Riley over the edge at Halloran Flats.

Jack Hart began talking about his Brussels trip, mostly cop-shop gossip, while the Jaguar purred on. Thane knew the signs. The Crime Squad commander was keeping his mind clear for the next stage, hearing from his deputy what the assorted mice had been up to while the boss was away.

It took about twenty minutes to get to Hart's choice of inn, a converted farmhouse called the Shearer which lay on the rat-run route between two busy golf courses. While the sergeant driver headed happily for a sandwich and a pint at the public bar, Hart led Thane through a corridor lined with old golfing prints, then into an oak-beamed and still almost empty dining room where the windows were small and the decor was a blend of sporting memorabilia and hard-sell display cases. They took an isolated table at the rear and their orders were taken by a young waiter in a golfing sweater.

Thane had visited the Shearer just once before. He grinned at the menu. The Shearer had to be one of the last inns that still proudly offered two sizes of individual steak pie – male and female, with male dominating in size. He glanced at Hart, saw Hart's matching grin, and they both ordered male-size pies. That came with a starter soup which was thick and vegetable, and with supporting pints of lager.

'Now,' said Hart as the food began arriving.

Thane told the story from the top while they ate, speaking quietly so that there was no risk of being overheard, pausing any time their waiter made a return trip. Time passed. Occasionally Hart had a question to ask, and he made no secret that Sir Andy Silverhill's visit still mattered.

But at last it was over. They turned down an apple pie sweet – the steak pie had left little room – and settled for two more pints of lager.

'All right, so mainly you get a gold star,' said Hart approvingly. 'Good practice for you, Colin. These damned Europeans love committee meetings, and I may have to do more disappearing acts.' He sipped his lager. 'One worry is this Wee Willie whatever his name is – we can't leave him to rot with the Transport Police, they won't like it. Lawyers could start doing sums about how long we've had him in custody.'

'Another talk with him, then we tuck him away on a court remand late this afternoon,' suggested Thane.

'Fine.' Hart toyed with his lager glass. 'And what about the Lazarus Widow? Do you believe we still pay attention to this coven of women out at Kirkintilloch?'

'Plus their friends – Adam Oliver and don't forget Gary Shaw.'

'Why?' asked Hart brutally. 'Because you've nobody else?'

Slowly, Thane nodded.

'Then I can't think of a better reason,' declared the Squad commander and lifted his glass. 'Drink up, let's get back to work.'

When they left the Shearer the September afternoon had settled into blue sky and warm sunshine. A dog was barking somewhere near. By the magic known only to their kind, the sergeant-driver was already out and waiting by their car. They started travelling back in toward the city, but were still only about halfway when a radio call came in on the Crime Squad frequency.

'I'll get it.' Leaning forward from the rear, Hart hauled the handset over and answered. When the reply came in, his eyes showed surprise. Then, curtly, he said. 'I'll tell him. Say he'll be there.' Then, ending the call, he tossed the handset into the front seat and faced Thane. 'Life has its little surprises, Colin. Adam Oliver has telephoned looking for you – your Baby Sergeant took the call. Oliver wants to see you straight away at his office and says it's urgent. Can you think why?'

Frowning, Thane shook his head.

'All the more reason for finding out,' declared Hart. 'We'll go in past Cadogan Street and I'll drop you off.' He raised his voice. 'That's if a certain damned sergeant stops driving as if he had the handbrake on!'

The sergeant driver grinned, then the Jaguar's engine gave a roar as the car gathered speed and the Glasgow skyline grew ahead.

Dropped off just around the corner in Wellington Street, Colin Thane walked the short distance to Cadogan Street, crossed over, then went into the building shared by Kingsley Estates and Rex Insurance Agencies. There was no sign of the uniformed door-man, but a young girl in a corporate blouse and skirt outfit in the same maroon colour took his name, used an internal 'phone, then guided him over to an elevator behind her desk.

The elevator door opened at the building's top floor and when Thane stepped out he found Adam Oliver standing there, wait-ing for him. The chief executive of Kingsley Estates Management wore a dark business suit with a white shirt and a striped red and blue tie, didn't smile, but offered an immediate strong handshake.

'Thank you for coming over, superintendent.' As he spoke, he was already ushering Thane along the corridor. He sucked an edge of his fair bristle of moustache. 'This won't take long, but it's important – and not just to me.'

They went through a door into a large outer office with staff at their desks, then from there into Oliver's own office where there was oak panelling, a boardroom table, upholstered chairs and smoked glass. The man pulled out two of the seats, and gestured Thane into one.

'Can I offer you a drink?' he suggested.' I've a couple of good malts in stock.'

'I'm working,' said Thane mildly. 'Sorry.'

'All right.' Oliver dropped into the other chair, rubbed a hand over his thinning fair hair as if trying to make up his mind, then went straight into it. 'Superintendent, this is not an official complaint – not yet.'

'But?' Thane raised an eyebrow. 'Tell me about it.'

The man shrugged. 'It's Liz Rankin. She's a – let's say a close friend of mine. Almost family. You're giving her a rough deal.'

'Who says?' asked Thane blandly.

'I do. And it has to stop.' Oliver's blue eyes met his own in the glare of a man used to being obeyed.' I've seen it for myself – you and your people are pressurising her, superintendent. Yet you know she's under a strain – her house broken into, all the rest of what she's been dragged into because of this man Baker being murdered.'

'She called Baker a pig of a man,' murmured Thane. 'Or was that Muriel Baker's description?'

'Does it matter?' The blue eyes had become angry. 'Baker's murder has nothing to do with any of these women. So I'm telling you and your people to back off. Or – '

'Or what, Mr Oliver?' Thane showed his teeth in a humourless smile.

'Or it becomes an official complaint.' One hand gestured around. 'This is an estate management company, Thane. I know some fairly important clients.'

'Most of my clients are in jail,' said Thane unemotionally. 'But I'll remember, Mr Oliver.' He had a thought. 'Will Liz be at her desk down in Rex Insurance? I could make some soothing noises.'

'She's out.' Oliver shook his head. 'I saw her this morning. She is visiting clients.' He scowled. 'Look, superintendent, I know you have a job to do. But stay away from her. You understand?'

'I think so.' Thane got to his feet. 'Thanks for the advice.'

Adam Oliver nodded but stayed seated. Thane went to the door, made his own way out from there and through the outer office, then rode the elevator down to the ground floor. When he got there, he stopped beside the girl at the reception desk.

'Where's the doorman who is usually here?' he asked mildly. 'His name is Tam, isn't it?'

She shook her head. 'Tam, yes. He phoned in this morning,

saying he was feeling sick and was taking the day off. Can I give him a message?'

Thane shook his head. 'I'll see him again.'

He thanked her and went out into the street. As he started walking, a car horn gave a soft peep and he saw Sandra Craig waiting further along in her white VW Golf.

'Good timing,' he congratulated her, getting aboard.

'Commander Hart's orders,' she said shortly, slamming the Golf into gear and starting it moving. 'He wants you back, in a hurry.'

'Did he give a reason?'

She nodded. 'We've had another 'phone call – I took it. Sir Andy Silverhill is on his way in to see you.'

Thane frowned. 'Why?'

'Your Sir Andy thinks the Lazarus Widow has grabbed another victim,' said his sergeant unemotionally, a fine moisture of perspiration on her upper lip. 'And Sir Andy knows who it is!'

Then she dropped a gear, accelerated hard, and began driving for real.

7

This time Sir Andy Silverhill did not have Daniel Wolfson to keep him company. He had already arrived by the time Thane and Sandra Craig returned to the headquarters building and was talking to Jack Hart and Phil Moss in a low urgent voice. He seemed to have aged ten years since their last meeting. No longer did he give an impression of boyish enthusiasm as he shook hands briefly with Thane. His cheeks were hollow and his eyes looked sore. It was as if all the energy had drained out of him. He had at last become an old man.

Thane did not waste time with introductory pleasantries. 'You have some information for us, Sir Andy?'

Silverhill nodded. He was breathing heavily. 'I'm afraid so.'

'Another approach has been made to you?'

'No, not at all,' Silverhill said irritably. 'Far worse than that. I was just explaining to Jack here . . .'

Hart said, 'Sir Andy is concerned that this time the Lazarus Widow has targeted Professor John MacMaster. With success.'

'The Professor? Yes, you know each other, don't you?' Thane remembered. 'Golfing buddies.'

Silverhill nodded. 'He isn't an easy man to get close to. A bit of a stickler, as you are no doubt well aware. But he and I go back a long way. I'm not sure John has too many friends, but I think I'd count myself as one of them.'

Phil Moss nodded. 'So when the Professor went missing, his wife called Sir Andy.'

'She is beside herself,' Sir Andy said hoarsely. 'Poor woman. They have been together a long time. He may not be easy, but he is totally reliable. He said he was going to tell these people that he'd changed his mind, then come straight home, but when she rang me, he was an hour overdue. She'd tried his mobile, but there was no answer. Out of character, she said.'

'No need to panic so soon, though, surely?' Thane asked.

'The MacMasters are thinking of moving house and they'd arranged to look around a place just outside Largs. It's simply not the sort of commitment he would break. She fears the worst. And so, frankly, do I.'

Thane thought about it and nodded. 'I take your point.'

The phone rang. Hart snatched it up angrily and said, 'Not now . . . oh, all right. I'll tell him.'

He turned to Thane. 'That was Doc Williams. He's in the process of re-checking, but he wanted you to know that he's starting to change his mind already. With the benefit of hindsight, there's nothing inconsistent with Betty Riley having been murdered.'

Thane groaned. What would MacMaster have had to say about a failure to spot a possible case of foul play? But upbraiding a former student might be the last thing on the Professor's mind right now.

He addressed Sir Andy. 'Let's take it in stages. What makes you think this is anything to do with the Lazarus Widow?'

Silverhill waved a hand dismissively. 'It was obvious as soon as she began to explain what had happened. Talk about history repeating itself. He's in much the same position as myself.'

'In what way?'

A sigh. 'John's wife reminded me that he too is a trustee of a charity. He set it up five years ago together with a handful of colleagues from other universities. Its prime purposes are two-fold. First, to promote research into forensic pathology. Second, to assist in training people in the field with bursaries, cash grants, and so on. In turn, the charity has attracted a great deal of funding. John's mentioned it to me himself. The University has been generous and there's been money from the Lottery, as well as Europe. The trustees are sitting on a very tidy sum. That's what the Lazarus Widow is after. She's planning to clean out the bank account, you can depend upon it.'

'Does the Professor's wife know the details?'

'As I understand, the story he's been spun is pretty similar to the yarn about Helena Bosso, except that this time the approach came from the Ivory Coast. At least John didn't make the mistake I did. He confided in someone. His wife's been nervous about the whole business ever since he told her about it, but he insisted on following it up. He's ambitious for the charity. You can never have enough funds for that kind of work, that's his argument. But he promised to take precautions. He insisted on a meeting in this country. He wasn't going to fly out to Africa without checking the whole business out pretty thoroughly. The people he's dealing with agreed to his request.'

Hart added, 'On reflection, though, he accepted that it all seemed too good to be true. His wife wanted him to call off the meeting, but he said he had to go. He's not short of guts. He wanted to tell them personally that he'd decided not to proceed. She said he meant it to take two minutes, no more, but he owed them the courtesy of breaking the news face to face rather than by 'phone.'

'Where was this meeting supposed to take place?'

Andy Silverhill frowned. 'That's the problem. All MacMaster told his wife was that they'd offered to talk to him at a cottage in Ayrshire. Apparently there was a man and a woman based in Scotland who were acting in a liaison capacity. Rather like Sam Fraser did with me, by the sound of things.'

Hart turned to Thane. 'As you came in, Sir Andy was telling Phil and me that the cottage is on the coast.'

'Yes, sorry. MacMaster did mention that. But damn it, you're talking about a pretty lengthy coastline.'

A man and a woman based in Scotland. Thane recalled that Liz Rankin was out of the office, allegedly seeing clients. Tam Reynolds was meant to be off sick. 'I don't suppose you have any names for the couple the Professor was supposed to meet?'

Sir Andy Silverhill gave a defeated shrug. 'Of course, but what's the significance? They'll be using pseudonyms. They call themselves Liz Browning and Bob Barrett, would you believe?'

Liz. Another pointer to Lizbeth Rankin, perhaps? But suddenly, Thane doubted it. He turned to Phil Moss and Sandra Craig. 'Phil. there's a call I need you to make. Sandra, it's time for us to do a bit of urgent house-hunting.'

By the time they heard from Phil Moss half an hour later, Thane and Sandra Craig were in the white Golf, leading a three-car convoy towards the Ayrshire coast. Thane made a note of the address and directions and repeated them to his sergeant.

'Another forty-five minutes, sir,' she said, keeping her eyes on the road. 'Assuming no major snarl-up with the traffic.'

'Before we left, I asked Jack Hart to speak to Andy Gallon from Ayrshire CID,' Thane said. 'Courtesy call, really, but if there is any excitement on Andy's patch, it's as well to give advance warning.'

'Do you think there will be any excitement, sir?'

She had been silent since they had got into the car, perhaps sensing that he was not in the mood to talk until he had put his own jumbled thoughts in order and yet at the same time unable to stifle altogether her resentment at being kept in the dark for a little while. He could tell from her body language, the rigid way her arms held the steering wheel, that she believed he was taking them on a wild goose chase. Her lips were pursed obstinately, her gaze unblinking.

'Who knows? Even though we have back-up, the odds are that we will never need it. Mind, this is the best lead we've got. Put it another way. It's the only lead we've got.'

'It seems like a pretty long shot to me, sir,' she said tightly.

'Not maybe quite as long as you might think.'

'Perhaps it would help if you explained it, sir.'

'Fair enough,' Thane said with a crooked grin. 'Though I'm still trying to think it all through. I've had a change of heart, you

180

see. Until now, I suspected that Adam Oliver was running the Lazarus Widow scam. I still believe he's been up to his neck in it in the past. But one thing's for sure. He can't be in two places at the same time and there's no way he can have been entertaining MacMaster. My bet is that he doesn't know anything about this meeting at the cottage.'

'Why not?' she demanded.

'If he did, why choose today of all days to draw attention to himself and his fancy woman by complaining about the way we've been treating her?'

'Double bluff? Trying to distract us, throw us off the scent?' She added doubtfully, 'Fixing an alibi?'

Thane said, 'Can't see it. Frankly, it would be an unnecessary complication. If Oliver's a villain, and I guess he is, he's been a successful one. Respectable businessman, loads of money. He's not got this far without being street-wise. He'll know that the smartest crooks keep their heads well below the parapet.'

'What's going on, then?'

'Don't tell him I said this, but Harry Cameron hit on the right phrase. He compared the Lazarus Widow scam to a franchising operation. My theory is that there's a new franchisee on the scene.'

'I'm not with you.'

Thane took a deep breath. 'Everything points to Adam Oliver as the original mastermind. Or co-mastermind might be more accurate. I'd say that he and Robin Rankin were in cahoots at the outset. From their African contacts, they learned that advance fee frauds were a lovely way to get rich quick. The question was: how to run the operation successfully? It takes a lot of planning. You need a certain amount of capital, there are underlings both in the UK and overseas who need to be paid. Rankin died before he could cash in, but through him Oliver had met his sister. She inherited his share in the scam and for good measure a statuette he'd brought back from Larnaca. Sort of a criminal's logo, I suppose. As an added bonus, she and Oliver fell for each other.'

'How do you think they set it up?'

'Oliver is obviously no mug when it comes to business. He's made a success of Kingsley, after all. But he needed access to the right sort of information. The scam depends on knowing who

181

the most likely victims are. He must have picked up some useful leads through Kingsley Estates, but maybe not as many as he needed. With the help of a bit of insider information and a few words in the right ears from Liz, he persuaded Rex Insurance Agencies to move into Cadogan Street. Result: he had immediate access to information about people who had money burning a hole in their pocket. A property company and a pensions and financial services outfit. It was a terrific combination. As an added bonus, his lover and fellow conspirator was right there on the spot.'

'They hired Sam Baker,' Sandra Craig said slowly as she overtook a heavy goods vehicle with not too much to spare. 'He and Liz went back a long way. She knew his failings, but she also knew he was a convincing liar and he needed money to keep Betty and Muriel happy, to say nothing of a pricey drug habit.'

'Correct. They needed a network of people they could trust around them. That's the one snag with this kind of scam. Two people can't carry it through all by themselves. I'd like to bet that Tam Reynolds was another cog in the wheel.'

'What about Trudi Andrews? You obviously think . . .'

'I was coming to her,' Thane said softly. 'She was in on it, too. I'm sure of that.'

'She's a sales negotiator,' Sandra said thoughtfully. 'She would be in daily contact with people buying or selling houses. Some of them would be worth big money. They were potential targets for the Lazarus Widow.'

'Spot on. As for Gary Shaw, he's in the travel business. Useful contact for people needing to operate internationally. I'd hazard that he was hired to organise Sir Andy's travel arrangements, for instance. More his line of country than Sam Baker's.'

'We know the MacMasters are planning to move house . . .' Sandra's mind was working fast even as she drove.

'And just before I followed you down to the car, I asked Sir Andy to put in a quick call to the Professor's wife. She confirmed their property is on the market with Kingsley Homes. Trudi was the person they have been dealing with. Mrs MacMaster left the business side to her husband.'

'So Trudi would have been able to find out about this hobby horse of his, the charity?'

'You can depend upon it. The Professor's an elderly man and

he's been married a long time. But most men are susceptible when an attractive young woman hangs on their every word. They feel flattered. Even if they don't make fools of themselves, they may be inclined to be – well, less taciturn than usual. The temptation to impress is overwhelming.'

Sandra Craig gave a scornful grunt and after a few seconds, Thane continued, 'Here's where I start putting two and two together and hoping I finish up with four. I think Oliver and Liz Rankin had given up on the Lazarus Widow. They'd made their pile. Let's face it, the Kingsley empire's probably profitable enough these days to keep them in the style to which they've become accustomed. So far they've probably had to be cautious about splashing out too much, for fear of making people talk. Now there are plenty of funds coming in from legitimate sources. No need to take any more unnecessary risks. Besides, Liz suffered from blood pressure. Muriel mentioned it, remember? She could do without the aggravation.'

'So what about this business with MacMaster?'

'Like I said, the franchise has been taken over. Without Oliver knowing, I suspect. Trudi and Gary Shaw fancied the idea of muscling in on his territory. Why let a good scam go to waste? Gary's maybe a bit of a dreamer . . .'

'You're prejudiced,' Sandra said. 'Just because he writes poetry in his spare time.'

Thane grinned. 'Bet I'm right, though. I'd say that they decided to take over the services of Tam Reynolds and Sam Baker. Funny thing, eh? Trudi used to work for Sam and he finished up acting as a go-between for her. As for Gary Shaw, he probably has contacts in the Ivory Coast through his travel business. It all looked like very easy money.'

'Until Sam decided to spill the beans to us, to save his own skin.'

'Sure. It explains something that's puzzled me. He was deeply implicated in the abortive attempt to dupe Sir Andy. Obviously he knew plenty about how Oliver and Liz Rankin operated. If he was planning to expose them, why did he take so long gathering the information to give to us? Far more likely that someone else was involved and he was intending to deliver them to us on a plate when they were about to move in for the kill with MacMaster.'

He could sense that his sergeant was turning it over in her mind, seeing how it all made sense. She said in a whisper, 'Instead of which, Trudi and Gary killed him?'

'Right. They found out he was playing a double game. Maybe it was something he let slip to Muriel, which she in turn passed on to Trudi. That seems the likeliest explanation. Anyway, the pair decided they were in too deep. Sam had to be kept quiet.'

Sandra waited until she had negotiated a sharp bend at speed before asking, 'What do you think happened?'

'Trying to lose our back-up, are you?' Thane asked.

'They'll catch us,' she said briskly. 'Now, you've built up the suspense long enough . . .'

'Okay, but this is pure speculation, you understand? Well, when Sam went to earth at first, Trudi and Gary had a couple of heavies out looking for him. But then maybe he got in touch of his own free will. Walked straight into a trap. My guess is that they used a property on the books of Kingsley Homes' Ayr office as a place to meet with Sam, maybe somewhere he could use as a base for his part in planning the MacMaster operation. It had to be somewhere off the beaten track.'

'Because they didn't want Oliver to cotton on to what they were doing?'

'Uh-huh. It was also a very convenient spot for committing a murder. Remember that Trudi has a record of violence. Either she or Gary killed Sam and then she drove him back in the car to Glasgow and tipped it in the river. But they weren't finished there. Before he died, they must have forced him to admit that Betty knew what was going on. Or perhaps he volunteered it, thinking of it as an insurance policy. But rather than not murdering him, they simply murdered his lover as well. He just didn't realise how desperate they were.'

'So you think Betty knew about the Lazarus Widow?'

'Certainly. I suppose he reassured her that if he told us what Trudi and Gary were getting up to, then he'd get off lightly so far as the smuggling scam was concerned. Which meant that Betty's mouth needed to be shut. When they turned the place over, they weren't bothered about money – just making sure there wasn't any compromising material which put the finger on them. They were ruthless, all right. Sam wasn't only playing a dangerous game, he was in the wrong league entirely.'

'He thought he'd be safe once he grassed up Trudi and Gary,' Sandra said slowly. 'But he wasn't going to be earning any more from the Lazarus Widow, so perhaps he was the one who burgled Liz. He knew she wasn't short of cash.'

Thane shook his head. 'No, my guess is that Trudi paid someone to turn over Liz's flat. She wanted to get her hands on the Lazarus Widow know-how. Names of prospects, overseas contacts. Stuff that would enable her and Gary to keep the scam going. It was a mistake. Liz would have been too smart not to destroy all the compromising data once she and Adam had decided to bury the Widow. And I shouldn't be surprised if she's started to wonder what her young friend has been getting up to. Perhaps she's persuaded Muriel to reveal the source of her new-found wealth.'

'A present from Trudi?'

'Depend upon it. A few pounds to tide her over, keep her in Jelly Joints for a while. The price may be hiked now that Willie Colston's business has been wound up. I suppose Trudi felt she owed Muriel. After all, the woman betrayed her husband, even if she didn't mean to.'

Sandra Craig bit her lip. 'So you think Trudi and Gary will be at this cottage? Barrett and Browning, the poetic lovers?'

The countryside was passing in a blur. Thane had always been fond of this part of the world, but he took no notice of the scenery as he said quietly, 'That's what I hope. As Phil said, when he spoke to the estate agency in Ayr, the only *empty* cottage on the coast which Trudi is responsible for is this place just past Culzean. Another long shot, maybe, but remember the National Trust pen cap that fell out of Baker's pocket? Maybe something he picked up while he was hanging around in the area, trying to get enough on Trudi and Gary to earn our gratitude.'

'I suppose that if they are there, the Professor will be too,' Sandra said.

'Let's hope so,' Thane said. 'The alternative is that he incurred their displeasure some time ago and that after dealing with him, they've made a hasty getaway.'

Sandra Craig said nothing more, but pressed her foot down hard.

*

Colin and Mary Thane knew Culzean well. They usually visited at least once a year. Occasionally they looked round the Castle, but often it was crowded and on a pleasant day they much preferred to wander around the country park. The castle was one of Robert Adam's finest achievements, and the most popular of all the National Trust for Scotland's attractions. Even as they explored the park, the Thanes would occasionally hear American accents – the Castle was a Mecca for tourists from the United States because of its connection with Eisenhower – and then they were apt to escape even further from their fellow visitors, relishing the solitude almost as much as the dramatic clifftop scenery. Every now and then they followed a circuitous path which led eventually to the shore. Thane recalled a trip years ago, slipping and sliding over the rocks as he chased Mary around. Maybe Sam Baker had taken a similar route and that was how he'd managed to get the rock slime on his jacket. He'd been killing time, little realising that soon he himself would be killed.

Today there would be no sight-seeing, no pleasant stroll through shady glades. Turnberry View Cottage was, according to Phil Moss, a short distance beyond the boundary of the National Trust land, an isolated building at the end of a long single track lane. Despite the lovely setting, it had been on the market for nine months. The previous owner had been an elderly woman who hadn't bothered with maintenance and it needed a lot of work, but her heirs were holding out for an unrealistic price. An ideally private headquarters for the resurrected Lazarus Widow. Thane wondered idly if Trudi had encouraged the owners to seek an over-the-top asking price as a means of guaranteeing the cottage's continued availability.

Phil's directions had proved, as ever, reliable and after a brief consultation with their colleagues in the following cars, Thane told Sandra Craig to start down the rutted track which led from the coast road. The track led through a densely wooded copse and then took a sharp turning before opening into a small clearing, with the cottage beyond.

Three cars were already parked by the dilapidated garden gate. One was Trudi Andrews' red Renault four-door, the second a familiar vintage black Daimler limousine. Thane might have been forgiven for a moment of self-congratulation. Instead he

186

uttered a brief and silent prayer. Partly he felt gratitude: his speculation had been bang on the mark so far. Partly he was apprehensive, unsure whether the Daimler's owner would ever be able to drive away from here again.

The third car was one Thane didn't recognise. A battered old Vauxhall saloon. Perhaps it belonged to Gary Shaw – but wouldn't he have come with Trudi? Thane frowned and turned to Sandra.

'Quite a party.'

'Pity we didn't have time to check out this place more thoroughly, sir,' she said. 'Puts us at a disadvantage. Do you think Andy Gallon could have . . .?'

'We'll manage,' Thane said. He knew she was criticising him for an uncharacteristic failure of foresight. Thane was a byword in the Crime Squad – and beyond – for meticulous efficiency.

But he'd been so engrossed in trying to fathom the mystery of the Lazarus Widow that his customary attention to detail had faltered. Perhaps in truth he had not really believed he would find Trudi and the Professor here. Besides, he simply hadn't had the time to plan the operation as thoroughly as usual. At the time they began their journey, he was still putting the pieces together in his mind. The lack of a carefully conceived plan was a drawback; they had no choice but to overcome it. He added grimly, 'We always do, sergeant.'

There was little room left in the clearing. The Golf was blocking the exit and the back-up vehicles lined up along the track behind it. At least Trudi and Gary – if he was here – would not be making a dash for it by road. Their best hope of escape lay in nipping out of the back of the cottage and heading for one of the coastal paths. If they got a good start, catching up with them would be far from easy.

As he quietly closed the door of the Golf, Thane wondered if the birds might already have flown. But he thought he saw a curtain twitch at one of the windows. He hurried back for a word with Maggie Donald. 'The chances are that we have a hostage situation on our hands. Call for support. Negotiators, marksmen, the full works.'

'You're assuming the Professor is still alive, sir?'

'What other assumption can we make?' he asked bleakly.

He returned to the Golf and Sandra Craig said, 'What next, sir?'

Thane felt the reassuring weight of his .38 in its holster. 'I'll approach . . .'

He was interrupted by the crash of a door opening and the sound of raised voices. Lizbeth Rankin appeared, with Trudi Andrews right behind her. They were arguing fiercely. Trudi seemed to be trying to pull the older woman back inside.

'It's gone too far!' Liz Rankin shouted. 'Can't you and lover boy see that? Why in God's name did you have to get such big ideas?'

Trudi swore at the woman who had been her friend. 'What do you know, bitch? You fell for the soft life. You turned your back on a fortune. What did you care about the rest of us?'

'We've argued long enough.' Liz called back into the house. 'Come on, we're leaving.'

She turned her head and waved at Thane. In an ironic tone, she said, 'We meet again, superintendent.'

Thane was in position behind the Golf. He could not guess how this would end. 'Is Professor MacMaster inside the cottage?'

Liz Rankin took a couple of steps down the crazy-paved path which curved through the wild and overgrown garden towards him. 'Yes, he is.'

'Safe and well?' Thane held his breath, waiting for the answer.

She shrugged. 'He could do with seeing a doctor, I'm afraid.'

Thank God he's alive, though. Thane shouted, 'Trudi, this has gone on long enough, hasn't it? Are you coming out? We need to talk.'

'She won't come,' Liz Rankin said. 'She's lost it. Completely lost it. And as for her feller . . .'

She took another two or three paces forward. Thane saw a movement of the curtains, spotted the barrel of a rifle poking out of the open window.

'Look out!' be bellowed.

Even as the words left his lips, a shot rang out. The bullet caught Liz Rankin in the back. An expression of puzzlement creased her face as she crumpled to the ground. A scream came from inside the cottage. Trudi Andrews ran out down the path and cradled the head of the other woman in her hands. She looked back in the direction of the window and raised a small fist.

'Look what you've done! She was my friend! You're mad, I tell you. Stark raving . . .'

Thane heard the roar of the second shot, watched as Trudi fell. Her body sprawled across that of Liz Rankin. He crouched behind the bonnet of the Golf. Gary Shaw might be a poet, he thought, but that didn't mean he wasn't also a psychopath.

Even as he forced himself to think logically, trying to work out the next step, he heard a third shot. His stomach lurched. MacMaster? He and the Professor would never be soul-mates, but he suddenly realised how desperate he had been to save the old man's life. That was why he had rushed here, casting caution to the winds, compromising his reputation for unemotional effectiveness. Then the man inside fired yet again.

'Sir,' Sandra Craig hissed. 'I saw something through the window. I couldn't see clearly, but the man turned the gun on himself, I'm sure of it.'

Thane closed his eyes for moment. 'Sure?'

She didn't hesitate. 'Absolutely positive.'

He straightened, cautiously putting his head above the level of the bonnet. The clearing was silent. Neither of the women were moving. God, what a mess. He had to get a grip of himself, remember that none of this was his fault. It was all right for villains to lose it. Thane didn't intend to join their number.

'Gary!' he shouted. 'If you're in there, now's the time to come out. With your hands up, all right? There's nothing more you can do.'

No answer. Thane exhaled. Slowly, he began to shuffle around the car. The garden gate was perhaps ten metres away. The front door was twice as far. He could wait, play for time. But if MacMaster had been shot, the best that could be hoped was that he was wounded. Time wasn't on his side. He simply could not afford to hang back until reinforcements arrived.

'Sir,' Sandra Craig whispered. 'He shot himself, I swear it.'

'I wasn't doubting your word, sergeant,' Thane said.

He emerged from his zone of safety. This was it, he told himself. If Sandra was mistaken and Gary Shaw wanted to fire again, he was dead meat. And she might be wrong. Suppose Tam Reynolds had turned up here, together with Liz Rankin? Maybe the Vauxhall was Tam's and Liz had asked him to accompany her while she confronted Trudi. Gary might have shot first MacMaster and then Reynolds. Gary might, Thane thought, simply be lying in wait. But he trusted Sandra. Until this moment, he'd never realised quite how much he trusted her. She would never let him down.

Keeping his eyes on the window, he strode briskly forward. Within a few moments he had reached the garden gate. Still no sign of movement within the house. When he pushed the gate, it swung on creaking hinges. He stepped over the bodies of Liz Rankin and Trudi Andrews, all the time fixing his gaze on the cottage, his mind empty of everything except determination to survive. The front door was open. He stepped inside.

He found himself in a narrow hall. A door to his left was ajar. It gave on to a small sitting room. He saw two corpses lying on the floor. One belonged to Tam Reynolds. The other was Gary Shaw. The rifle was by his side. He'd blown part of his own head off.

'Poetic justice,' Thane muttered to himself.

Where was MacMaster? And had he been killed before the latest bout of shooting started? There were two more doors off the hall. Thane opened the first. A dining room, cobwebbed and empty. He tried the second.

Suddenly he was looking into an old-fashioned kitchen with a black and white linoleum floor.

At the far end, seated on the ground with his back to the wall was Professor MacMaster. He was gagged and bound and his forehead was badly bruised. His watery eyes were looking at Thane. The expression in them was one Thane had never seen before. The Professor was terrified and pleading with him, pleading to be released. He had heard the shooting and been unable to move a muscle. He could not have expected to leave the cottage alive.

Sticky tape had been stuck across the Professor's mouth. Thane had to crush the irreverent thought that generations of students who had felt the lash of MacMaster's tongue would relish the sight, regarding it as sweet revenge. Thane moved swiftly over to the old man and peeled off the tape, none too gently.

MacMaster sucked in air greedily. For a few moments he said nothing. Finally he lifted his head so that he was looking into Thane's eyes and spoke in a hoarse whisper.

'You took your time.'